Enchantment of Silver and Sea

Tara Straight

Cover by MIBLART
Developmental edit and copy edit by Megan Records

ISBN Paperback: 979-8-9987426-0-6
ISBN Hardback: 979-8-9987426-1-3
ISBN Ebook (EPUB): 979-8-9987426-2-0

To David

CONTENT AND TRIGGER WARNINGS

If you prefer not to read content and trigger warnings due to possible spoilers, feel free to skip this page at your discretion.

Please note that this work includes the following potential triggers – character coping with mental illness (PTSD, depression, anxiety), death, violence, graphic language, and explicit sexual activities that are shown on the page.

CHAPTER ONE

I woke gasping for air, my heart pounding, smothered in a sickly sweat.

Leaping out of bed, I landed on legs that felt unsteady, as if they weren't a part of me anymore. I ran to the balcony door, flinging it open and dropping to a seated position, calling on my five senses to bring me back to the present.

I forced myself to see the city below me, the dark silhouettes of buildings against the muted purple of the morning sky. I breathed in the sweet smell of baking bread drifting from above me and knew Brielle was awake one story up. I tuned in to the mournful song of the doves, cooing from their perches on the edges of windowsills and gutters. My mouth, I forced myself to observe, was filled with the sour flavor that lingered each time I woke from a nightmare. And I felt the cool morning breeze ruffling my hair. The rough concrete beneath me. The uncomfortable cling of my sweat-drenched nightgown.

Slowly but surely, my galloping heart slowed. The vice grip on my lungs loosened, allowing them to expand.

At this point, I had calming my post-nightmare panic down to a science. And even just knowing this—that I had a plan each time, that I was in control—aided in bringing me back.

It hadn't always been that way. Countless times, I had awoken in throat-constricting terror, certain I was dying. But after so many years, I suppose I had become as used to it as a person could get. Now I could even pinpoint what triggered the dream each time.

In this instance, it was the woman at the living quarters' market the previous evening. That confident gleam in her emerald eyes as she made her friends roar with laughter. The way they looked at her like it was both a joy and an honor to be in her presence. The way she swaggered from aisle to aisle with her chocolate-brown ponytail swishing behind her, plucking items off the shelves and adding them to her basket, while they trailed behind, hanging on her every word.

She was just like Irene.

And I suppose in some respects, like me. Even though my green eyes also contained a hint of blue, and my figure was more petite than Irene's, my dark hair and heart-shaped face had only grown to look more like her as I aged.

Now, here I was. Twenty. The same age she was when she died.

I continued inhaling deeply. In through the nose for ten seconds. Out through the mouth for ten seconds.

In. Out. In. Out.

Exhaling all thoughts of Irene.

I stood carefully, feeling the blood flow return to my legs as I shifted on my feet. I stretched my arms overhead and released another cleansing breath. The sky was fading from that deep purple to a softer periwinkle. The rest of the living quarters would enjoy a few more hours of sleep before we were expected to report for work assignments. But knowing Brielle was up and about in her kitchen was a small comfort.

After one more moment to steady myself, I turned to go inside.

Then spun back around.

I scanned the city again, but this time with more intent.

What was this feeling? It had nothing to do with the nightmare or the panic that was still seeping out of my veins. It was more...an awareness. But of what?

Finding nothing out of the ordinary, I headed back into my apartment. But I still couldn't shake the feeling that something was off.

That skin-prickling feeling stayed with me as I tossed and turned for the next two hours, my pulse still hammering a staccato that ensured sleep would not find me. It stayed with me as I finally flung off the clammy sheets and readied for my work assignment. And it was still with me, making my scalp tingle, as I met Brielle outside my apartment to walk to the Knowledge Center.

"For you!" Brielle said with a flourish, presenting me with a neatly wrapped package as we walked down the carpeted hallway.

We strolled across the seventh floor, sidestepping copies of The Cyllene Sentinel that had been deposited outside our doors before sunup, until the hall of identical white doors became the open atrium that was the most impressive feature of our living quarters. Massive windows spanned all ten floors, flooding the space with light. Beyond the glass, the city streets had already begun to fill with a steady stream of people.

Brielle's honey-colored hair was tied back in her usual loose braid, her hazel eyes bright. My own hair was braided similarly, but I had always thought the style looked prettier on her.

I took the package, knowing without even opening it that it was a loaf of the banana bread I had smelled earlier. "You're the best!"

It was true—there was no beating Brielle's cooking and baking. This was due in large part to her training in the Culinary Preservation department, but it also didn't hurt that her work assignment afforded her access to rare and exotic ingredients. I knew from my own work in the Library that there was a time when bananas could be found in every market. But thanks to The Awakening, they were now a luxury.

"I could smell this when I was out on the balcony earlier," I said, taking another whiff.

"I thought I heard you out there." Brielle took her own loaf out of her knapsack, tore off a piece, and popped it in her mouth. "You should have Maintenance do something about that creaky door. Anyway, I almost popped my head out to say hello."

I wasn't sure she meant that. But I played along. "You should have."

"Maybe I will next time."

"If you do, toss some banana bread over the railing."

She giggled politely, and I chuckled along with her.

Brielle was, without question, the sweetest person that I knew. After six years of friendship, I was still amazed that she maintained such kindness. But I often found myself wondering if she understood just how hard life could be.

We never discussed incidents like what happened this morning. Times when she could hear me burst out onto the balcony before the sun was up, gasping for air as if I had been submerged underwater. Our interactions were lighthearted and surface level, and I preferred to keep them that way.

"Hey, Mai! Brie!" a familiar voice called from behind us.

We both turned to see Zander approaching. With his long stride, it was only a few moments before he fell into step with us.

I bit my lip. Something about the way Zander shortened my name had always irked me. I liked the name Maila well enough, but every time he called me Mai, I couldn't help but think of the word "My" and feel like there was something too intimate in it.

And anyway, Zander lived on the tenth floor—what was he doing on the seventh? Was he purposely trying to run into us?

"How are you ladies doing today?" he asked.

Much like Brielle and her trademark braid, Zander's appearance didn't change much from day to day. As an Enforcer, he was required to keep his sandy hair close-cropped and his face clean-shaven. His navy-blue uniform was equally well-maintained, without so much as a stray thread, much less a wrinkle or a stain.

"We're doing fine," Brielle replied brightly. Her delicate skin had begun to turn a flattering shade of pink, like it always did when Zander was around. "How about you?"

"Great, now that I'm walking with the two of you," he replied. Even though he was only joking, a mockery of being smooth, it still had the desired effect. Brielle's blush deepened. "How about you?" he continued, giving me a playful nudge. Since we were still in the living quarters, he was allowed to be a little more relaxed and informal.

"Can't complain." When my gaze drifted to his, our eyes locked.

I wasn't thrilled to see him this morning. But I would also be lying if I said my cheeks didn't heat a bit too when he stared a beat longer than he should have.

"It's so nice outside," Zander said after a moment. "Perfect weather."

He wasn't looking out the windows. His eyes were still fixed on me.

"I might take lunch on the deck," he continued, a hopeful suggestion in his voice.

I turned to look at the approaching wave of people at the other end of the hall, getting ready to converge with us as we all headed down the central staircase. Maybe it was immature, but I pretended something there had caught my attention.

But thankfully for Zander, he still got a bite from Brielle.

"We take lunch there every day. You should join us." Both her braid and ankle-length skirt bounced as she twisted to face him more fully. "Unless you're having lunch with Trena."

She tucked a stray strand of hair behind her ear, her tell for when she was nervous.

"Oh, no. Definitely not." Zander cleared his throat. "We went out a few times, and it was fun. But Trena and I are better off as friends."

I could almost feel Brielle's sigh of relief beside me.

"She's an amazing woman, though," he added enthusiastically.

Typical Zander. Even if Trena were the most disliked person in the Knowledge Center, he would never speak an ill word about her. Or anyone, for that matter.

"She is!" Brielle agreed. She and Zander continued to make small talk while we descended the staircase to the first floor.

The living quarters housed almost everyone whose work assignments were in the Knowledge Center, plus the Enforcers. Our apartments and other shared living spaces were located here, along with a small market that stocked essentials like nonperishable food, basic first aid items, and toiletries.

I had heard that prior to The Awakening, the building used to be a hotel. It was an interesting concept...a dwelling that you only lived in for a night or two at a time.

From the main building, many other buildings branched out, forming a self-sufficient network that was practically its own world. Considering that all our needs were provided for here, and our lack of free time due to the rigor of Knowledge Center work assignments, Zander and his fellow Enforcers were typically the only ones who even bothered venturing out into the heart of Cyllene.

It was ironic, really. We were an isolated city within an isolated city.

"So maybe I'll see you two at lunch then," Zander said as we reached the foot of the stairs. He continued walking backwards toward the heavy glass doors that led into the city.

"Yes! See you then!" Brielle waved as we turned to head in the opposite direction, toward the Knowledge Center.

A few seconds passed. I realized they were waiting on me to say something. "See you then," I echoed. Awkwardly.

As soon as we were out of earshot, Brielle grabbed my arm with a strength that could only come from endless hours of kneading dough. "Maila Gray!" she half-scolded, half-whined. She only used my full name when she meant business. "When are you going to just accept that he likes you?"

"He doesn't like me," I said lamely. He did, and we both knew it.

I gave her a sheepish look. Then we dissolved into laughter.

"What are you so afraid of?" Brielle demanded between giggles as we stepped through the back entrance of the living quarters and into the courtyard.

The Knowledge Center loomed roughly half a mile ahead, beyond immaculately maintained gardens. Every mass of magenta bougainvillea, every smattering of Blue Daze, every cluster of bubblegum pink pentas were meticulously tended to by the Wildlife Preservation department.

"I don't know," I answered honestly. The sweet scent of the flowers filled my nostrils, mingling with the salt air.

The salt from an ocean that we weren't allowed to see.

Thank goodness I had my books. I sometimes wondered what the general public imagined when they heard of this mysterious ocean that lurked beyond our walls. Then again, maybe it took a lifetime staring at old photos in books to make a person even care about such a thing.

"Don't you think he's just…painfully handsome?"

I laughed again at Brielle's wistful sigh. "Of course I do."

But I didn't, and that was the problem. Handsome? Absolutely. *Painfully* handsome? Not so much. Not to me, anyway.

My logical mind could look at Zander and appreciate all the things that made him nice to look at. But the girl who had grown up with Irene and her books of fairytales wanted more than "nice to look at."

I didn't ache for Zander. And I wanted someone who made me ache for them, in more ways than one.

"Is he not your type?" Brielle pressed.

I shrugged. "I don't think I've ever really had a type. It's not like we have a lot of options here."

Brielle scoffed. "You need to start living in the real world, Maila! Even if we were born hundreds of years ago, before The Awakening, it's not like all the men on the planet would be lining up for you to take your pick. All those stories you read mess with your head."

She was probably right. Again.

"Eventually Zander's going to get bored of pining for you, and some other woman is going to lock him down. And with any luck, it will be me." She sighed again.

I could certainly picture Zander walking hand in hand with Brielle, like two beacons of warmth and light that were always meant to find one another. I knew that deep down, it hurt Brielle that Zander had never considered her in that way.

"He doesn't like me like that, though." It was as if she read my thoughts. "He's asked out just about every single woman in the Knowledge Center. Including Trena now, apparently. But I think he must see me like a sister."

"I actually hadn't heard about the Trena thing until you mentioned it earlier."

"I know you didn't." Her smile was smug. We were at the front doors of the Knowledge Center now, and I held the door for her as we walked inside. "I have to keep track of these things for you since you refuse."

"Thanks," I said, my voice thick with sarcasm. "I don't know what I would do without you to keep me up to speed. It's a shame Cyllene doesn't have gossip magazines like the old ones in the Library. That could have been your work assignment instead."

"Absolutely!" Brielle exclaimed, so animated that her braid flipped around and dropped over her chest. "Who truly needs my cooking when you have my juicy gossip to sustain you?"

We paused in the main hall. The Library was on the right-hand side of the compound, the Culinary Preservation department to the left.

"Well," I said after a moment. "I guess I'll see you and Zander at lunch then."

I took a step toward the Library. But just like earlier on the balcony, I suddenly had a strange urge to turn back around.

I stared through the glass doors at the courtyard and the path we had just walked. I scanned the faces of the people passing through the doors, headed to their work assignments.

Some were waving as they parted ways. Others were walking by themselves, a few at a quick pace that told me they were running late. No one was looking at me.

"Is everything okay?" Brielle asked, and it took me a second to process that she was still standing there.

"Oh, yeah, sorry," I said with a dismissive wave of my hand.

"Are you sure? You looked a little pale earlier. When we first met up, I mean."

Her hazel eyes were full of concern as she searched my face. All the lingering humor and cheer from our conversation about Zander was gone, replaced with something more serious.

I couldn't remember the last time she had looked at me that earnestly. As if for once, her walls were truly down, and she was ready to tackle whatever I threw at her.

Somewhere far away, a little voice told me that I didn't deserve a friend like her.

"I didn't sleep well for some reason. But I'm fine. I'll probably just take a long nap after work." I instantly hated myself for the lie. But I hoped she would accept it and not push any further.

She stared at me for a few seconds more.

"Got it," she said finally, and a wave of guilt and relief washed over me. "Someone was being super noisy on my floor last night, so I can relate. See you at lunch!"

"See you at lunch," I echoed.

She hurried off to the kitchen, and I headed for the Library.

This time, although I didn't turn around, I was certain that someone's eyes were boring holes in my back as I walked away.

This was my happy place.

Breathing in that comforting scent of paper. Feeling the rays of sunshine gently warm my skin as they poured through the windows on the sixth floor. Knowing that with only a handful of us assigned to the Library, I was probably the only person even on this floor at the moment. If there was anywhere that felt like home to me, this was surely it.

The Library was safe. It was silent. It existed outside of the day-to-day, outside of the Knowledge Center and Cyllene. It existed outside of the nightmares that plagued me, and the events that caused them.

As I sat tucked into an overstuffed armchair, alternately leafing through the stack of books on the wooden end table beside me and gazing at the view of the courtyard below, I wished for the millionth time that I could always be here.

It was normal in Cyllene for The Council to choose your work assignment for you. On a citizen's thirteenth birthday, they were told where their assignment would be, and what specifically they would be doing within that department. However, The Council was proud of the fact that in this process, they "took each individual's interests and strengths into consideration." Hopefully, a person would be pleased with their assignment, considering they would be spending most every day of their life there.

My situation was rare in that I not only began my work assignment at ten years old, but also got to choose where I worked. The understanding was that I would be provided with work that I found meaningful and the basic necessities I needed to survive, as long as I kept my mouth shut about what happened to Irene and to our home.

The story told to our fellow citizens was that Irene had tragically perished in a grease fire that incinerated our home. An unfortunate accident.

Except in a Post-Awakening world where magic was rampant outside the safety of Cyllene's walls, you could never be too careful. Instead of pitying the orphaned girl who had lost her only remaining relative, the people of Cyllene saw two Enforcer parents killed years ago in the line of duty, and an Enforcer sister lost in a freak accident, and drew their own conclusions.

My personal favorite rumor was—that an enchantress cursed our family during one of my parents' team's supply runs outside the walls, and we were all doomed to die tragically.

I knew the truth of Irene's death. But both things could be true. Maybe our family *was* cursed.

Rubbing my eyes as though I could physically rub the exhaustion right out of them, I examined the thick book in my hand. A collection of crumpled notes, handwritten musings, and pencil sketches that together made a guide to the habits of marsh wolves. As I skimmed each line, my attention occasionally catching on the drawings of the scaly beasts, I wondered for probably the millionth time what Pre-Awakening people would think of our attempts at books. In comparison to the hundred-year-old hardcover reference guide on normal, Pre-Awakening wolves that I was using for comparison…well, I could compare the two species of wolves all I wanted, but there was no comparison between the books.

After I finished skimming through the guide, I jotted down a few notes in my spiral notebook and moved on to the next one. My assignment today was to gather information on the mating habits of marsh wolves, and I was relishing it.

The only thing better than a day spent reading was a day spent reading about magic.

As my eyes flitted over page after page on the wolves, I questioned if this project was in preparation for one of the

Enforcers' supply runs. It only made sense that they would request this research from the Library because they were venturing beyond the walls and were concerned about a potential marsh wolf encounter.

Just like that, the thought had those dreaded connections snapping into place. Expeditions beyond the wall. Enforcers. My parents. Irene.

A spike of dread tried to claw its way from my stomach into my throat.

I shoved it right back down.

"Fucking typical," I mumbled to myself, forcing a breath out through my nose.

I could tolerate having an Enforcer as a friend. I'd had no choice but to desensitize myself to Zander and his work assignment back when he first started taking an interest in me. But that was the key—desensitization. One reminder of something that didn't quite fit the mold of my usual, Maila-approved ruminations…a thought that slid under the mental armor I'd built at just the right angle that I couldn't defend against it…and the panic was right there. More than eager for the opportunity to tear me to shreds.

I set all the books aside and stared out at the courtyard again. As I tried to regain control of my own brain, I felt the urge to stretch. No, not just to stretch. To take a lap around the sixth floor, to get some of that anxious energy out. Weaving through aisle after aisle of books and allowing myself to imagine that I was the only one in the entire Library, the only one in the world even, was something that often helped me to clear my head.

But I stayed glued to my chair, watching people strolling through the gardens below.

The Knowledge Center was created to preserve the knowledge of humankind. The Council felt it was crucial for us to protect what our ancestors had worked so tirelessly to compile over millennia, encouraging all of us not to lose hope in the fate of the world. One day, they assured us, we would return to life as it once was, and humankind would continue making scientific, technological, and artistic advancements that would carry us into a future that was beyond imagination. Brielle always said that she felt the weight of that responsibility every time she stepped into the kitchen in the Culinary Preservation department. I suppose I typically felt it, too. But as I wrangled my panic into submission for the second time that day, what I felt more than anything was deeply tired.

Tired of dread. Tired of memories. Tired of everything. Tired of it all.

I continued to stare out the window until the occasional person meandering through the gardens became several people, then pairs walking together, then groups with reusable bags and containers in hand. It was nearly lunchtime.

I forced myself to stretch my arms and legs, willing the dull soreness from sitting in the same position too long to dissipate. I wondered if Brielle and Zander were already out on the deck off the Knowledge Center kitchen, waiting on me. If I didn't arrive soon, Brielle would come looking for me.

I reluctantly vacated my spot in the armchair, steeling myself to face the world again.

Later that night, I savored the feeling of my cotton sheets against my skin, grateful to be in bed. In spite of the nightmares, my bed was still my other safe place. On nights when the nightmares stayed away, sleep was my escape.

I curled up on my side, pulling the sheets and comforter partway over my face and snuggling deeper into my pillow. Through the glass door to the balcony, I watched from under drooping eyelids as the lights from candles and lanterns began to blink out in the city below, its inhabitants climbing into their beds for the night as well.

My mind drifted back to lunch with Brielle and Zander.

On top of our assigned lunch from Culinary Preservation, we had snacked on more of Brielle's banana bread, earning us some jealous glances from the people sitting around us. Brielle's navy blue Culinary Preservation department apron was, as always, the only thing that deterred them from questioning us.

It was ironic, really, that Brielle's work assignment seemed to afford her that respect. Even if I'd had a uniform that signaled my role in the Library—and therefore, my unrestricted access to some of the most crucial information for keeping our city afloat—something told me I'd still be treated like an outcast and loner.

After Brielle, my thoughts moved to Zander. Having just finished a morning patrol of the city, his skin was coated in a glistening layer of sweat. His hair, perfectly styled at the start of the day, was slightly mussed. And his face, already tan from time spent outdoors, had a fresh pink glow to it. In between bites of sandwich and conversation with Brielle, he had noticed me noticing all of this.

He had looked at me then with an intensity that made me set down my own sandwich. Not hungry anymore.

Now lying in bed, with that memory replaying in my mind, I could feel heat flooding me again. I let out an exasperated sigh and flipped onto my back, flinging my arms over my face as though they could protect me from my own thoughts.

It was always at night, wasn't it? When the loneliness would creep in and start screwing with my thoughts.

A soft thud sounded nearby, yanking me out of my own head so fast that I could almost feel the physical sensation of whiplash.

I sat up. My heart was still racing, but for an entirely different reason.

On the other side of the glass door, there was a dark shape.

A person.

A roaring erupted in my ears.

A person. There was a person on my balcony.

Adrenaline and fear exploded through me at the same time. I needed to leap out of bed, to run, to grab something to use as a weapon, to call for help. I could fight the person, or run from them, or bargain with them, or…was there even anything in my apartment that they would want? It could only be me, right?

I heard the lock click. I should have been more surprised that it was being unlocked from the outside. But that was the kind of luck I had, wasn't it?

The figure stepped into the room. I sat in my bed, frozen with terror. My lungs were too tight to breathe.

The figure took a few steps toward me, stopping a foot away. A voice rang out in the darkness.

"Get up."

CHAPTER TWO

The voice sounded like it belonged to a female. It was deep, and there was something melodic in it. But above all, it was commanding.

I did as it ordered and scrambled out of bed.

The figure spoke again. "Are you listening?"

I wasn't sure my voice would work. "Yes," I managed to choke out.

"Good. I'm not here to hurt you, but I will if I have to. There's something that I need from you, and it involves us having a calm, civil conversation. Are you following me so far?"

"Yes," I repeated.

"Obviously, it would be ideal that we continue this conversation in the darkness, to conceal my identity. But there are some things I need to show you, so that isn't an option. Are the candles on your desk the only means you have for light?"

"Yes."

Most Cyllene citizens used lanterns. But even after losing my home to fire, I still preferred candles. They reminded me of how Irene and I would read by candlelight every night before bed. She was always bringing home new books, and as far back as I could remember, I understood they were something secret and special and forbidden. I knew better than to ask how she came to be in possession of them.

I tried to visualize that I was back with Irene on one of those nights, curled up under our comforter with a tattered paperback. It seemed as good a memory as any to be my final one, fresh in my mind when this woman killed me.

"I'm going to light the candles," the woman continued. "But I need you to understand that trying to remember my face to identify me later is only going to backfire on you. As I said, I don't want to hurt you, but I will if I have to. If you tell your Enforcers anything that happened here tonight, including what I look like, myself or one of my partners will come right back here, and we will not hesitate to kill you. Do you understand me?"

As terrified as I was, my thoughts still snagged on her choice of words—"your" Enforcers. What did she mean by that?

I wasn't about to question her. "Yes."

At that, the woman stalked over to my desk, yanked a match out of its box, and began lighting the candles.

With each flame that flickered to life, I began to get an idea of what she looked like.

She appeared to be in her early twenties and was tall for a woman. Her toned arms and legs looked like they had carried her through many years of physical exertion. She was wearing a green tank top and tan cargo shorts, both of which were faded and rumpled. Her ankle-high boots had a slight heel on them, adding to her height. Her raven black hair was gathered into many braids, which in turn were gathered into one thick ponytail that hung down her back. Her rich brown skin was nearly the same shade as her eyes, which regarded me impassively. Although her clothes had seen better days, her face had the glow of health and vitality that comes from time spent in sunshine and fresh air.

"Sit down," she ordered, pointing to my desk chair. "And I'll show you what I need your assistance with."

I did as she instructed.

"Okay," she began as she slid a faded blue backpack off her shoulders. "I'm going to show you a map." She cleared her throat. "I apologize in advance for how rudimentary it is."

The woman pulled a giant sheet of paper out of the main pocket. It had been folded and crumpled in several different ways in order to make it fit. She tried to spread it out in front of me, but all the creases and wrinkles prevented it from lying flat. She sighed.

"While I'm straightening this out," she continued as she tried again to smooth it out. "Go ahead and tell me what you know about marsh wolves. And how to take down a pack of them."

A long silence followed.

"I'm sorry…what?" The first words I'd said other than "yes."

"Marsh wolves," she repeated. "Tell me what you know about how to take down a marsh wolf pack."

The terror I had been feeling dissipated for a moment, replaced by utter confusion. "I don't understand. Is this related to my research assignment?"

"No." Her tone made it clear that no further explanation would be given.

I was pushing my luck, but I couldn't help myself. "The nearest marsh wolf pack is at least twenty miles from here," I said. "Has there been a recent sighting?"

The woman looked like she was considering how she wanted to respond when there was another thud on the balcony. I jumped at the sound. She just narrowed her eyes.

"You've got to be kidding me," she muttered, stalking to the door. She reached to open it, but the person on the other side opened it first and brushed past her.

At first glance, I saw it was a man wearing all black—a loose black T-shirt, black jeans, and black boots. Like the woman, he was somewhere in his early twenties and had a tall, athletic build. But his skin, while having something of a healthy glow, was pale. His hair—also black—was short, but had a tousled look to it, with strands hanging over his brow and past his ears.

Then he turned to face me.

He had high cheekbones and full lips, with thick, dark lashes that were the perfect complement to his inky hair. And all of that came together like a perfect picture frame to accentuate the most striking eyes I had ever seen.

The irises were silver. Not pale blue, or even a shade of blue that took on a silvery hue, but pure, metallic silver. The candlelight reflected off them as if they were solid chrome.

He smiled at me. A lazy half-smile that somehow made his face even more spectacular.

"Ugh. Kill me," the woman spat, snapping me out of my trance.

"Aw, you're no fun," the man said to her, still not taking his eyes off me. His voice was low and deep.

"Kieran is the most beautiful man in the world!" the woman exclaimed, throwing her hands up in the air. "He amazes us all daily with his beauty." She turned to me. "Have you beheld his majestic face? Do you want to rip his clothes off and make sweet love to him?"

I gaped at her.

"I'll take that as a yes," she said decisively. "Unfortunately, she has more important things to do right now. So get the hell out and go keep watch."

I couldn't even begin to know what to say.

The man, who I now understand to be Kieran, winced. "She knows my name now. I think you just broke one of the most important rules of our mission, *Nyathera*." He said the last part with emphasis.

The woman— Nyathera?—gave him one of the most terrifying expressions I've ever seen. If looks could kill, he would have been dead a thousand times over.

"Don't worry, Kieran," she said calmly. "It doesn't matter that she knows your name. Because when we get back, I'm going to kill you myself."

They stared each other down.

I sat there wordlessly.

Nyathera was the first to look away, shaking her head. She walked back to me and went back to wrangling with the map.

Kieran's eyes flicked to mine. He grinned.

"If you're going to tell your Enforcers about me," Nyathera said tightly. "Tell them my name is *Nya*. I don't answer to Nyathera."

There was a beat of silence. I glanced over to find that she was staring at me, waiting for confirmation.

"Okay," I blurted out.

"Anyway," Nya continued. "The marsh wolves."

The map was still wrinkled, but I could make out crudely drawn shapes of trees, wavy lines for water, and squiggles that I assumed represented other plant life. There were gray smudges where someone had sketched and erased lines several times. In the right-hand corner, there was a lumpy blob with some lines drawn through it. Another tree? A bush that was the size of a tree?

No, I realized upon closer inspection. It was someone's attempt—a pitiful attempt, unfortunately—at mapping out the interior of a cave.

Everything suddenly clicked into place.

"You guys aren't from here," I said quietly. "You're from outside the walls. Strangers."

I slowly looked up at them. Kieran had moved to stand next to Nya, and they were both regarding me with unreadable expressions.

Then they burst out laughing.

"'Strangers?'" Nya wiped a tear from her eye. "Is that what they're calling us now?"

Kieran shrugged. "Apparently so."

"Sorry if I offended you," I said quickly.

"You didn't." Nya waved her hand dismissively. "But yes, you're correct. We don't live here in the city, and that's the absolute last thing"—here she shot a look at Kieran—"that we're revealing about ourselves tonight.

Now, since Kieran has decided he's not going to keep watch, we're in even more of a time crunch. I'm going to request one more time that you tell us how to take down this pack of marsh wolves, and the next thing out of your mouth had better be an answer."

All traces of laughter were gone. Kieran's expression returned to being unreadable.

"Okay," I said, looking back at the map. I went to flatten a crumpled edge and realized my hands were slick with sweat.

I took a deep breath and let it out slowly. I just needed to pretend that this was a Knowledge Center request. Like it was a part of the marsh wolf assignment I was working on.

In fact, regardless of what Nya said, that *had* to have been why they were here. They knew, somehow, what my work assignment was. The kind of information I had access to.

"What kind of weapons do you have at your disposal?" I asked in my work voice. I could do this. I could compartmentalize. This was just another job.

"We can't answer that," Nya responded quietly.

"Then what is the purpose of this endeavor?"

"We can't answer that, either."

I blinked. "How am I supposed to help you if I can't know any details?"

Nya and Kieran exchanged a look.

"How about this?" Kieran said after a moment, as Nya eyed him warily. "We need to take down this marsh wolf pack. But we need to kill them in the least messy way possible, leaving their bodies mostly intact."

I considered his words.

"Got it," I said finally. "You need their pelts."

Nya huffed and leaned against the wall. Her reaction was the confirmation I needed.

"Their meat has an unpleasant taste," I explained as I studied the map some more. "So it only makes sense that you need their pelts."

Silence.

"The problem is," I continued. "Unless something has changed in the last six months, the pack local to this area has gotten out of control. At last count, there were upwards of thirty wolves sharing that den." I scanned the lines of water. "Assuming this is the Eridanus Marsh. It is, right?"

Nya nodded. Her full lips were pressed into a thin line.

"The marsh wolves are at the top of the food chain in this area. There's nothing out there keeping them in check. Again, unless something has changed. Magic makes things unpredictable." I paused. "Have you gone up against them before?"

"Yes," Nya replied.

Kieran added, "It didn't go well."

"It would really help if I knew what weapons you had available to you," I repeated, and was met once again with silence. "But I guess, not knowing, I would start by recommending that you catch them in the middle of a hunt. Marsh wolves typically hunt at night, and even though they're pretty organized about it, they'd still be relatively distracted. If you can take them by surprise, that will give you a small advantage."

I pulled out my desk drawer and grabbed a pencil. I also grabbed a sheet of paper, unsure if I should mark on their map.

I made a quick sketch of a marsh wolf. The powerful body with rough, scaly skin. The long jaw with intimidatingly large teeth. The massive paws with claws that arced upward before digging into the ground in sharp points. Its eyes and ears were unremarkable, but as intimidating as all of its other physical attributes were, that wasn't much comfort. I added a few scruffy lines here and there, to represent the smatterings of waterproof fur that stuck out in certain spots against the scales. Around the face, on the back of the legs, a bit on the stomach. And of course, the tail.

"The weakest spots on a marsh wolf are the furry spots," I explained, using my pencil to point to each in turn. "That's not to say that you can't puncture the scales. But depending on what kind of weapons you're using, you may not have anything sharp enough. Going for the face is risky because their reaction time is already quick as it is, even without them seeing you coming. And their bite, as you probably know, is deadly. There are three thousand pounds of force behind it."

Nya made a noise in the back of her throat, sounding equally impressed and intimidated.

"Honestly," I said, playing out the potential confrontation in my mind. "I think your best bet is to observe them for a while and get a good understanding of their hunting patterns. Once you know where they tend to go and how often, you can set a trap of some kind. Again, something that goes for the face would be most effective in killing them instantly, but would be easiest for them to dodge, and therefore most risky. I would recommend something that injures or snares their legs."

I glanced at Nya and Kieran, and they were both nodding, following my train of thought.

"Depending on how many people you have to help with this"—I assumed they weren't going to share that, either—"you may have to do this in parts. If you ensnare, let's say, five wolves at once, that still leaves fifteen to twenty wolves that you have to face. Assuming a handful have stayed back to guard the lair. You could ensnare a few at a time, hang back and wait for the rest of the pack to leave them to their fate, and then move in and finish the kill. It would take some creativity, especially once they start to catch on that you're hunting them. But it's probably the safest approach if you're trying to minimize your casualties."

I returned to the map and scanned the waterways that had been sketched through the marsh. I found a spot where several intersected and gestured to it.

"A lot of fish and other prey that the marsh wolves feast on tend to gather at intersections like this. I would be willing to bet that this spot is part of the wolves' hunting rotation. It would be a good place to start when looking for where to lay the trap."

Kieran let out what sounded like an incredulous laugh. "You know all of this from books?"

That confirmed it, then. No one but the Library researchers and temporary, permitted visitors had access to Cyllene's books. They knew about my work assignment.

"I have nothing else to do but read," I responded. It seemed like a safe enough answer. And it was true.

Another thought occurred to me.

"It should go without saying, though," I said. "To not, under any circumstances, have a physical confrontation with the marsh wolves in the water. Laying traps in the water is fine, but don't try to fight them there. If all else fails, confront them on land."

Nya and Kieran were quiet. Almost as if they were hesitating.

Eventually, Nya tilted her head to the side. "Why don't we want to confront them in the water?"

"Marsh wolves are dangerous on land," I began. "But in the water, there's no contest. Even though they get by just fine on dry land and even make their lairs above water, they also have all the key characteristics of a creature that lives exclusively in the water. When necessary, they can swim at speeds of up to thirty miles per hour. They can stay submerged underwater for twenty minutes at a time. And most terrifying of all, they have the ability to completely disappear in murky water. Even water that's relatively shallow. Since they stand as tall as a human if up on their hind legs and are hard to miss while on land, we assume the disappearing underwater part is aided by magic."

Nya crossed her arms. "Makes sense."

I sat back in my chair. "I don't know if I'm helping much. I assume a lot of this is stuff that you already knew, especially if you've confronted them before. And I mean… you see creatures like this a lot, right? Out there?"

Nya's brown eyes narrowed. "We get gored, mutilated, and sometimes eaten by creatures like this a lot, if that's what you mean."

Her words were like a slap across the face. These people were Strangers, and they were intruders in my home. But that had nothing to do with why I suddenly couldn't make eye contact with them. I felt…ashamed.

"Hey," Kieran said, his rumbling voice sounding almost gentle. "We appreciate the help. To answer your question—no, most of the information you just shared isn't stuff we already knew. When you're trying to survive out there, you don't have time to do an in-depth study of the behavior of a marsh wolf." His expression was grim. "You don't have time to calculate how fast they swim, or observe them enough to know that they can disappear even when the water's shallow. You just see a friend fall into water that seemed clear a second before, and they get dragged under before you even realize what's happened."

"Kieran." Nya's voice was low. A warning.

Kieran glanced at Nya, and his mouth quirked up into that half-smile again. His gaze shifted back to me.

"You have beautiful eyes," he said quietly. "Have you ever noticed that the shade of green changes slightly with your mood?"

I hadn't. I also wasn't expecting this change in conversation.

"They were clear and light when you were in the zone, telling us about the marsh wolves. But they got darker after Nya made you feel bad."

"I didn't 'make her feel bad,' I just said the truth," Nya mumbled.

I swallowed. "Your eyes," I said nervously. "Are the ones that are really exceptional. Did one of your parents have eyes that unusual color?"

Kieran's smirk turned into a broad grin, like I had said something funny but wasn't in on the joke. "Yes," he said, crouching down so his face was only inches away from mine. "One of my parents did."

Up close, I could see his eyes even more clearly than before. They were still that bright silver, but they also took in every color around them. Reflections of the flickering candlelight, myself, Nya, the slight glow of moonlight peeking through the window above me, and even the darkness itself danced in them.

They were utterly mesmerizing.

Nya made a gagging noise. "And on that note," she said, jerking Kieran up by the arm. She snatched the map off the desk, stuffed it unceremoniously into the backpack, and stalked toward the balcony. "I think we have what we need. Like Kieran said, we appreciate your help."

She yanked open the door and stepped outside. It was a humid night, and warm air seeped into the room.

"Wait," I found myself saying. "I still don't understand. Why did you come to me for this? How did you even get into Cyllene?"

Kieran gave something between a salute and a wave, then followed Nya out onto the balcony.

I stood up from the desk and walked to the door, which they were at least polite enough to close behind them. I peered through the glass.

They were gone.

CHAPTER THREE

I was useless at work the next day.

Naturally, I had spent the rest of the night and into the early hours of the morning sitting motionless on the edge of my bed. Head spinning.

Had all of that really just happened to me? Who were Nya and Kieran? Were they truly from Outside? And most importantly, why of all people did they seek *me* out?

Sure, I was knowledgeable about a lot of things from years spent working in the Library, and had access to information that everyday citizens of Cyllene didn't. They clearly knew that. But considering my unusual history and my tendency to spend every moment that I wasn't eating or sleeping holed up in the Library, I wasn't well-liked or even well-known in the Knowledge Center community. And even if, for the sake of argument, the Strangers had talked to someone like Brielle or Zander, they wouldn't have known enough about the specifics of my job to recommend me as an expert on marsh wolves.

I turned the encounter over and over in my head until the sky was gray with the first light of morning. By that time, my head ached, my mouth was dry, and my stomach gurgled with hunger. I had folded my hair into a braid, dressed in my usual tunic, loose pants, and sandals, and headed out the door earlier than was necessary. Even though it gave me a pang of guilt, I had had too much on my mind to wait to walk with Brielle.

Now I sat in one of the Library's plush chairs, this time on the second floor, with yet another stack of books in front of me. These were books about love, and the genres were varied. With the goal of finding meaningful passages for a workshop on love and romance that the Human Interest department was putting together—the not-so-discreet purpose of which was to encourage all of us to pop out babies and keep population growth steady—I had grabbed everything from poetry to self-help books. And of course, novels that featured images of men and women on the covers in various states of undress.

One cover consisted of only an attractive man, staring intently into the reader's eyes. Clearly, his seductive gaze alone was supposed to motivate someone to pick up the book and start reading.

The memory of Kieran's eyes, so close to mine as he crouched beside my desk, flashed into my mind. It wasn't possible for a human to have eyes like that, was it?

Something tugged at my brain. Something else I had seen before. No, something I had read. Or perhaps it was both—something I had read, but with an illustration that reminded me of Kieran's eyes.

Like a flower unfurling its petals, the memory opened up to me a bit more.

It was something I had read once in the basement.

I stared out the window at the courtyard but saw nothing. I would find Cato after lunch and see if we had any pending research requests that involved the basement. Once I was down there, I was going to find that book.

I told myself my curiosity about the origin of that strange silver hue was the only reason why I had thought of Kieran's eyes.

"Where were you this morning?" Brielle asked as she cut into the charred slab on her plate.

Today's assigned lunch of smoked meat and potatoes felt heavy on a day when the air was thick and the temperature high. We were sitting at our usual table on the deck off the Culinary Preservation kitchen, and sweat was already beginning to trickle down the back of my neck.

"Sorry," I replied around my own bite. "I had to get to the Library early to get a head start on a project."

Nya had been clear about the consequences if I told anyone about her and Kieran's visit. If only she knew that she had nothing to worry about. I still allowed my best friend to believe that my father and sister had died in a house fire. It seemed I was too much of a coward to be truthful about anything in my life.

"Where's Zander today?" I asked to change the subject.

"I'm not sure. I saw him this morning, but only at a distance." Brielle leaned in and added conspiratorially, "He's not as eager to walk together when it's just me and him."

I made a face at her and continued eating. She just grinned in return.

Above us, thunderheads were moving in, casting a shadow over everyone on the deck. Thunderstorms were frequent in Cyllene at that time of year, in that space between spring and summer. Normally I didn't pay much attention other than to praise myself for remembering— or curse myself for forgetting—an umbrella. But today as my mind wandered, I thought about how Nya and Kieran would fare during the storm. Did they have adequate shelter?

My stomach clenched.

They wouldn't try to take on the marsh wolf pack today, right? They had seemed to be listening closely the night before. Surely, they wouldn't skip the step of surveilling the marsh wolves for a while first before taking any action. And I had put a lot of emphasis on not confronting them in the water. They had to know that in the rain, when visibility is poor and the marsh is likely to flood, they wouldn't stand a chance.

Right?

"What are you thinking about?" Brielle asked, snapping me out of my ruminations. I looked down at my empty plate and realized just how long I had been silent.

"I was thinking about Zander." For some reason, that was the first lie that came to mind. "Wondering if he's out in the city today, and if he's going to be able to stay dry during the storm that's coming."

Brielle grimaced. "Those are some dark clouds," she agreed emphatically. "But you have to admit, the thought of Zander out there…drenched in the rain…in his Enforcer uniform…it's a pretty nice thought."

The mental image popped into my head before I could stop it. My face gave me away, and Brielle collapsed into giggles.

We stood and carried our trays to the drop-off station near the doors to the kitchen. Brielle would likely be back to clear it later.

"Since you had to go in early, do you have to stay late, too?" Brielle asked. "Or can we walk home together?"

"Let's walk back together."

The genuine happiness in Brielle's answering smile gave me a pang of guilt. She waved and bypassed the main doors to the cafeteria, taking the side door to the kitchen.

Around me, others were hurrying to finish their lunches and get back to their respective work assignments before the rain began. I was anxious to get back to mine, too, but not because of the rain.

I needed to find Cato.

I finally tracked him down on the fifth floor. He was standing next to a cart that was piled high with books. As I got closer, I realized he was shelving them.

"I can do that," I said hurriedly, reaching for a stack.

"Don't worry, I've got this!" he insisted. "Every now and then, I just need a simple task to help me clear my head." He added with a laugh, "Don't take that away from me."

I couldn't help but laugh, too. He just had that effect.

Cato spent most of his time in the Library, but he was the Mentor of the entire Knowledge Center. Which technically meant that he was our leader, but The Council tried to avoid using terms like that. Much less terms like "boss," which were absolutely out of the question.

As Mentor of the Knowledge Center, Cato oversaw the Library, the Culinary Preservation department, the Agricultural Preservation department, the Wildlife Preservation department, and the Human Interest department. Considering the weight of his responsibilities, I often wondered if he himself was a member of The Council. But considering the strict anonymity that The Council maintained, I knew better than to ask.

His head was shaved, his skin a deep umber, and his dark eyes always held a mischievous twinkle. Although he was happily married, there were women in the Knowledge Center who stood up a little straighter and became a little more animated whenever he was around.

To me, though, Cato was a mentor in the truest sense of the word. Sometimes, much like with Brielle and Zander, I wished that I could truly let him in. Just once.

"What's on your mind?" Cato asked as he examined the spine of a novel.

"I was just wondering if we had any outstanding projects that required the basement."

I hoped my voice sounded as nonchalant as I intended. When Cato's eyes cut to mine, I instantly worried that it had not.

"Why?" he asked simply.

Lying to Cato was more nerve-wracking than lying to Brielle. However, I had read once that the most convincing lies were ones that had some truth woven into them.

"The research assignments that I've been working on lately have been a little…straightforward," I began. "It's been a while since I've had the opportunity to work on a more serious project. One that involves a bit more mystery and intrigue."

"Marsh wolves aren't intriguing enough for you?"

I rocked my head from side to side, as if considering. He seemed to buy my indecisiveness.

"We do have a couple meatier assignments in the queue." He found the shelf that he was looking for, tucked the novel into its rightful spot, and continued down the aisle. I trailed behind him. "I can grab you the details on one."

"That would be great!" My enthusiasm was genuine.

He abandoned the cart, and we descended the staircase to the ground level, where his office was located. He unlocked the door, and as I did every time I stepped inside his office, I marveled at how it was like stepping into his mind.

His mahogany desk was piled high with stacks of paper, books of all sizes, and multi-colored folders. The far wall featured a garden window that normally bathed the room in a pleasant glow, but today just looked out on the rain-soaked courtyard. The remaining walls were covered by floor-to-ceiling shelves, which were crammed to capacity with more books and curios.

Somehow, even though there was not a free surface to rest an elbow or write on, there was still an organization to things. A system, as Cato would say.

He unlocked the top drawer of his desk with a click. The neon yellow folder he pulled out was one that I was very familiar with. It was where he kept notes on pending basement-level projects, before they were finished and ready to be filed away. He leafed through a few packets held together by paper clips. Finally, he made an approving sound in the back of his throat as he landed on one that he liked.

"Here," he said, hand outstretched. "Take this one."

I opened the packet and skimmed over the first page. Enforcers who had ventured Outside on reconnaissance had encountered what they described as a "wind" or "breeze." They had thought nothing of it at first. But, in what they estimated was about thirty seconds after the encounter, one of the men had gone mad. Screaming, clawing at his face, lunging at the others…I felt increasingly sick to my stomach as my eyes traveled down the page.

"Not too much for you, I hope?"

When I looked up, Cato was studying me carefully. "Not at all," I assured him. "Gruesome, but…hey, I asked for something more intriguing, right?"

In the silence that followed, Cato crossed his arms and regarded me with a furrowed brow. "Maila," he said after a moment. In my ten years working in the Library, I had rarely heard such a serious tone from him. "Is everything okay?"

"Yes, of course," I said quickly. "Why do you ask?"

"You just seem off today. Don't get me wrong, I'm glad to see you enthusiastic about your work." When I gave him a puzzled look, he clarified, "You always do a great job. You know this Library like the back of your hand. But you tend to keep your head down and do what you're asked. You've handled plenty of projects that had meat to them, but only when I assigned them to you. You've never taken the initiative to ask for one."

I wasn't sure how to respond. What *was* up with me lately? And not in the sense that Cato was referring to, but in the fact that everyone kept questioning me about my feelings. Was I suddenly wearing every emotion on my face?

"I'm not sure," I finally replied. When the crease in his brow deepened, I added, "I'd like to keep learning as much as I can and make myself as valuable to The Council as possible. Maybe hold a position like yours one day."

Once again, I wove some truth into the lie. There wasn't much left that I hoped for in life, but I figured if I still had many years ahead of me and time to fill, becoming the Mentor of the Knowledge Center after Cato was an admirable goal.

He shut the drawer and relocked it, then moved around the desk to make for the door. I turned to follow and almost ran into him as he spun to face me.

"If you ever need someone to talk to, about anything, I'm here. You know that, don't you?"

The sincerity in his voice made my chest tighten. "I do. Thank you, Cato."

He grinned. His teeth were perfectly straight and so white that they almost glowed. He pulled his keyring out of his pocket, slid the key to the basement off of it, and tossed it to me. I almost dropped the packet I was holding to catch it.

"Good! Now get to work."

You would think that the section of the Library that contained our most crucial—and often most frightening—findings on magic would have an air of importance about it. Something that signified its potential to cause mass hysteria in Cyllene if the specifics of what existed just outside the walls was ever released to everyday citizens.

The books on marsh wolves on the sixth floor? Those struck fear in citizens, which reinforced that they should never disobey the law regarding leaving the walls. But they also satisfied some of their curiosity about what lies Outside.

Books on an evil wind that makes you go insane before you even know what's happened? According to The Council, that was the terrifying shit that everyday people didn't need to know.

But considering the gravity of its contents, the basement level was nothing special to look at. Through an unassuming beige door, down a flight of concrete stairs, at the end of an equally bland concrete hallway, was the entrance.

Which, unsurprisingly, was another unassuming beige door.

When I stepped inside, the familiar musty smell filled my nostrils. It was the scent of an obscene amount of paper crammed into a room with limited air flow. And mixed in with that, the damp, earthy scent of mold.

Even without the lantern in my hand, I could have followed the path to the other lanterns, placed strategically around the room, by memory. I clicked on each one and watched as the room began to fill with light.

Much like Cato's office, the basement was encased in wall-to-wall books, except with no window to break it up. The door had the appearance of being crammed in the middle of it all. In the center of the room were four sets of wooden tables and chairs, arranged in a square. On top of each table was a lantern and scrap paper for scribbling notes.

Despite the smell, it was an effective room for perfectly quiet, focused research. Nothing contained in it was archival quality, but we made do with what we had. Those with the expertise to design something on that level for us, with conditions perfect for long-term preservation, had likely all perished since The Awakening. A perfect example, as Cato would say, of why our task to preserve any and all Pre-Awakening knowledge was so crucial.

On the table to the left, in the row closest to the door, sat a massive black binder. So heavy that in a crisis, you could probably use it as a weapon. Inside was an ever-growing index that Cato had created. It acted as a guide to the many shelves, which contained notes, compilations, guides, and drawings. Most of which were compiled in notebooks or stapled together by hand.

A couple books of actual published content could be found in the mix, but they were few and far between. Those had been released by a few fast-acting universities and research groups when The Awakening first hit. Studies that contained initial observations about the strange creatures and phenomena—everyone had resorted to simply calling them "magic" at that point, having no other rational way to explain them—that suddenly appeared in the world seventy years ago.

Magic-wielding beings, seemingly magical occurrences, and magic-ripe locations…despite how drastically the world had changed since The Awakening began, and the countless limitations that cities like Cyllene had to navigate, we had managed to expand on many of those initial observations over the years. Mainly thanks to the Enforcers, since they were the only citizens whose work assignments required them to venture beyond the walls.

And thus—the collection of spiral-bound notebooks and hand-assembled guides.

I sat down and began flipping through Cato's giant index, looking for terms that seemed relevant to the project in my hand. Terms like "wind." When I couldn't find "madness" in the index, I ran through a mental list of synonyms.

I checked again, and was pleased to find an entry for "psychosis."

Once I had a list of ten or so items that referenced those terms, I began scanning the shelves and gathering the corresponding books. Then I plopped back down in the chair, flipped my braid over my shoulder, and got to work.

After two hours and a few more trips to the shelves, I had three full pages of other possible occurrences, similar phenomena, and anything else that seemed relevant.

Was that enough to ward off any suspicion if Cato came down to check on me?

I scanned my notes again.

It was.

With a deep breath and a jolt of anticipation, I returned to the index.

I had been turning the memory of Kieran's silver eyes over and over in my head all day, and my brain had finally offered up a mental image that nearly had my hands trembling. It was a colored drawing of eyes very similar to Kieran's looking out from beneath a dark hood.

My search began with the terms "hoods" (this word was not in the index) and "darkness" (over thirty books referencing this one), as well as "eyes," which I figured would make reference to any creatures or beings with exceptional eyes.

I spent over an hour looking through the corresponding books.

No luck.

Some books were instantly familiar when I glanced at their covers. But once my memory was refreshed of the contents inside, I already knew they didn't contain the drawing.

I rested my elbows on the table in front of me, face in my hands.

I had seen those eyes before. Or at least the closest you could get to recreating them with a set of colored pencils.

Savoring the knowledge that I was truly alone in the basement with no one around to hear me, I threw my head back and let out a growl of frustration.

It was here. I *knew* it was here.

I returned to the index yet again, this time reading every term, one line at a time. It was completely inefficient, I knew. Reading the entire index like this would take hours. But I couldn't think of another option, and I was not giving up.

I made it all the way to the letter M. I was powering through a sickening twist of my stomach at the word "mutilation," remembering a few unfortunate books on that topic, when it hit me.

I flipped furiously until I reached the page with the letter U. And there it was.

"Unexplained."

Technically, everything to do with magic was unexplained in one way or another. But the situations referenced under this label were ones in which we were truly clueless. There were several titles jotted in Cato's handwriting, but I already knew which one I was looking for. I made a mental note of the name and description, then practically ran to the shelf on the far wall.

When I pulled down the small leather journal, my pulse was thundering so loudly that I could feel it in my ears.

Only eighteen pages contained actual content. The rest was blank. The title scribbled onto the front cover in Cato's handwriting read "Matthew's Travel Diary."

According to Cato's notes pasted carefully onto the inside cover, Matthew was a man in his thirties who was alive at the start of The Awakening. He was an avid hiker and nature enthusiast, and in those initial months of Post-Awakening chaos before the walls went up, he decided that he wanted to do something useful. He and his team of ten other men and women bravely set out from the city on foot with the goal of traveling around the continent and documenting their findings on magic.

But only a few short days after Matthew's departure, one of his team members reappeared at the old police station—now Enforcer headquarters—in Cyllene. The man was mute. Eyes glazed. Practically catatonic. He could not speak of what happened to Matthew and the other members of their team.

He was still wearing his backpack, and although it looked as weathered as he did, it provided a few clues. One was on the eighteenth page of Matthew's travel diary.

The last page with content.

I flipped to page eighteen, and my earlier appreciation of being all alone in the basement dissipated. A chill ran down my spine.

No one knew how this man, who lived for only a few weeks more before dying of unknown causes, came to be in possession of Matthew's diary. But on that last page, there was a sketch of a figure in what appeared to be a black cloak. The rough sketch didn't include any details of the body, limbs, or anything that would give a better understanding of the size and shape of this being.

With the exception of the eyes.

The person who made the sketch—assumed to be Matthew—was not a skilled artist. But he had managed to capture the being's piercing stare. Its irises were colored in a blend of gray and metallic silver.

The sketch was captioned:

Saw something like this in the forest tonight. Was standing in clearing, but disappeared under shadow of tree when I approached. Just vanished. Felt like I was being watched after? Can't say for sure.

That was the last entry Matthew made.

I tried to swallow away the growing tightness in my throat.

Nya was human. I felt relatively confident in that. But was Kieran? And if not, what exactly was he? If he wasn't human, wouldn't the wards on the walls have prevented him from entering the city?

I closed the book, hiding those eyes between its covers.

Would I see him again? And if so, how afraid should I be?

CHAPTER FOUR

A week passed. I spent every night tossing and turning, staring at the ceiling or out the balcony door into the early hours of the morning.

Another week passed, and I started to find sleep again. But I still jolted awake at the slightest noise.

By the third week, I was convinced that if Nya and Kieran were going to return, this would be the time. Three weeks was sufficient to surveil the marsh wolves and lay a trap. Then I remembered with dismay that I had told them they may need to lay multiple traps, to whittle away at the pack a few at a time versus taking them on all at once. I kept this thought in mind as it hit the one-month mark.

By five weeks, I was convinced that Nya and Kieran had gotten everything they needed from me. I would never see them again or be able to satisfy my curiosity about why they sought me out.

The days dragged on as they always did. Brielle and I walked to our work assignments every day, ate lunch together, and walked back to our apartments together. We didn't see much of Zander, and eventually Brielle learned through the rumor mill that he was seeing someone. But the relationship was short-lived, and it wasn't long before word around the Knowledge Center—once again, according to Brielle—was that he was single again.

One stormy morning, as Brielle and I were staring out the glass doors of the living quarters, dreading our necessary walk through the courtyard, Zander appeared beside us.

"Well," he said with a sigh. He held up two umbrellas. "I was going to offer these to you ladies, but it's practically raining sideways. I'm not sure what good an umbrella's going to do."

"Oh!" Brielle exclaimed at the sight of him. "That was so thoughtful of you."

He waved away her praise. "It's nothing. I just have a few spare umbrellas and always figure on a day like today, I'm going to run into people who could use them."

I had my compact umbrella tucked away in my bag and knew Brielle did as well. But I also knew she wasn't about to tell Zander that. Not if it meant an opportunity to get her hands on something that belonged to him.

"How have you been, Mai?" Zander asked. Even in the darkness of the storm, his amber eyes were bright. And the shadows cast across his face highlighted his dimples.

"I've been fine. How about you?"

"Eh, could be better." An awkward pause. "I'm sure you two heard that I was seeing someone for a while."

"We did," I agreed, wincing slightly.

The corner of his mouth turned up in a grim smile. "Yeah, it didn't end very well."

"I'm so sorry to hear that," Brielle chimed in. "She'll be hard-pressed to find someone as great as you, Zander. Seriously."

My eyes darted back and forth between the two of them, gauging Zander's response.

He just shrugged and shook his head. Either he really didn't hear her words as anything other than the appreciation of a good friend, or he was making the conscious choice not to hear them as anything more.

"It's not like that," he said. "I was the one who ended it. I thought she was feeling it, too…that we're better off as friends. But I guess I really hurt her."

If it were any other guy telling us this, I would have thought he was boasting about breaking some poor girl's heart. But that wasn't Zander.

He was staring out at the driving rain, absent-mindedly knocking the umbrellas against his leg, his jaw flexed.

"Why did you end it?" I found myself asking.

His eyes shifted back to mine. He let out a long sigh. "I just wasn't feeling it. She's…not the one for me."

"Since we're not heading out into *that* anytime soon," Brielle said abruptly, gesturing to the rain. It was coming down so hard now that in the gardens, only the first row of raised beds was visible. "I'm going to run to the restroom. Be right back."

She touched my arm as she walked away. A touch that conveyed that she didn't have to go to the bathroom that badly. Or at all.

I swallowed.

"So," I said as Brielle's footsteps echoed down the hallway. "Are you going to get in trouble for being late?"

"No, our Mentor will understand," he said with a smile.

My stomach lurched.

I didn't doubt his Mentor would understand. I didn't doubt that he would show that almost fatherly understanding that would make Zander let his guard down. That made a person trust that no matter what, he would always have your back.

I wanted to scream at Zander that he was a fucking fool. The desire was so overpowering, so intense, that I felt my throat start to close.

Breathe.

Focus.

"What about you?" Zander asked, oblivious. "Will Cato expect you to wade through this torrential downpour?"

"No," I managed to get out. I stretched my arms overhead, hoping the movement would disguise the true reason my voice was strained. "Cato will understand."

"Cato's a good guy." Zander had stopped fidgeting with the umbrellas, but was now shifting his weight from foot to foot. "How are things going in the Library, anyway?"

He was reaching for something to talk about. And the fact that we were both aware of it made me feel on edge in an entirely different way. I pretended that I was a magical being and willed Brielle to hurry back.

"Things are fine. Just the usual stuff. Mostly just researching things for other departments."

"Sounds interesting. I wish everyone could check out books from the Library whenever they wanted, like you hear about from the Pre-Awakening days. I'd love to be able to read more."

I nodded sympathetically. I couldn't imagine not being able to read all the books I wanted. But then again, my experiences were a little different, being a reformed rule follower. My memories of reading with Irene—always fiction, always a paperback that was tattered from overuse, and always something that was very much *not* a Council-approved pamphlet—were some of my favorites.

If only she could see all the books that I had access to now.

"It really is a shame," I said. "But I understand the thinking behind it. We have limited copies of each book and no way to replace them."

"Right," he agreed. "Not worth the risk." He had become still for a moment. Somber. But he must have realized we had hit another dead end in our conversation because he started shifting his weight from foot to foot again.

A thought struck me.

"Zander," I began. "Have you ever been Outside?"

He stilled again. Then he looked up at the ceiling, tongue pressed to the inside of his cheek. As if considering how to respond. After a moment, he said simply, "I have, yeah."

"What was it like?" I knew I was pushing a boundary, almost fully crossing it, by asking this.

In Cyllene, the extent of our discussions about the world outside the walls was the conversations that Cato and I had as they related to research projects. It was an unspoken rule that you didn't discuss Outside with fellow citizens, in case your speaking about it manifested some sort of connection between Inside and Outside into existence. A tether that would cause the horrors out there to suddenly take interest in all of us in here and motivate them to disrupt our peaceful existence.

As an Enforcer, Irene had of course been required to go on supply runs Outside. And even in the quiet darkness of our bedroom, before we fell asleep, she wouldn't share what happened there.

Discussing this was ratcheting my heart rate back up. But for some reason, I felt strangely motived to keep going.

Zander sighed through his nose. He turned away from the window to face me fully.

"It was like a jungle," he began slowly. "Everything was overgrown. It felt very…alive. It's hard to explain. We had to wear gas masks, which felt kind of silly because I don't think magic is something you inhale. But then, what do I know? I guess there was some incident recently."

The Enforcer who went mad after experiencing that wind-like phenomenon.

"So this was recent, then?"

I knew as soon as the words came out that I had pushed too far. His eyes searched mine, and I suddenly became aware of how close we were standing to one other.

"Yeah," he said finally. "It was relatively recent."

An uncomfortable silence followed, in which all we could do was stare at one another.

Zander's hair, while Enforcer-short, accentuated his strong jaw and the toned muscles of his neck. And his eyes…well, they may not have been an indicator that he was some terrifying Outside creature. But for a human, they were an interesting shade. This close, I could see the way that caramel and gold feathered out and around his irises, blending into one another.

He broke the silence first. "Mai –"

"Zander!" A male's voice echoed through the high-ceilinged room.

We turned to see several Enforcers clustered near the back of the staircase, grinning with amusement.

"Come on," one of them goaded. "The rain looks like it's letting up, and we're going to make a run for it."

Zander's eyes narrowed, but he was smiling. "Well, guess I've got to go." He held out the umbrellas in a final offer.

"We brought umbrellas. But thanks anyway." I hadn't realized until I opened my mouth to speak that I had been holding my breath.

He waved and headed off in the direction of his fellow Enforcers.

If I were Brielle, I would've taken the opportunity to watch him walk away. Instead, I found my attention drifting back to the window, watching the paths of the raindrops as they raced one another down the glass.

"Well, I tried."

Brielle's voice was so close that I jumped. "Where were you?" I demanded.

"Close enough to see you two gazing into each other's eyes!" she exclaimed, and I clamped a hand over her mouth.

I twisted around and was relieved to find that Zander was already out of earshot, headed toward the main entrance and out into the city. When I pulled my hand back, Brielle continued talking as if nothing had happened. "He was about to ask you out, you know."

"No, I don't 'know.' He could've been about to say anything." I'm not sure why I bothered disagreeing with her. As usual, she was probably right.

"One of these days, Maila," she said in a sing-song voice, wagging her finger at me. She reached in her bag to pull out her umbrella, and I did the same. "You two lovebirds are finally going to get together, and I'm going to take all the credit."

I rolled my eyes and followed her out the door.

She was right, wasn't she? Zander was attracted to me, and I could acknowledge that he was handsome. Considering how much time I had spent alone over the years, I should be jumping at the opportunity for companionship. Not only that, but at twenty years old, the extent of my romantic experience was a fumbling first time with a guy from the Agricultural Preservation department and a brief relationship with a colleague of Brielle's in Culinary Preservation that was equally anticlimactic.

Did reminiscing on those experiences feed my late-night fantasies? No.

But were my experiences pretty standard considering our limited options? Yes.

The fact that I would even think of our choice of partners in Cyllene as being "limited" was a glaring sign of Irene's influence. I should have considered myself fortunate to have someone I found even the slightest bit attractive interested in me.

Rather than dreaming of an all-consuming romance like the stories from Irene's books, I needed to focus on reality. On what—and who—was right in front of me, presenting a perfectly attainable, and probably perfectly pleasant, opportunity for companionship.

As I braced my umbrella against the rain, feeling the mist against my cheek, I wondered why I still couldn't quite convince myself of that.

That evening, Brielle invited me over for dinner at her apartment.

The meal was incredible, as always. Chicken stuffed with ham and goat cheese, which Brielle claimed was the perfect hearty entree for a rainy day. Roasted broccoli, which only Brielle could prepare in such a way that it rivaled the main course. And, keeping with the theme of warmth and comfort, fresh oatmeal cookies for dessert.

The cookies were so rich that I could only eat two before I had to admit defeat.

As I walked down the stairs and back to my place, I marveled again at how fortunate I was to have a friend who had a fully functioning kitchen in her apartment. It wasn't exactly standard, even for someone who worked in Culinary Preservation. But considering how I gorged myself at her table on a regular basis, I wasn't about to question it.

I unlocked my door, stepped inside, and relocked the door behind me. When I turned back around, I noticed immediately an unfamiliar shape in the darkness.

A scream was just rising in my throat when I lifted the lantern I had borrowed from Brielle. I gaped at what it illuminated.

It was Nya. Sitting at my desk. An ankle crossed over a knee.

"Finally!" She threw her head back, braids swishing. She was dressed the same as last time—tank top, tan cargo shorts, and ankle-high boots. The only difference was that her shirt was a faded tangerine instead of green. It was a color that would have looked atrocious on me, but it complemented her dark skin.

The wall to my left was partially obscuring my view of the room. I held my breath as I hurried to the edge of the kitchen.

There he was.

Sprawled across my comforter, arms crossed behind his head, was Kieran. He was dressed the same as last time, except he thankfully had the decency to take off his shoes before climbing on my bed. Due to his height, his black-socked feet nearly hung off the bottom. Plastered across his face, exactly as I remembered it, was that smug smile.

"Welcome home," he said cheerily.

I grinned in spite of myself, glancing between the two of them. "You're back! How did everything go with the marsh wolves?"

They exchanged a look.

"Don't tell me you're actually happy to see us," Nya said slowly, uncrossing her legs and leaning forward.

"I don't know if 'happy' is the word," I said. Although it was, strangely. They didn't need to know that. "But I've been wondering how things turned out for you."

I walked around Nya and began lighting candles. When I was finished, I realized she and Kieran were both staring at me incredulously. Kieran, no longer the picture of relaxation, was sitting up in the middle of the bed.

I almost asked the two of them how they had fared in the rain earlier, which had continued on and off throughout the day. But considering I had spent the day warm and dry in the safety of the Library, something felt wrong about that. I swallowed the question.

Then I remembered what was tucked into my bag. I couldn't pull it out fast enough.

"Here," I said, thrusting the plastic containers into Nya's hands. "I'm sure you're hungry."

I cringed inwardly at my word choice. Of course they were hungry. They lived Outside.

I went to the cabinet where I kept my small stack of plates and pulled out one for each of them. I also grabbed silverware from the drawer and two cloth napkins that I was certain I had never used.

When I returned to where Nya was sitting, she was still staring blankly at the containers. I took them back from her and set them on the desk, pulling the lids off all three. A container for the chicken, a container for the roasted broccoli, and a container of oatmeal cookies. Brielle had loaded me up with leftovers, and I'd never been so thankful for her concern about my eating habits.

I divided everything until two heaping plates sat in front of me. Then I once again shoved the plate of food, silverware, and a napkin into Nya's hands. Then I turned to Kieran, arms extended.

He stared at the plate. After a long moment, he reached out and took it from me.

Nya spoke first.

"We're not hungry," she said. It was clear from her tone that her words were both a statement, and a command directed at Kieran.

Kieran snorted. "Like she believes that."

"Fine. How about 'We're not up for being poisoned today?'"

I glanced between the two of them, horrified. "You think I would try to poison you?"

"We're from the spooky, evil *Outside*," Nya said slowly, as if I was missing something important. "We broke into your home. Again. We're about to insist that you help us. Again. Under threat of…death, I guess."

"You were doing good there until the end," Kieran said with a sympathetic shake of his head.

For the first time since I walked in the door, I allowed myself to really look at his eyes again. They were the same—gray right now, but with that glint of silver where the light hit them—and yet somehow more breathtaking than I remembered.

"I didn't know you two were in my apartment," I pointed out, trying to stay focused. "When would I have had time to poison this food?"

"I don't know," Nya admitted. "But maybe—Seriously, Kieran?!"

Kieran was stuffing his face.

He held the entire piece of chicken up in the air, speared on the end of his fork, as he devoured it. Cheese and creamy sauce dripped on his plate.

"This is better than sex," he sighed, closing his eyes. His mouth was so packed with food that it took me a moment to even process what he had said.

The mental image of him having sex popped into my mind before I could stop it. I turned my gaze to Nya, as if the image was a real thing that I could look away from.

"That's saying a lot for you," she snapped. She was still glaring down at her food.

Something in her expression was like a cold shower, washing away the image of Kieran having sex. And the decidedly less enticing sounds of Kieran inhaling his food, for that matter.

It made something in me crack.

"Nya," I said quietly. "Please trust me. It really is safe to eat. I know you all think you've put me out by showing up at my apartment, scaring me half to death, threatening me, forcing me to help you, and…I mean, that does all sound terrible when you spell it out like that." I swallowed. What *did* it say about me that I wasn't terrified of them? I continued, "But it's really not. I live alone, and things are pretty uneventful. You aren't putting me out as much as you think."

She seemed to consider my words. "How old are you?"

"Twenty."

"Does your family live nearby?"

"No."

"Where are they?"

The answer was on the tip of my tongue. *My mother and father served as Enforcers, and gave up their lives for the good of Cyllene I was three years old. My sister died in a house fire when I was ten.* I opened my mouth.

"My mother and father were Enforcers, and they died in the line of duty when I was three. My sister was executed by The Council, the entity that governs Cyllene."

"The Council executed your sister?" Nya repeated, her eyes widening momentarily. Then she blinked, and whatever I thought I had seen on her face was gone. "So you just, what…live alongside the people who killed your sister? Fear for your life every day?"

There was no judgment in her tone, only genuine curiosity. I think that's why I found myself speaking truthfully again.

"I don't fear for my life, really," I said. "I mean, I guess I must to some extent. I was scared the first time you two showed up here. But aside from that, I don't think I care enough about my life to be that fearful. I just do what I have to do to get by. Put one foot in front of the other, move from one day to the next. Because it's what my sister wanted. It's…it's what she, uh…she—"

It's what Irene begged for, in her last moments. She begged for my life.

The words were stuck in my throat. Every syllable I forced out was released on a wave of white-hot terror, like a faucet that couldn't release water without pushing out dirt and grime from the pipes. I tried to swallow, but the muscles in my neck weren't cooperating.

The clink of Kieran setting down his fork was the only sound in the room. It was shortly followed by the low rumble of his voice. "You don't have to say it," he murmured. "Whatever it is. We get it. Trust me, we get it."

Nya's dark gaze shifted just over my shoulder, and I knew she was exchanging another look with him. When her eyes returned to me, they were full of warmth.

"I'm sorry about your sister," she said finally. "And your parents. All of it."

It took a moment of quiet self-soothing, of reassuring myself that I wasn't going to have to talk about Irene's death after all, before I could find the ability to respond. "Me, too," I said finally. "It's not easy being alone."

"No. It's not." Nya's response was as soft as my own.

She picked up her fork and knife and began to cut into the chicken.

I lowered myself onto the carpet and leaned against the strip of wall between the desk and the balcony door. As my body continued to come down from the panic, the gravity of what I had just shared with two Strangers hung in the room between us. Why did I tell them the truth? Was it a betrayal to Cyllene to share something like that with people from Outside?

These were people whose mere existence disgusted The Council, disgusted Cyllene citizens. Wild, animalistic people, and many of them exiled criminals. As intensely as Cyllene feared magic, the city would celebrate if magical beings actually did the job they had been expected to do and wiped the Strangers out of existence.

Nya and Kieran didn't speak as they polished off everything on their plates. I knew that Nya had to be as hungry as Kieran, but she still cut her food into polite, bite-sized pieces and swallowed each mouthful before moving on to the next.

Kieran continued to cram as much as possible into his mouth at once.

He finished eating first. Then he flopped back on the bed, sighing contentedly, and closed his eyes.

When Nya finished, she grabbed Kieran's empty plate and carried both dishes to the sink. She turned on the faucet to rinse them.

"Just leave them," I called over the running water. "I'll wash them later."

Nya obliged and sat back down at the desk.

"Since you shared something with us," she began carefully. "I'll share with you that we followed your advice, and we got what we needed from the marsh wolf pack. With no losses on our end."

A smile spread across my face.

She added quickly, "Don't make me regret telling you that."

"I won't," I promised. My body felt suddenly light, as if releasing tension that I hadn't even realized had been there. "So what can I help with this time?"

"One second, let me grab the map." Nya reached under the desk and pulled out her same blue backpack. She began digging through it. "I'll go ahead and warn you that this map is as skillfully drawn as the last one."

I chuckled.

While she was doing that, I felt a chill coming from the glass door beside me, creeping in between the shoddy weather stripping. I tried to remember another time when I had had a reason to sit on the carpet, against the wall like this.

I couldn't think of one. I had never had to make space for guests before.

I began to unravel my braid. I ran my hand through the roots a few times, loosening the strands against my scalp, then let the soft waves fall over my shoulders, savoring the warmth.

A rustle on the bed caught my attention.

Kieran's eyes were open now, and he was staring at me.

I was so surprised that I couldn't stop myself from staring back at him.

His eyes narrowed almost imperceptibly, and the corner of his mouth turned up.

Heat flooded my cheeks. Then it proceeded to flood my whole body.

I had tried to write it off as curiosity. As the piqued interest that anyone would have observing someone with such unusual features. But in that moment, I knew it was time to be honest with myself.

I was incredibly attracted to him.

And I suddenly, overwhelmingly, did not want him to know this.

"Your eyes," I blurted out. "I did some research on them."

His smile widened. He rolled lazily onto his side, propping his head on his hand. "You researched me, huh?"

"No," I said quickly. Too quickly.

His eyes were an almost shimmering silver now, dancing with amusement.

"What I mean is that your eyes are very…interesting. And I kept thinking that I had seen eyes like those before, in one of the books in the Library. Turns out, I did."

"Did you?" he asked, his voice dripping with the over-the-top enthusiasm that you might use when speaking to a child.

Annoyance prickled in me at his tone. "I did. Years ago, a citizen of Cyllene saw a being with eyes like yours outside the walls. Right before he and almost everyone in his party disappeared."

"No way."

I don't know what I had expected his response to be. But the sarcasm made me wish I had something to throw at him. I was more than just annoyed now.

"Kieran," Nya said reproachfully. She had the map out and was carefully moving my candles to make room for it on the desk. "You're being rude."

Kieran laughed. A deep, rumbling sound that traveled up from his chest. I wanted to tell him to shut up and never stop. "No, *you're* being rude. Be quiet and let Maila finish telling me about my own family."

In spite of myself, I felt a thrill at the sound of my name on his lips. Of course they both knew my name. How else would they have tracked me down? And yet, it was the first time he had spoken it.

I was aggravated with him, though. More aggravated than I probably should have been. But I couldn't quite place why that was.

"Never mind," I said, standing to go look at the map.

Kieran caught my arm. His hand was warm and rough from what felt like many years' worth of calluses.

"Hey," he said, his already-low voice dropping an octave. The humor had vanished from his face. "I'm not making fun of you. I just hate talking about my family. If you even want to call them that."

"So you really are…" I swallowed reflexively. "Whatever that being was, that that group encountered in the forest. That's what you are? What your family is?"

"I'm half that," he corrected. He sat up and threw his legs over the edge of the bed. He was still holding onto my arm, and I struggled to process his words while every part of my brain zeroed in on that contact. "My mother was human."

A thousand questions boiled up in me all at once. "Your mother married a…" Again, I searched for the right words, not wanting to offend him. "A magical being?"

He laughed. "No, they weren't married." His voice had resumed that patient tone, like he was speaking to a child. "That wouldn't have even been a possibility. My father was absolutely forbidden to marry a human woman. And I doubt he wanted to, anyway. But they did like each other."

His grip on my arm tightened a bit, and his thumb grazed my skin ever so slightly. A movement just subtle enough that Nya, leaned over the map at my desk, didn't take notice of it.

"Apparently," he said with a grin. "My mother couldn't resist my father's eyes."

I tried to swallow, but my throat wouldn't cooperate. I scrambled for something witty to say back. My mind was blank. Apparently my entire body was going to fail me in this moment. To my horror, what suddenly escaped my mouth was, "I think your eyes are really nice."

"I know you do," he said, chuckling softly. His laugh wasn't mean-spirited or poking fun at me this time. It was more like…like we were sharing a private joke.

We were staring at each other again. But this time, the heat that flooded me wasn't from nervousness. And maybe I was just seeing what I wanted to see, but I could have sworn it was matched in his eyes.

The silence was broken by a gagging noise coming from my desk. "I'm going to start requesting that someone else accompany me on these missions," Nya said without looking up.

"You know you don't mean that," Kieran replied, but he still let go of my arm.

Not wanting to continue standing there awkwardly, I resumed walking over to the desk. My head was tilted toward the map, but my eyes were unseeing.

"I do mean it. In fact, maybe I'll bring Xiomara." Nya finally looked up. She was the one smirking now.

"You're no fun, Nya," Kieran sighed. I had my back turned to him, but I could tell he wasn't smiling anymore. There was a soft thump as he flopped back down on the bed.

I wanted to ask who Xiomara was, but something told me I wasn't going to get an answer.

"What we need this time," Nya explained, her voice all business now, "is assistance with raiding a cave devil lair."

I thought at first that I hadn't heard her correctly. "A cave devil lair?"

She nodded, her mouth twisted into a grimace.

"I want to make sure we're talking about the same creatures. As far as our Library is concerned, 'cave devils' are huge, nasty, humanoid beasts who build their dwellings in the sides of rocky hills and mountains."

She nodded again.

My eyes flitted over the map, and this time I actually took in what was before me. Drawings—crudely done, as promised—of trees and other foliage, rocks, something that I took to be dirt paths. And taking up almost the entire top half of the map, a sketch of what looked to be a colossal rock formation, with multiple…holes? Windows? No, doors. Entrances.

"There's a cave devil lair near here?" I couldn't hide the disbelief in my voice. Did The Council know about this? And if so, were they taking any precautions? Sending

Enforcers on a supply run when cave devils had settled in the area was like sending them straight to their deaths.

"It's not that close," Nya reassured me, and I nearly sagged with relief. "But a week's travel on foot will get you there."

That was still closer than I had hoped. I studied the map some more. "So this isn't really a map…but more of a sketch. A true-to-life sketch of the front of their lair."

"Correct."

"And you said 'raid,' so…you're not necessarily trying to kill them this time. You just need something from their stash. Weapons?"

Nya shook her head as if in defeat. "You know what? Sure. We need their weapons. You obviously know too much about all these creatures for us to try to conceal what we're after."

I did know too much about a lot of things. But especially about cave devils. The first time I had to read up on them for a basement-level assignment, the cave devils replaced the humans in my recurring nightmares, making for an especially horrific night's sleep.

It was easy to see why my brain would do such a thing. The cave devils were interchangeable with the human monsters of my memories.

I crossed one arm over my chest and rested my other elbow on it, pressing a finger to my lips. I ran through different scenarios of how this could play out. The scenarios that were the most realistic were all ones that I disliked.

"Cave devils are horrible," I murmured. "We have an account from one of our citizens from around thirty years ago. And accounts from cities that The Council maintains limited communication with."

There were a few other cities besides Cyllene that were still holding on Post-Awakening. But they were few and far between. Beyond the fact that they were out there, and The Council oversaw some minor trade and knowledge exchange with them, I couldn't have said what they were like or how they compared to Cyllene.

"Cave devils are carnivores, yes…just like the marsh wolves. But they engage in surplus killing, which means they don't just kill for food. They actually seem to take pleasure in ripping people apart. Disemboweling them. Tearing their heads off. Atrocities that are practically beyond description. And then they just leave the body to rot. But sometimes they take all the belongings that the person left behind—armor, weapons, food, any other trinkets—and add them to their stash of treasures."

I thought back to the descriptions I had read of muscled, beast-like beings that were nine and ten feet tall. With jagged teeth and nails just sharp enough to tear into someone, but just dull enough that it wouldn't be quick. The sound of their roar alone was enough to make one explorer lose hearing in his left ear. At least he had lived to tell the tale, though.

Shuddering at the thought, I added, "Some say that they embody true evil."

"We know." Kieran's footsteps padded behind me. I felt his body heat as he looked over my shoulder. "We don't have a choice. We need their weapons."

"Why?" I demanded. The thought of he and Nya going up against cave devils made me want to vomit.

"We already told you," Nya said. "Things are different Outside. We're barely scraping by out there. Our people have been barely scraping by for years, actually. Not once since The Awakening have our people been able to feel confident in their homes, their food supply…their ability to provide for their families." Her face hardened with determination. "But we have an opportunity to change that now. We have the strongest group we've ever had. Mentally, emotionally, and physically. We can do things that haven't been done before. And provide a better future for generations to come."

Her words humbled me. But I still couldn't shake the fear I felt on their behalf.

"And there's nowhere else that you could get the weapons from?" I asked, even though I already knew the answer.

"No." It was Kieran who replied. "There's not."

I sighed.

"Okay. If you're set on stealing from cave devils, then I guess all I can do is give you my best possible advice on how to pull it off."

I was angry.

I had given Nya and Kieran every piece of information on cave devils that I could pull from every corner of my mind.

I told them about an explorer from Ymir, to the north of us, who somehow made it in and out of a lair without getting ripped to shreds. It was challenging without her journal in front of me, but I described the sketch she had made of the layout of the lair, what she observed about cave devils' habits, and how, after hiding under a pile of rotting carcasses—both human and animal—for two terrifying days, she ultimately made her escape.

I told them about the brief account from a group of hunters to the west, near Pyxis, who were unknowingly pursuing the same herd of deer as three cave devils. When the groups encountered one another in a clearing, one hunter found that the beasts were wary of his flamethrower.

At this, Kieran remarked dryly that it sure would be convenient to have access to a flamethrower.

I gave Nya and Kieran any and all details that I could recall, no matter how insignificant. We talked into the early hours of the morning.

When the sky began to take on that purplish glow that indicated sunrise was soon to come, they thanked me for the meal and for my help. Then they left as unceremoniously as they had the last time.

Once again, I tried to watch their departure through the glass. And once again, they disappeared as if into thin air, leaving me staring at nothing but the sleeping buildings below.

And that was when the anger began to set in.

I was angry at Kieran for distracting me once again with flirting, before I could ask more questions about his family. Who were they? Were they truly a danger to humans? How did his mother and father meet? And what happened to the two of them? Were they still alive? Or was he like me? Alone in the world.

I was angry at both Kieran and Nya for still refusing to tell me why they had sought me out.

I was angry at them for not telling me how they kept getting in and out of Cyllene so easily.

I was angry at them for refusing to take the additional food that I had offered them. Yes, it was only bread, crackers, dried fruit, and some other simple items that hardly made for a feast. But it was something, and they needed it.

I was angry at Kieran for reasons that I couldn't quite explain.

But most of all, as I stared up at the ceiling, replaying our conversation about cave devils over and over, my throat aching and eyes burning, I was angry because this time, I knew I would never see either of them again.

CHAPTER FIVE

The next week was agony.

I couldn't shake the irritability that had settled in after Nya and Kieran's departure, making every minor inconvenience feel like the most insufferable thing I had ever had to endure. I could feel myself being short with Brielle, Zander, and even Cato. And yet I couldn't stop myself. I lost the sensation of hunger, and when the time of day dictated that I should eat something, I only managed a few bites here and there.

Despite what poor company I was to Brielle, she snuck me bowls of soup from Culinary Preservation's kitchen for lunch each day, insisting that I must be coming down with something. I forced myself to eat as much as I could to satisfy her. Even though it was the middle of summer, and I would've been miserable trying to shovel down hot soup on a sweltering day even if I were well.

What I dreaded the most was going to bed at night. Or rather, attempting to go to bed at night. It was almost laughable. Did I really need more difficulty sleeping?

I struggled to shut my brain off, my skin crawling and limbs jittery. After several days of tossing and turning, my body was so desperate for rest that I finally managed to fall unconscious for a few hours here and there. But that turned out to be even worse than not sleeping.

I was plagued by two types of dreams. For once, neither of them involved reliving Irene's death, which I suppose was a small mercy.

The first dream was of Nya and Kieran, and others whose faces I had never seen and would probably never see, getting gored by cave devils. My brain got increasingly more creative with each nightmare, to the point where I didn't know if I should be more horrified at the prospect of what cave devils could do, or horrified at myself for being able to concoct such deplorable scenarios all on my own.

The second dream that plagued me was somehow better and worse all at once. I dreamt of Kieran, back in my bed, but this time without Nya present. My brain was just as creative with the scenarios it presented for this one. A mixture of things that I had experienced before and things that I hadn't, but all of which felt brand new under his silver gaze. Each time, I woke up with my heart pounding, sweat drenching my sheets. Aching for something that wasn't even real. Feeling empty and alone in every possible way.

Several weeks passed. Eventually, my mood started to improve. But there were still times throughout the day when my mind would drift as though caught in a current, floating downstream, bouncing off rocks and fallen trees that held unanswerable questions. When Brielle or Zander directed a question to me or tried to include me in their conversations, it felt like I was looking up at them from far away. Two specks on a distant shore.

One day, after a particularly painful lunch where I couldn't hide the fact that I had tuned out of their entire conversation, I returned to the Library to find Cato in his office. This by itself wasn't out of the ordinary. But his demeanor was.

He seemed to be searching for something. Brows furrowed, mouth a grim line. Every drawer that was closed and stack of papers that was set down had a sharp smack to it that confirmed he was not in a good mood.

I knocked politely on the open door, poking my head in. "Is everything okay?"

"Maila, good. You're back," he said. "I know something's been up with you lately, and I also know you're not going to share with me what it is. That's fine.

But I need your help with something, and I need you to be a good sport about it."

Clearly, we weren't mincing words today.

"Of course." I walked the rest of the way into his office. "What can I help you find?"

He waved a hand dismissively. "No, not this. The folder I need is around here somewhere." He continued picking up things, examining them, and dropping them in frustration.

I wiggled my toes in my tennis shoes, unsure what I should be doing.

I was just opening my mouth to ask if I should come back later when he paused and looked up at the ceiling. He spun on his heel and dug into his leather messenger bag. A few seconds later, he let out a sigh of relief.

"It was already in my bag." He held up a manila file folder with something I couldn't quite make out scrawled across the tab. "Not like me to be so forgetful, huh?" he went on, voicing my exact thoughts.

"We all have those days." I had been having those days more often than anyone lately.

"Come with me," he ordered, slinging his bag over his shoulder and striding past me with a sense of urgency.

I had no sooner stepped across the threshold, and he was already locking the door behind me. I trailed after him for a few steps before I realized we were heading straight out of the Library.

"What about the messenger from Agricultural Preservation?"

There were a few books that the Agricultural Preservation department needed, and we had agreed to lend them out for a few days. With the grave understanding, as always, that if anything happened to those books, everything contained within them could be lost to us forever.

"I left a note for Trena. The books are behind the front desk," Cato called over his shoulder, not slowing down.

It wasn't my place to question him. I jogged until I fell into step behind him.

We walked out of the Library, across the main atrium of the Knowledge Center, and out the front entrance.

The courtyard was bustling with activity. People were strolling a bit more leisurely than usual between the Knowledge Center and the living quarters, soaking up the warm afternoon sunshine. We had endured so many midday storms lately that everyone seemed happy for a change of pace. Breaking up the humidity was a cool, refreshing breeze. A reminder to me, and anyone else who spent their evenings alone and reading about our climate—in other words, no one—that the ocean was nearby, just out of view.

I had read that Pre-Awakening, when Cyllene was known for being a lively seaside city, people used to visit at this time of year to see the ocean at its most beautiful shade of turquoise.

"I bet the ocean's nice today," Cato said conversationally, as if reading my thoughts again. Had he ever gone to the ocean? Did The Council permit Mentors to do things like that, in secret?

"I wish we got to see it more often," I mused. It would have defeated the purpose of having walls around the city if we left ourselves wide open on our eastern side. Walling ourselves off from the dangers Outside meant truly walling ourselves off, including from the beach. The most we could hope for was to stand atop a tall building on a clear day and see the hazy smudge of blue in the distance.

"It's the price we pay for our safety," Cato muttered a bit more darkly than the conversation warranted.

I nodded, then felt silly as I remembered he didn't have eyes in the back of his head. "Yes, it is."

We passed through the greenery of the courtyard, especially lush from all the rain, and entered the living quarters. I was more than a little curious now where we were headed.

Before I had time to process it, we had passed out of the other end of the living quarters and were headed down the front steps, into the city. I felt a familiar prickle of anxiety as I took in the buildings ahead. Much more…

solid and real up close than they were when I looked down at them from my balcony.

People were walking and riding bicycles down the main drag. A few in the distance were taking the streets on horseback. The shouts and squeals of children echoed from the vacant lot a few blocks to the left of us. I was never at my apartment during the day, able to sit out on my balcony when the sun was still shining. The sounds of children playing was foreign to me.

"You probably don't get out into the city much, do you?"

Okay. If I wasn't already used to Cato being so perceptive, I would have been wondering at this point if he had some magical mind-reading abilities.

"No," I said simply. "I don't." I hoped my tone conveyed the appropriate amount of respect and also deterred him from asking any follow-up questions.

To fill the silence that followed, I said, "I can't remember the last time I rode a bicycle."

Even with the limited options that we had in comparison to Pre-Awakening bike shops, the people pedaling past us rode bicycles in a variety of colors and styles. Neon red and electric blue and chrome black and countless others zipped by. Some had baskets that were laden with grocery bags, lunch pails, and other essentials.

"Funny you should say that," Cato said, turning to face me. He grinned.

I blinked. And saw what was right in front of my face. "We're riding bikes?"

"Sure are!" He circled to stand beside the white beach cruiser that was the bigger of the two bicycles. "I hope you like green, because that's what I chose for you."

My bike was really more of a light shade of teal, and I couldn't help but feel touched as I stared at it. It was one of my favorite colors, one that Irene had always said went perfectly with the pale blue-green of my eyes.

As I toed the kickstand up and climbed onto the seat, I wondered if Cato's polite concern for me lately was something more. Like actual worry from someone who genuinely wanted to see me happy.

"Where are we headed?" I asked. I was bouncing from side to side on my toes, trying unsuccessfully to steady myself.

Cato was circling nearby. He pulled up alongside me.

He hopped off his bike with practiced ease. "Get off for a second."

My own dismount was…not graceful.

Cato kneeled down and proceeded to adjust something under the seat. Then he stepped back, motioning for me to try again.

"There we go!" he said as I planted both feet on the ground. "Now follow me."

He was off again, coasting leisurely around the road to give me time to catch up. I pushed away from the curb and pedaled after him, muscle memory kicking in. I had almost forgotten what it felt like to ride a bike, to do something physical for once. The days of long rides around the city with Irene felt like a distant memory, and yet suddenly not so distant.

I felt a smile beginning to spread across my face as the wind gently whipped loose strands of hair against my cheeks.

My smile faltered at what Cato said next.

"To answer your question," he called over his shoulder. "I wish we were headed somewhere else."

"Whose house is this?" I asked quietly. I wasn't sure why I felt it necessary to keep my voice low, but somehow the situation felt like it warranted it.

On the other side of a well-kept lawn was a ranch-style house. The white siding looked like it had received a fresh coat of paint sometime in the last year or two, and the same could be said for the front door, which was a pleasant chestnut. Windows covered most of the front of the house, and there were no curtains to block the view inside. As if whoever lived there had pulled them back to let in every possible ray of sunshine.

"The name isn't important," Cato replied, in a tone that told me it was. "What matters is what's inside the house."

He began walking his bicycle up the driveway, and I followed.

Driveways weren't much use to us since cars—along with buses, trains, and airplanes—were not a usable mode of transportation. Our lack of reliable fuel and consistent access to electricity ensured that. But some houses that were built in Pre-Awakening times still had them.

We parked our bicycles in the shade against the side of the house, then strolled up the front walkway. A clean white cement path that, like the yard, gave the impression that it was well-tended.

When we reached the front door, Cato pulled out his keyring and began flipping through an intimidating collection of keys. "This may take a moment," he joked.

While he was busy with that, I tried not to think of the last time I had stood on the front stoop of a house.

Tried not to remember stepping through the front door and almost running right into Irene. Her face red and dripping with sweat, her bike tossed in the grass in a hurry.

Tried not to remember the whirlwind of confusion and terror as we packed a bag. How I still had no idea what was happening or where we were going when the Enforcers set fire to our home. How Irene tried to break down the door so we could escape through the back yard, and her shriek when she dislocated her shoulder.

The memories were coming too hard and too fast.

I focused on steadying my breath, calling on my five senses. Dragging myself back to the present, even as my mind tried to resist.

I made myself see Cato standing in front of me, his shirt slightly damp with sweat from our bike ride. The brown door ahead of him.

I smelled the earthy scent of naturally growing grass and bushes and trees. Things that only existed in the concrete labyrinth of the Knowledge Center when they were carefully cultivated.

I heard the sounds of children playing in the yards of neighboring homes. Children playing just outside the Knowledge Center, children playing here in this neighborhood…I suppose it should have been encouraging to see that so many couples were comfortable enough in our situation and confident enough in our safety to reproduce.

I tasted only sweat, but that was preferable to the bile that had been rising in my throat only a moment before.

I touched the white paint of the siding with my left hand, skimming my fingers across the smooth surface.

Through the soles of my shoes, I could feel the solid ground beneath me. Holding me upright.

I inhaled a breath, held it for ten seconds, then let it out. With it, I let out all the unwelcome thoughts. I nearly jumped at the click of the key in the lock and tried to school my face into a mask of polite curiosity as I followed Cato over the threshold.

I gasped.

The inside of the home was unremarkable enough. An open floor plan with ceramic tile, a white kitchen, and simple but functional furniture. But what immediately caught my attention, impossible to miss, were the books.

So many books.

Not only on the walls, packed tightly into built-in shelves that covered all available wall space, but also piled high on every surface. The end tables that flanked either side of the cushiony sofa, the glass coffee table, the dining room table on the far side of the house, even the ground. Outside of the Library, I had never seen so many books in one place.

"Incredible, isn't it?" The awe in Cato's voice matched what I felt inside.

"Are these yours?"

"I wish." There was that note in his voice again. Something heavy.

"Whose are they?" I demanded, no longer willing to accept his short, cryptic answers. This was a personal library the likes of which I could only dream of. The likes of which most everyone in Cyllene could only dream of. I had to know who had the pleasure of owning it.

And who in their right mind would be so bold, so brave, so fuck-you in their approach as to hoard illegal books right under The Council's noses.

"They belong," Cato said. "To someone who doesn't get to enjoy them anymore, unfortunately." After a pause, he added, "Someone who won't be returning to them."

I could feel my face fall. "So someone who passed away, then?"

"No."

I raised my brows at him.

He huffed out a sigh. "The books belong to someone who The Council had to release outside the walls yesterday. Someone who obviously didn't want to follow the law, or care to understand how Cyllene's laws protect each and every one of us."

Cato was always reading people's tics and the nuances of their behavior, usually in a way that was discreet. But his warm brown eyes searched mine openly, gauging my reaction to his words.

I was trying my best to project acceptance and neutrality.

And I must have failed miserably at it because he frowned.

"Things aren't like they used to be," he went on. "Before my time. And long before your time. There were jails, prisons…ways of keeping someone confined. Our government could afford to do that. Just keep someone in a cell, feed them, clothe them, provide them with life's essentials. We don't have the means to do that anymore. When someone does something unacceptable, we have to do something about it, right? You know this, Maila. People can't just do whatever they want."

I bit my lip.

There were few things in life that I wouldn't have given to have this many books. Even from a distance, I could see that the genres were many and varied. The weathered bindings of old biographies. The dark, ominous jackets of mysteries. The swirling, intricate fonts gracing the covers of romances. Without even knowing this person, I understood that "devastating" was probably not a big enough word to describe the loss of this private world of books that he had so lovingly built.

"Our job today is to divide all of these into two piles," Cato explained, already starting to sift through a stack on the counter. "Books that should be transported to the Library, books that should be disposed of, and books that we can make available to the public. The Enforcers will be by tomorrow to begin moving everything out of the house, including the books, so we don't need to worry about actually hauling them anywhere. Just separating them." When I remained silent, he added, "Making some of these books available to the public was my idea. Yes, we probably won't have copies of most of these, and we have to protect what's contained in each of them." He grabbed a book at random from the pile and held it up for emphasis. "But you and I won't be around forever. We need to make sure we're instilling a love of books in the next generation. Otherwise, who will protect the books when we're gone?"

I was beyond curious to know what books, if any, The Council was going to be willing to make available to the public when this was all said and done. But something about the sincerity in Cato's words had me opening my mouth. "Cato, do you ever think about the people Outside? How they get by? What they go through in order to survive?"

He set down the book. "I have two answers for that."

I dipped my head in an almost imperceptible nod, willing him to continue.

"My first answer is yes. I do think about them. I think about them when I'm enjoying the safety of the walls. When I'm reaping the benefits of thousands of years' worth of knowledge in the Knowledge Center. And when I'm kissing my wife and kids goodnight, taking comfort in knowing that they have a roof over their heads and food on their table every day."

His throat bobbed.

"My second answer is—don't ever ask me that question again."

CHAPTER SIX

I practically collapsed onto my bed that night. My hair was still wet and tangled, and my skin chilled from the shower. I had barely made it into my nightgown.

After riding the bicycle across town, then back again, plus over five hours of leafing through book after book after book, I was spent. Every part of me ached.

Literally every part of me, thanks to the bicycle seat.

For the first time in weeks, my mind was pleasantly quiet, too tired to even form a thought. I savored the feeling, snuggling deeper into my pillow and pulling the blankets up to my nose. The warm fuzziness of sleep began to drift over me, like a leaf floating slowly downward from a branch.

A knock sounded at the door.

Not my front door. The balcony door.

I catapulted out of bed and jerked the door open.

There they were.

I couldn't stop myself from flinging myself at them, wrapping them both in a giant hug. Nya grunted in surprise. Kieran just laughed, and a comforting warmth enveloped my back as he snaked his arm around me.

"As much as I'm enjoying this," Nya said dryly. "I think we'd better get inside before someone spots us."

She was right—if Brielle could sometimes hear me out there by myself, surely she or someone else would hear us now. I let go of the two of them and stepped aside so they could enter.

Nya strode in, making for the chair at my desk.

Kieran lingered on the balcony. His eyes were alight with that amusement that seemed an almost permanent fixture on his face. But there was something else, too. His eyes flicked down my body, then back up to meet my gaze.

Was he that bold? He wasn't even going to hide the fact that he was checking me out?

Then it hit me.

I spun on my heel and brushed past Nya to my closet. I found a cotton jacket and yanked it down so hard that the hanger flipped around and fell off the rod. Then I tossed aside my wet hair, pulled my arms into the sleeves, and zipped it as high as it would go, concealing where the thin fabric of my nightgown, soaked from my hair, clung to my skin.

More specifically, clung to my breasts. As Kieran had already observed.

He was shutting the door behind him when I reemerged. His mouth was tilted upward in that same smirk, but it transformed into a self-satisfied grin at the sight of my jacket.

"Don't cover up for my sake." He kicked off his shoes and laid back on my unmade bed.

"Cover up for mine," Nya muttered. "Or let me step outside for five minutes so you two can bang one out and get it out of your system."

Kieran sputtered out a laugh. "Five minutes?"

Nya batted her eyelashes. "Sorry, you're right. Two minutes."

"Wow," Kieran laughed, propping my pillows behind his head. "Nya, you're a terrible wingman."

Nya jabbed a finger in his direction. "See, that was your first mistake. Thinking I'm your wingman."

My head swiveled back and forth as I listened to their banter. The words were on the tip of my tongue, and pride be damned, I was going to voice them.

"I'm so glad you're both alive."

They had to have known that I felt that way, considering the bear hug I had sprung on the both of them. But the emotion in my voice had them gaping slightly.

Nya broke the silence first. "You never had to worry about me. This one, on the other hand…" She gestured to Kieran, then shook her head.

"I said it once, and I'll say it again: if someone hadn't distracted the cave devils when Cecil tripped over that rock, we would all be dead." Kieran stretched and yawned. He closed his eyes. "You all can joke all you want about my little game of tag, but they never caught me, and you all survived. Really, I'm kind of a hero."

Nya rolled her eyes. "You're delusional, is what you are."

I thought about settling into the same spot as last time, on the floor. Instead, with a decisive flick of my still-damp hair, I sat down on the edge of the bed.

Kieran opened one eye, assessing, then closed it again.

I tucked a foot underneath me. "How long have you all been friends?"

"What makes you think we're friends?" Kieran sounded like he was already half asleep.

"We've known each other since our group found Kieran, which was…when? When you were seven, right? Which would have made me six." Nya leaned against the back of the chair, looking up at the ceiling thoughtfully. "When we first met, Kieran yanked on my braids. And I punched him in the face."

"That doesn't surprise me," I said. Then I added, "Not that I know you two that well. But I could see that."

"And before you ask," Kieran muttered. "No, we've never been anything more than friends."

"Ugh. Kieran, for fuck's sake." Nya wrinkled her nose and feigned a shudder. "I hope she wasn't going to ask that. It should go without saying that I'm not one of your harem."

Kieran's eyes flew open. Two wide, silver discs that looked vaguely…alarmed? Embarrassed? I thought he was about to fire back with something sarcastic, but instead he said simply, "I don't have a harem."

He and Nya exchanged one of their long looks. This time it wasn't over something I said, at least.

"Right," Nya said at length. She turned to address me, but her eyes were still on Kieran. "That was a joke."

Something had shifted in the mood, but I couldn't quite place what it was.

"You know, I don't have leftovers from a big meal like I did last time," I offered, eager for something to say. "But I do have some basic stuff. I can throw something together for you two."

Nya blinked, and the strange look she had been giving Kieran was replaced with a smile. "Don't put yourself out. We're fine."

"I'm not putting myself out." I scrambled off the bed and over to my row of cabinets. I came to the immediate realization that the few edible things I had were not actually all that edible. Nya and Kieran may have been used to roughing it Outside, but the thought of serving them something stale was horrifying. Like a comment on their status as Strangers, declaring that they didn't deserve anything better.

The thought made my face burn.

I continued as I searched, "You're also welcome to anything else here. You can take a cool shower if you want. Or take a nap on the bed." Clearly, Kieran hadn't been waiting on an invitation for that one. "Anything you want."

Nya leaned forward, and I could hear the rustling sound that I'd come to recognize as her digging through her backpack. I wondered what scribbly mess of a "map" she had for me this time and almost laughed out loud. As predicted, she pulled a long, folded piece of paper out of the main pocket. "Before we do anything else, we need to do what we came here for. Which is to get your input on another mission."

I paused with a loaf of bread—more accurately, a brick of bread—in my hand. Suddenly, I couldn't move. Swallow. Breathe. And for once, it had nothing to do with panic.

It was a moment of clarity, the likes of which I hadn't had in a long time. Maybe ever. And it felt shockingly sudden, as if my own brain had been hiding something crucial from me. But also perfectly expected. As if I was always destined to make this decision, right now, right here, with two Strangers in my room and moldy bread in my hand.

"I'm not going to be giving you input on anything like that tonight," I said as an eerie sense of calm settled over me.

There was a stirring from the bed. I knew Kieran was sitting up now at full attention.

Nya was still holding the map in midair. "What are you saying?"

I set down the bread. Then I walked out into the bedroom, facing them fully.

Nya's expression was wary.

Kieran's eyes were twinkling, as if he found this turn of events entertaining.

"I'm saying," I started, gathering some courage before I continued. "That I'm not giving you advice or input or whatever you want to call it. At least not here, not tonight. Because whatever you're facing this time, I'm going with you. Outside."

I sat on the concrete floor of my balcony, knees tucked under my chin, arms wrapped around my legs. Obviously, this was my go-to spot to clear my head after nightmares. But the nightmares always seemed to come in the morning, right before waking, when the first rays of sun were lightening the sky. There was something novel about being out here at night, when the city below was just a mass of shadowy shapes.

Beside me was my usual book bag. But instead of my notebook and other items that I needed for work, it contained a toothbrush and several changes of clothes.

Three nights ago, I had announced that I was sneaking out of the city with Nya and Kieran. And three nights ago, Nya had been adamant that there was absolutely, positively, no way that I was going *anywhere* with them. Much less to face this latest challenge, which she insisted would be the riskiest of all—taking down a beast that they referred to as "Leviathan," after the biblical creature that was both sea serpent and demon. The name didn't sound familiar, but their description of it did. I found it in Cato's index under "sea monster."

"You'll be a liability," Nya had spat as she paced circles around my room. "This wasn't part of the plan."

Kieran had made a noise of disagreement in his throat. "Wasn't it, though? Eventually?"

They had exchanged a look yet again. And I couldn't resist saying, "Stop communicating telepathically or whatever the hell it is you two do when you look at each other like that. I want to be a part of this, so let me. Please."

"I wish we could communicate telepathically," Nya had grumbled. "There's a fucking lot I'd have to say."

In the tense silence that followed, I explained that I would need time to research the Leviathan further. This, I pointed out, gave them plenty of time to prepare for me to join them.

Nya's response was to plant her feet and declare that I was not coming with them. End of story. And she refused to hear anything else about it.

It was Kieran who finally asked what my reasons were.

It was difficult to look the two of them in the eye. But I had squared my shoulders and forced myself to hold each of their gazes in turn as I said, "I want to go Outside. I want to see what the world is like out beyond the walls. How you live. The magical creatures and beings that I've only read about. But most of all"—here I pressed on, despite a lump forming in my throat—"I can't sit here for a third time, watching the days go by, knowing you're risking your lives out there. And that I may never see either of you again. So you can follow through on your threat to hurt me or kill me or whatever it is you have to do. But I won't help you with this unless you take me with you."

At my words, Kieran's eyes had shifted in that way that only his could, darkening from that chrome silver to the deep blue-gray of the sky just after a storm. "We risk our lives every day," he had said, his voice surprisingly gentle. "The same creatures that we've been seeking out could randomly appear in our camp one night and slaughter us all in our sleep. There's a real possibility you could die out there."

The next words that came out of my mouth should have surprised me more than they did. But the same way it becomes easier to lie the more you do it, it becomes easier to admit the truth the more you do it. Or at least, that's how it felt to someone who had spent the last decade being dishonest.

"Magical beings and beasts aren't the only things that can kill you," I said. "People kill, too. And besides, having your life taken in that manner isn't the only thing to fear." My voice had become so soft, it was barely above a whisper. "Having to continue living when you've lost everything that you loved, everything that gave you purpose, everything that made you look forward to the future…that's its own version of death."

I'm not sure how much time passed before Kieran spoke again. "And if we decide not to do either one—take you or hurt you—but just leave and never come back here again?"

"You won't?" It was meant to be a statement. But the question was there in my voice.

Kieran's slow smile, closely followed by Nya's exasperated sigh, was my answer.

It was decided. I was going with them.

Nya and Kieran said they would have to return to the Strangers to present my terms. Which, despite Nya's concerns, they were fairly certain that the other decision-makers in the group would accept. Just that word, "terms," made me feel like a child roleplaying as someone important. But I suppose there was no other way to describe the agreement I presented:

- Nya and Kieran would sneak me out of Cyllene for two days, to return at the end of the second day.
- In exchange for meeting these people I had been assisting and getting to see the Outside firsthand, I would not stray from what I was instructed to do, would not take unnecessary risks, and would keep my distance during the confrontation with the Leviathan.
- I would never speak of what I saw or experienced Outside, but would use that knowledge to fuel my continued support of the Strangers from inside Cyllene.

That last part had settled heavily over me. Cyllene may have been a city of rule-followers, but I hadn't spent my childhood staying up late into the night, reading mysteries and thrillers with Irene for nothing. I knew well the concept of a double agent.

And that's what I was now, formally and willingly, agreeing to be.

While Nya and Kieran did their part, I did mine in turn. I found an excuse to be sent down to the basement level of the Library again. Just like before, while researching the actual project Cato had given me, I soaked up every bit of information I could on the Leviathan.

Near the end of the third day, I steeled myself to find out just how skilled ten years' worth of lying had made me. With palms sweating, I found Cato in his office. I confirmed that I had had a lot on my mind, as he had guessed. I told him I didn't want to talk about it, but I thought I could benefit from a few days to myself. In my decade working in the Library, it was my first time making a request like that.

The conversation ended up being both easier and harder than I had expected.

Easier, because Cato believed me right away and didn't probe. Harder, because I had to sell it like I finally trusted him enough to admit what I needed in order to feel like my old self again. I could tell, by the compassion in his eyes and the reassuring pat on the shoulder that he gave me as I left, how much that meant to him.

Maybe one day I would tell him the truth.

And maybe one day I would tell Brielle and Zander the truth, instead of feeding them a lie about working in my room on an extremely important Library project and asking that they please not disturb me for several days. Thank goodness the two of them never had a reason to cross paths with Cato to confirm.

Everything had gone according to plan. But there was one step left, and it was going to be the most challenging one.

Nya and Kieran had to sneak me out of Cyllene.

I was dressed in my most comfortable T-shirt, black jeans, and black sneakers. My hair was pulled back in a smooth ponytail instead of a braid, which helped cool the sticky sweat that was already forming on my neck. Whether it was from the humidity that lingered after another sweltering day or from my nerves, I couldn't say. Probably a combination of both.

As I was getting ready, I had allowed myself to look at my reflection for the first time in, well, I suppose I couldn't even guess at how long it had been. Not a quick glance, but a truly intentional moment of observing myself. Seeing the person before me. Even the parts that reminded me of Irene.

Where did this person come from? This person who would demand to go with two people she barely knew beyond the walls of Cyllene?

As I fidgeted now on the floor of the balcony, I decided I must have been waiting for an hour or more. But in spite of the anxious energy that kept my legs bouncing and my feet tapping, I wasn't concerned.

Nya had forewarned me that they could only give an estimate of when to expect them. One patrolling Enforcer could mean the difference between crossing the wall and having to hang back until the coast was clear.

However, I had been staring at the dark cityscape for so long that the buildings were starting to look like they were moving.

No. That was actual movement.

The shadowy shapes weaved and bobbed, all the while drawing closer. As they neared, I realized they were leaping from rooftop to rooftop. How was that possible?

When the shapes reached the edge of the high-rise directly across from my apartment, they paused.

I stood and walked to the edge of the railing, holding my breath.

One of the shapes moved quickly across the rooftop. Faster and faster, until it sailed over the edge, across the street, and onto the living quarters' lawn. I could make out now that it was Nya. She sprinted up the incline until she was in line with the column of balconies that led to mine. I had assumed she would climb from balcony to balcony, but instead she launched herself into the air.

She landed right beside me, the soles of her boots smacking the cement. That, I realized, was the thud I always heard from inside the apartment.

Kieran wasn't far behind. He followed the same path as Nya, who stepped aside to make room for him. He landed in a crouch, straightened, and flashed me a grin.

"Okay." Nya's voice had that commanding edge that it took on when she was focused. "Maila, you're with Kieran."

"To do *that*?"

I had known we were going to have to do some running and climbing to sneak out of the city, but I hadn't expected what I just witnessed. Leaping inhuman distances and arcing through the air like giant crickets.

Kieran lifted his shirt sleeve to reveal a diamond-shaped marking on his left deltoid. It was about two inches long and one inch wide, the lines contained within too intricate to make out fully in the dark.

"Congratulations! This is your first encounter with *magic*." He said the last part in a mock ominous tone, waving his hands in the air.

Nya rolled her eyes. Then she lifted the cuff of her shorts to show me the identical marking on her right thigh.

The realization made my chest constrict and my pulse start hammering, but in the best possible way. Kieran was right. I had spent most of my life reading about magic and researching magic. Now I was witnessing it firsthand.

Starting with these tattoos, which I assumed were the work of an enchantress. I adored enchantresses, mostly because some research I had done on them a few years back had led me to this eloquently written line from an Enforcer's field journal: *"Holy fuck these people look like people, but I don't think they ARE people."*

Turns out, they were people. Just not "our" people. They arrived during The Awakening.

"Luck is on our side tonight," Kieran continued. "The wards are disabled in one section of the wall."

There was one burning question answered. Finally. "Who disabled them?"

Kieran's smile was the definition of smug. "I did."

"Both of you be quiet and come on." Nya's chastising whisper came from the other side of the balcony. She had slung my bag over her shoulder, where it hung against her backpack, and she was already perched on the railing.

Kieran turned his back to me and squatted down.

After a beat, he spoke. "The magic only works on me. So unless you've been concealing some magic of your own, you'd better hop on."

Right. I lowered myself toward him, wrapping my arms around his neck.

In one swift movement, he stood, caught my legs in his hands, and pitched my weight forward so that my chin was resting on his shoulder. Our cheeks pressed against one another.

His body was warm despite the cool night air, and I could feel the rounded muscles of his shoulders, back, and arms against me. There was something about the way his hands cradled my thighs that was both firm and gentle.

"Ready?" With my face and neck against his, I could feel the vibration of his voice in his throat.

"Ready," I confirmed, a bit more breathlessly than I would've liked. My heart was hammering again, but it had nothing to do with the fact that he was climbing onto the railing next to Nya, about to free-fall from my seventh-floor balcony.

Nya jumped first, sailing to the ground with the grace of a cat.

Kieran dropped his hands from my legs, holding out his arms to steady himself.

All my feelings about being this close to him abruptly vanished. I was going to be sick. I squeezed my eyes shut and tightened my legs around him.

"You know," he said, turning so his lips brushed against my ear, making me shiver involuntarily. "That shirt looks great on you." His tone told me he wasn't referring to the fabric or the color. "But I think your look the other night is my favorite."

The stupid nightgown.

My eyes snapped open just in time to see the silver twinkle in his eye. Then we were falling.

It was over quickly, yet also seemed like it would never end.

As soon as I felt the rebound from Kieran's feet hitting the ground, I took stock of myself. My stomach was in my throat. I tasted blood…I must have bit my lip. My arms and legs were shaking violently, wrapped as tightly around Kieran's neck and waist as humanly possible.

Kieran gagged and yanked my hands down to his clavicle. "This may come as a surprise, but if you choke me out while we're falling, our chances of survival decrease drastically."

"Sorry," I muttered. I wondered what our chances of survival would be if I vomited on him mid-fall instead. My throat tightened as if in preparation.

"No worries," he called over his shoulder, jogging across the grass.

Nya was already on the other side of the road, in front of the brick high-rise. She ran straight at the building, then jumped at the last second, using her momentum and magic to catapult her up ten stories.

"I don't think I'm going to handle this jump any better than the last one," I said, dreading every step that brought us closer.

"You handled that last one just fine." Kieran scanned the street, checking for patrolling Enforcers before sprinting across. "Besides, this isn't so bad on my end. The feeling of you trembling and gasping, legs wrapped around me—"

"You may have distracted me the first time with that," I interrupted. "But it's not going to work again."

Kieran laughed, the movement bouncing both of us. "Who said I was trying to distract you?"

That irritability that I felt the night of his and Nya's second visit creeped up again. It only intensified as Kieran pushed off the ground and we catapulted through the air, landing so hard on the roof that my teeth clacked painfully against each other.

Jumping upwards had been better than falling, but I still felt nauseated and dizzy. My discomfort made me suddenly bold.

"You know," I said. Taking a page from his book, I tilted my head so my lips brushed against his ear. I lowered my voice to a whisper. "It's no fun being toyed with. That is what's happening, right? Are you teasing me, Kieran?"

His steps faltered, and his breathing hitched. When he spoke, his voice was hoarse. "Which would offend you more—if I was messing with you, or if I was serious?"

I didn't know. And I was suddenly terrified to know the truth. "What would offend me most," I said, creating as much distance between us as I could with him still carrying me, "would be if you dropped me because you're screwing around. Pay attention."

I was being a coward, and we both knew it. But as we reached the other end of the roof, he said, "Noted."

We continued in silence.

Kieran bounded from rooftop to rooftop, somehow managing to keep Nya within view. I wondered if it was the magic or his own strength and endurance that allowed him to do this so effortlessly.

I tried to maintain an awareness of where we were in the city. But by the eighth jump, I was staring at the inside of my eyelids and wishing for it to be over.

"Doing okay?" Kieran asked after a particularly long leap.

I realized I had groaned out loud. Normally that would've embarrassed me, but I was too miserable to care.

"I'm fine." It felt like the right thing to say, but I couldn't find the strength to make my voice sound convincing.

"I guess it's safe to say that you get motion sick." Kieran's chuckle was comforting somehow. "No jumping from cliffs or diving from waterfalls for you."

"You actually do all of that?"

"Sure. Not a lot of cliffs in this area, but if you keep heading north, you'll come across some great spots."

I thought about all the things he must have seen and experienced Outside, all the life he had lived. And then he was picking up speed again.

I braced myself.

We must have descended to a shorter building, because we sailed forward but also fell for much longer than I had anticipated. I pressed my face against the solid expanse of his shoulder, willing the contents of my stomach to stay put.

"I would stop if I could, to give you a break." His voice was near my ear again. "But we have to keep moving."

There was nothing teasing in what he said. But despite how awful I felt, my body still reacted to the rumble of his voice and the feeling of his breath against my skin.

I stifled another groan of misery. I was a ball of frustrating and uncomfortable sensations, and I needed them all to stop. Immediately.

Kieran must have sensed how I was feeling because he said, "Hang in there. We're about to jump down onto the street, then it's up and over the wall."

The wall. We were going to cross the wall.

Nya was still about fifty feet in front of us, but she had paused to balance on the cornice. I opened my eyes just in time to see her hold her arm high, flash a thumbs-up, and fall soundlessly. Beyond where she had been standing, the silhouette of the wall loomed. Closer than I had expected.

"Hang on." Kieran reached his left arm across his body and over my shoulder, holding me against him. His grip was tight to the point of pain. Not a good sign of what was to come.

I buried my face in his shoulder again, this time to stifle a scream.

When I felt the resistance of the ground, I could have wept with relief.

Then we were at the base of the wall.

One hundred feet tall, the pride and joy of Cyllene.

The wall was constructed at the beginning of The Awakening. Television channels, radio stations, and written publications had foregone all other news in favor of reporting on the strange happenings around the planet. The stories both frightened and fascinated the public, and people speculated about what all of this meant for humankind. There was a running joke that maybe another ten years would find us all riding on the backs of our unicorn steeds.

Then the reports of deaths start trickling in. Corpses mutilated in ways that baffled authorities. Encounters with creatures who were initially enchanting, but went on to suck the very life out of their victims. Phenomena like the wind that I had researched for Cato, where one gust brought madness and violence. These occurrences started to snowball, overwhelming police and filling hospitals to capacity.

Then the floodgates opened. People were dying by the thousands.

And thus…the wall. A desperate attempt to keep the now-hostile world at bay.

Every construction company, every individual with skill in building, and even citizens who were unskilled but willing to learn…they all banded together to erect the wall. Other cities did the same, and the remaining news outlets reported on the ventures with mixed opinions. Some questioned how a concrete barrier was going to keep out magic. In most cases, people could neither physically see nor understand the mechanics of how magic worked. But others questioned what else, exactly, they were supposed to do in order to keep their families safe. And that question was met with silence.

In an astounding two years from the day the team broke ground, a one-hundred-foot-high, forty-foot-thick cement wall encased the whole of the thirty miles of Cyllene. One massive, drawbridge-style gate sat on the western side. Wards—protection spells deployed by an enchantress who was willing to offer her services to Cyllene for a price—were placed around the top of the wall in the form of special inscriptions on the surface. Protection against leaping, climbing, crawling, and other wall-breaching things. As an additional safety measure, steel spikes were also adhered to half of the perimeter of the wall, with the remaining half left empty due to a shortage of steel.

Long before the wall was completed, but especially once it was, everyday people were forbidden to come and go from the city. Those who wished to enter Cyllene could only do so under special circumstances. Those who wished to leave were told they could never return. Enforcers were the only exception. However, if they displayed unusual behavior or symptoms upon their return, even they could be declined reentry. Patrols along the perimeter of the wall could be irregular at times, but the gate itself was heavily guarded.

All of this and more on the history of the wall, I knew from the Library.

Yet none of that prepared me to cross it.

Kieran paused for a moment under the wall's massive shadow. Ahead, Nya slowed to a halt as well. She lifted her arms in the air in exasperation, questioning what we were doing.

"This is going to get rough," Kieran whispered. Even in the shadows, I must have looked terrible, because he gently brushed a few loose strands of hair from my face, tucking them behind my ears. "The Springing Spell is really going to kick in here to help us achieve the jumps onto and down from the wall. I'm not going to lie, if the other jumps were hard on you, these two are going to feel brutal. But just try to focus on the fact that this is the last hurdle—literally and figuratively—and then we're going to be over the wall. Alive."

"Okay." I could hear how pitiful my voice sounded.

Kieran seemed to be considering something. "Also," he said after a moment. Before I knew what was happening, he had moved me off his back and around to his front. Like a rag doll, he adjusted me into the same position I had been in before—arms draped over his shoulders, legs wrapped around his waist. "I want you facing this way so you're not fighting against the drag on the way up. And…you know…in case you pass out."

"This is a great pep talk," I mumbled against his chest, my words almost inaudible.

Through the clenching of my sour stomach and the rising of bile in my throat, I couldn't help but notice how hard his chest and abdomen were against me. My body had gotten used to the sensation of being on his back, but the adjustment made me feel the heat that radiated from him, and that his neck and arms were slick with sweat. I swallowed against a wave of nausea, and…something else.

What an uncomfortable and confusing experience.

Nya's anxious hiss carried across the grass.

"Ready?" Now that I was hugging Kieran's chest, his voice resonated through my whole body.

I opened my mouth to respond, but we were off again.

The rustling thud of Kieran's footfalls grew louder, and the flexing of his muscles against me became more rapid.

We were accelerating. Fast.

I closed my eyes, clenching my hands and legs and every muscle in my body until I was a solid, unmoving thing.

Then we were airborne.

The wind we were creating, rushing past us, was deafening. I tried to suck in a breath and instantly had it knocked out of me. Instead of rocketing toward the sky on Kieran's momentum alone, it now felt like we were being jerked up by a giant's hand. Although I was beyond forming an actual thought, some part of me understood that this was the Springing Spell kicking in.

We slammed down on top of the wall, and Kieran stumbled a few steps before righting us. I hadn't even processed until we landed that his arms, rather than being outstretched to steady us, were wrapped tightly across my back and hips.

In the distance, I heard the smacking of the soles of shoes against concrete. Nya. When the sound disappeared, I knew she had jumped.

Forty feet. Less than that, at this point. Under forty feet, and we were going to be following Nya down the other side.

"Almost there!"

Kieran's enthusiasm did nothing to soothe me. A deep, primal kind of terror formed in my gut. It had me unintentionally loosening my grip around his neck as my vision swam. I flailed desperately for a handhold, my palms connecting with his deltoids and grabbing on for dear life.

"Careful," he barked. He jerked my hands from his arms and wrapped them around his neck again.

The rebuke in his tone was so sharp that it snapped me out of my suffering for a moment. "What—"

The words fell away as he tightened his grip around me, bracing us.

I tilted my nose upward slightly, just enough that I could look over Kieran's shoulder and see Cyllene receding in the distance. Then the ground went out from under us.

It felt like we were falling to our deaths.

All my senses went dark.

At some point, I had the vague awareness of something pushing against us, slowing us.

Then everything went dark again.

I couldn't say how much time had passed when I became aware of an itchy, burning sensation against my cheek.

I lifted my head. Dark, twisting shapes came into focus. Grass. Tall grass, smashed down by my weight. And Kieran's.

Kieran was flat on his back, and I was draped over him, my head hanging over his shoulder. I pushed up on tremoring arms to look at him.

Other than tousled hair, he appeared perfectly normal. His expression must have mirrored my own. Wide eyes searched my face to confirm that everything was as it should be.

"Feeling okay?"

"Yeah, I'm fine." I turned my head and vomited.

Kieran maneuvered me off him just in time.

"There it is," he said sympathetically, barely hiding his amusement.

I would have said something witty back if I wasn't busy emptying my stomach.

My ponytail disappeared behind me with a gentle tug. A large hand rubbed circles across my back. "There, there." Kieran's voice held a barely stifled laugh.

Crunching footfalls sounded behind us.

"Damn." Nya's voice. I heard the shuffling of her sifting through her backpack, then the sound of liquid splashing on the grass. Wet fabric pressed against the back of my neck. "The water's not cold, but hopefully this helps."

Tears were streaming down my face, but I was dry heaving now at least.

"I wonder," Nya began. "Would we have convinced her not to come if we had just told her what leaving the city actually entailed?"

"No," I croaked, but I wasn't sure that was true.

I wiped my watery eyes and mouth on the back of my arm. Then I willed myself to stand, to prove to them that bringing me along was not a mistake. When I stood, finally taking in my surroundings, everything I had just endured was worth it.

I was Outside.

CHAPTER SEVEN

"Is it how you pictured it?" Nya asked softly, coming to stand beside me.

There was a crunch as Kieran stepped gingerly over the spot where I'd just been sick. He appeared on my other side.

"I don't know," I answered honestly.

I was used to Cyllene's salt air. But out here, the scent mingled with an earthy musk.

A vast field of tall, untended grasses lay ahead of us, lit up by the moon overhead. The moon was unchanged, and yet at the same time, bigger and brighter out here. Before me were so many different species of grass and weeds, I wouldn't have known where to start in identifying them all. The land was wild, untamed. No one waking up at dawn to water and trim and shape it, and yet it was full and lush and very much alive. Just like Zander had described it.

On the horizon were the looming shapes of trees. The forest. I could hardly wait to see it up close.

"We're basically in the clear now," Nya said. She grabbed the wet cloth off the ground where it had fallen and shoved it back in the main pocket of her backpack. Then she handed me my own bag. "But it's still a good idea not to stand around out here in the open. You never know."

With that, she began wading through the waist-high grass, headed toward the forest.

I waited for Kieran to fall into step behind her, but he gestured for me to go ahead of him. "Tread carefully," he warned. "You can't always see when there's a hole or a rock underfoot. Or an animal."

"An animal?" I glanced around quickly, as if just the mention of an animal would cause one to appear.

"Yeah. Like a marsh wolf."

When I whipped around, he was grinning. "That's not funny."

"Sure it is." He chuckled. "Really, though. Most animals will take off as soon as they hear us stomping their way. It's the holes and rocks that can leave you with a twisted ankle."

As we walked, I tried to follow Nya's exact path. I figured as long as I did that, there was little chance of falling. The grasses were stiff and brittle in some parts and soft and pliant in others. I ran my hands along the tips of the blades, marveling at the feeling.

When we approached the trees, I was awestruck at the size of them. I had seen trees in Cyllene, of course. But none were as tall and imposing as these. I recognized cypress and maple and palm. Thick tangles of gray moss covered many of them, cascading over the branches like small waterfalls. Some of these trees had observed the last seventy years of chaos from the beginning. Some were old enough to have seen much more than that.

Also in the mix were a few species of trees that didn't quite fit with the rest. They stood just as tall and fit neatly in between the others, as if they had always been there. Like imposters, trying to blend in.

Trees with magical properties.

Such as the eventide locust. While nothing like a sunset in appearance, this tree captured the same sense of foreboding that comes with nightfall. True to what I had read, the clusters of spiky thorns that covered its surface resembled a regular honey locust, except they were larger. More menacing. Smothering the tree until there was no smooth bark visible. The tree was fine enough when left alone. But it was sentient and had a nasty temper. When disturbed, it could release those thorns like deadly projectiles.

Further down the tree line, a ways from where we were entering, I also spied a gemstone willow. The eventide locust and the gemstone willow—I couldn't have picked two more opposite trees. And yet here they were, towering and tangible and absolutely magnificent. Even from a distance, I could see the cascading leaves of the gemstone willow glittering in the moonlight, like strands of peridots. I hoped at some point while on the other side of the walls, I would have an opportunity to see one up close.

We stepped under the canopy, leaving the field behind. Now we were trading stepping carefully through the tall grass for stepping carefully over roots, fallen branches, and scrub.

The same as before, I watched Nya's steps and tried to mimic them. Her long legs carried her easily across the forest floor, and I was reminded again of the effortless poise of a cat. Although considering Nya's personality, she was more lion than cat.

"Stay close," she said over her shoulder.

I picked up the pace, trying to close the distance between us. But the ground was uneven, and I stumbled forward, arms flailing.

Kieran's firm grip encircled my arm, steadying me. I hadn't realized he was walking that close.

"Thanks," I mumbled.

"You know, I can always carry you again," he offered, his deep voice sickeningly sweet.

"You'd like that, wouldn't you?"

He was still laughing when I resumed trudging through the underbrush. "I wasn't sure at first how I felt about this side of you that I've seen tonight, but I think she's growing on me. Like a squirrel that chatters at you when you get too close to its nest."

A squirrel?

I whirled around to face him. But my comeback died on my lips when I saw his grin. He had gotten under my skin again, and he knew it.

I gave him my back again. "If I'm a squirrel, what does that make you?" I asked.

"Hmmm…a lion, maybe?"

"That won't work. I already decided that Nya is a lion."

"And you two are my whining cubs," Nya said without missing a beat.

The crack of a branch echoed to the left of us.

We fell silent.

Instantly, as if it were second nature, Nya stepped back and Kieran stepped forward, filling in the gaps between us. Kieran turned toward the noise and crouched slightly, as if in a fighting stance. Nya did the same, but facing the opposite direction. In case we were being hunted. Surrounded.

I was afraid to swallow, to breathe. We stood like that for several minutes. Waiting.

"Well?" Nya's whisper was barely audible.

"I don't see anything," Kieran replied.

They straightened at the same time. Nya resumed her position at the front of our little line and started out again.

Reluctantly, I trailed after her. "What if it's that evil wind?"

I shouldn't have been surprised when the sound of laughter burst out from behind me. "Evil wind?"

"We don't have a name for it yet," I explained. "But it's a wind-like phenomenon that apparently makes people go mad."

Ahead of me, Nya made a noise in her throat and continued walking.

"Have you all ever encountered something like that?" I pressed.

"Nope." Nya paused, holding a low-hanging branch so that I could pass. "And even if something like that does exist, doesn't sound like there's a whole hell of a lot we can do about it. If we venture out to hunt, and an evil wind gets us, then I guess that's just what fate has in store for us that day."

Well, she had a point there.

Sensing that the subject was dead, I decided to broach another. This was my opportunity to learn from them, to get more questions answered. "It's getting darker the deeper we go. It must have taken a lot of practice to be able to see so well at night."

Nya scoffed. "Or no practice, if you're Kieran."

I looked back at him with raised brows.

He pointed at his eyes. They were shadowed under the treetops, but whenever we crossed under a gap in the canopy, they flashed that shade of silver that rivaled the moonlight. "A gift from my father," he said. "They're not just for looks." He considered a moment, then added, "On second thought, *looks* are exactly what they're for, huh?"

Nya sighed. "You're becoming absolutely intolerable."

I ignored them both. This was the opening I had been waiting for, to find out more about his family. "So your eyes—the eyes you share with your father—allow you to see clearly in the dark?"

"Yes."

"Can they do other things, too?"

"Probably," he snorted. "But being a half-human bastard doesn't exactly earn you a spot as a student or acolyte or whatever the fuck they call their offspring who still need training. I know next to nothing about my own abilities, and I imagine they would prefer it stay that way. We have a nice unspoken agreement where they pretend I don't exist, and I live out my life as a human."

His situation was so different from mine. And in some ways, so eerily similar.

The tree trunks and foliage closest to us were shadowed, but beyond them, unidentifiable shapes twisted and collided into something foreboding. After considering, I asked, "Is it possible that we could run into"—I almost said "your father," but decided against it—"others with those eyes while we're out here?"

"Are you planning on burning down the forest?" he asked flatly.

I weighed his words. "So your father's people are protectors of the forest? If I were to do something crazy and destructive, like set fire to the trees, they would intervene?"

"Something like that."

I gathered from his tone that I still hadn't quite hit the mark. A thought bubbled to the surface. "Matthew, the explorer who disappeared—whose whole team disappeared after seeing a hooded figure with silver eyes. Are you saying he was a threat?"

"I don't know who this 'Matthew' is," Kieran said, sounding bored. "But based on what you just said, it would seem that way, wouldn't it?"

I whirled around again and let out a startled cry as I smacked into his chest.

"Everything okay back there?" Nya's footfalls paused.

"Yeah, sorry." I rubbed my nose.

The corner of Kieran's mouth tugged upward. He inclined his head expectantly, as if to say, "Go on."

"I was just wondering what sort of threat Matthew would have to have been. Would they have not liked the fact that he was exploring? I mean, this land used to belong to humans. And to animals. Regular ones, I mean. Explorers like Matthew were, and still are, just trying to understand how the world has changed." As I said the words, angry heat flared in me. On behalf of this man I had never met. On behalf of the others on his team who were apparently killed along with him. "For fuck's sake, the world has always been like this for our generation, and yet even *we* are still trying to make sense of things. It's not so bad to want to understand this world around us, is it? To brave the unknown, for the sake of knowledge?"

I wasn't so sure I was talking about Matthew Hart anymore.

Kieran's lips were still turned up in smirk, but something in his expression softened. "Don't take this the wrong way, Maila. But you're very naive."

"Then tell me what I don't understand," I challenged.

He opened his mouth, and my chest tightened. "Keep walking. We've got a lot of ground to cover tonight." With that, he grabbed my shoulders, spun me around, gave me a gentle nudge forward.

We walked the rest of the way in silence. At first, I didn't speak because I was frustrated with Kieran, his insults, and his evasiveness. But after a while, I was too exhausted to have spoken if I'd wanted to. I may have had a naturally slim frame, but a sedentary life had left me with exactly zero endurance.

The terrain was unchanging for most of the journey. The only highlight was when we had to cross a narrow stream, which we did by leaping—did everything out here involve jumping?—from one side to the other. I refused to be carried by Kieran again, so I gave it a shot on my own and came up short, landing in several inches of water. Afterwards, my footsteps elicited two sounds—a wet squishing noise, closely followed by laughter from Kieran.

After what I estimated to be two hours of trudging through the underbrush, the forest began to feel less coastal. Towering palms became less frequent, and bristly pines began to make an appearance. We emerged onto a hill, looking down into a shallow valley.

I glanced between Nya and Kieran, eyes wide. "Is this your camp?"

"Yes," Nya answered simply. "This is home."

Sitting at the bottom of the valley was a neighborhood. Or rather, what was left of one. Rows of houses sat in various states of decay—ceilings caved in, gaping holes where walls once stood, and some lots reduced to nothing but rubble. Each row was separated from the next by crumbling remnants of road. Weeds, vines, and other greenery burst through the cracks in the pavement, with some sections of concrete entirely split in half.

This had once been a peaceful suburban neighborhood, like the few that were preserved within Cyllene. And now, like so much of the world, it was a graveyard.

Without another word, we descended the hill and entered the once-neighborhood.

Upon closer inspection, there were items of all kinds strewn across the remnants of yards and scattered across the broken chunks of pavement. A rusty skeleton of what I assumed was once a bicycle. A blackened shape that resembled a child's toy. Even, I realized with awe, a crumbling mass that looked like it was once a car.

We walked straight for several blocks, then turned left.

It was immediately apparent that this street was different than the others. First, by the barbed wire fence that we passed through. Then, as we made our way down the road, I noticed spots that looked like they had once been giant holes were filled with carefully packed dirt. As if to prevent a stumble or fall. The houses that lined the street were still falling apart, but there were also signs of life in them. A front porch and walkway that, despite cracks, looked recently swept. A clothesline tied between sections of roof.

I started as my eyes landed on a bonfire up ahead, burning in the center of a cul-de-sac. Then I caught sight of the dark shapes gathered around it. People. Dozens of them.

And one headed down the street, right for us.

"There you guys are!" a booming voice exclaimed.

The man who stopped in front of us appeared to be in his mid-thirties and was well over six-foot. He not only towered over us all, including Nya and Kieran, but had a wide, stocky frame. In the moonlight, I could see that he was blue-eyed and fair. His hair fell in wild waves to his shoulders, and he had a bushy beard to match.

I expected him to address Nya and Kieran, but instead he extended a hand to me.

"Hey, there!" he said with sincere enthusiasm. "You must be Maila. I'm Cecil. As you can see, my name doesn't really fit me, so you can call me 'C' if you want."

Nya looked to the sky. "Literally not a single person ever has called you 'C.'"

I held my hand out, and he shook it vigorously while giving a hearty laugh. "Every nickname has to start somewhere, Nyathera."

Kieran chortled as Nya punched Cecil in the arm.

"Welcome to Ersa Estates," Cecil continued. "That was the name of this neighborhood once, and we loved the irony." He gestured to the ruined street around us.

"So we decided to keep it. It's not much compared to what you're used to, but it's somewhere to call home. For now, at least."

"Thank you for having me."

I suddenly felt uneasy. Why had I insisted on coming here? On intruding in Nya's and Kieran's lives? I shifted on my feet, looking past Cecil to the crackling bonfire. I wondered if the fire was for warmth or to keep animals and other creatures at bay. Or if it was just a way to make the dark, dying streets feel a little less lonely.

Two women approached just behind Cecil. One looked to be in her late twenties and was short and curvy, with cropped dark hair that framed her face. In contrast to the tapered edges of her hair, I could see that she had soft features, a pert nose, and wide copper eyes.

The other woman also looked to be in her mid- to late twenties. Her body had the same tone and definition as Nya's, and her chest-length hair cascaded down in natural curls. Although her dark features were sharper than the other woman's, the two were clearly related.

"Maila, let me introduce you to my wife, Rubi," Cecil said affectionately, wrapping an arm around the shorter woman's shoulder and squeezing. Their height difference was so drastic that he had to stoop just to reach her.

Rubi smiled, creating charming dimples in both cheeks that reminded me of Zander's.

"And this," Cecil continued, gesturing to the other woman. "Is my sister-in-law, Xiomara."

I had heard that name before. Xiomara smiled, but unlike her sister, the smile didn't quite reach her eyes. My attention shifted back to Cecil as he began asking about our trip, but not before I saw Xiomara's eyes flick up and down my body.

In the same moment, something soft brushed my arm.

The fabric of Kieran's shirt. As he and Nya filled Cecil in on our journey, he had stepped forward to idly stretch his leg, moving almost imperceptibly in front of me.

Cecil was just remarking on what good fortune we had that the skies were clear and cloudless, when something else caught my attention. I couldn't stop myself from interrupting.

"A baby."

The bundle in Rubi's arms had escaped my notice somehow. Now it was all I could see.

Rubi tilted the bundle forward, allowing the blanket to slip down and reveal a small, sleeping face. "Her name is Filimena." It was the first time Rubi had spoken, and her voice was gentle and sweet. I had also never heard a voice so full of complete and total adoration. "She's three months old."

As if aware that she was being talked about, Filimena flung a pudgy arm out of the blanket, revealing more of her tiny body, and let out a snuffling noise.

Everyone was quiet, mesmerized by the little sleeping person.

"Have you ever seen a baby before?" Rubi asked, gently rocking her from side to side.

"No," I said quietly. Almost reverently.

"Surely you've got babies in the city." Cecil patted the downy fluff on Filimena's head. The baby didn't even stir.

"We do, but—" I stopped myself.

I was about to say that maintaining our population was one of The Council's highest priorities, so babies were kept in a special facility on the southern end of the city until they were at least a year old. According to The Council, babies needed to be carefully monitored and protected at all costs during their most vulnerable time of life.

It was a reality that I had heard was almost unbearably difficult for the mothers, whose visits were scheduled and supervised closely by assigned caretakers. I still remembered Irene's wistful recollection of the day she and my parents got to bring me home.

After seeing the conditions that the Strangers lived in, that this baby lived in, I couldn't bring myself to say any of that to Cecil or Rubi.

"It's late," Xiomara spoke up suddenly. Where Rubi's voice was warm spring sunshine, hers was a cool summer storm. "What's the plan for tomorrow?"

All eyes turned to me.

I swallowed. "According to everything I read, the Leviathan tends to hover around the coast this time of year. Which I think you all already know and were hoping for. But it has never been spotted before late afternoon or after sunset. We have a short window of time if you want to lure it to shore." I paused. "Then again, there also aren't many accounts of people going out on the water after dark. I guess we can't really say for certain that it's not still out there at night."

"So...what? We go to the beach in the afternoon and wait around for it to show up?" Xiomara's arms were crossed in front of her.

"We don't have to wait around." I meant for my response to be reassuring, but Xiomara's cheek rounded as she pressed her tongue against it. Had I said something wrong? "We can summon the Leviathan to us while it's close to shore. We just need to chum the waters, so to speak."

"That, we can do!" Cecil clapped his hands together. "What are we hunting?"

"We need the blood of a creature that has magic."

Nya circled behind me and grabbed Kieran's arm, lifting it in the air. "Hunt's over."

Kieran sneered at Nya, then turned to me. "We just need blood, right?"

I considered. "I mean...yeah, that should be fine. The stories I read didn't specify that entrails had to be included, and they also didn't say that the creature had to be dead."

"Well, sounds like you're up, Kieran!" Cecil crowed. "We'll lure it in, give it a sound beating and a nice descaling, then be on our way. Hopefully those scales are all they're rumored to be. I'll spread the word, and we can head out tomorrow morning."

At the finality in his tone, everyone moved to part ways.

"Come on." Nya motioned for me to follow her to a house on the opposite side of the fire. "I hope all those years of living alone haven't made you territorial, because there are ten of us that share this house."

When I saw that Kieran was headed in the opposite direction, I gave him a small wave. "Goodnight."

"Goodnight," he replied sweetly, waggling his fingers at me. Apparently, there was nothing I did that he didn't find amusing.

I sighed inwardly. Then I followed Nya across the square of dirt that had once been someone's front yard and into the house.

CHAPTER EIGHT

"Are you okay?"

Nya's voice carried from across the room.

I blinked away the last remnants of the dream world. The room came into focus. The cracked walls, the carpet stiff with layers of residue. Nya was pulling a shirt over her head. Through the glassless window behind her, I could see that the sun was rising, casting the small bedroom in a dim glow.

"Yeah, sorry," I said, even though I didn't know what exactly I was apologizing for. I didn't remember sitting up. I didn't remember opening my eyes. But here I was. And if I had screamed or even called out at the end of my nightmare…how humiliating.

Nya gave me a smile that had an undercurrent of sympathy to it. But didn't put me out of my misery by telling me what she had witnessed.

Well, at least I wasn't waking in a full panic this time. Small victories.

I stood and began making the bed. The mattress was thin and sat directly on the floor, and the blankets reeked of mildew. But it was somewhere to sleep, and Nya had insisted on letting me have the mattress to myself.

I had tried to tell her that wasn't necessary, especially as I noticed most everyone else who lived in the house shared beds. Including Nya's roommate and bedmate, Wren, who Nya explained had gone to sleep in another room while I was visiting, to allow me some privacy.

But Nya was adamant, and I had gotten the feeling it had less to do with ensuring my comfort, and more to do with the fact that she didn't know me well enough to trust me fully. When she had settled into her sleeping bag across the room, I had caught her slipping a knife under her pillow.

Once the bed looked as presentable as I could make it, I dug in my bag and pulled out my outfit for the day, a forest green V-neck and jean shorts.

"I know you brought a few changes of clothes with you," Nya said as she loaded a few things into her backpack. Although she was trying to be discreet, I noticed yet again that one of those things was the knife. "But did you bring a bathing suit?"

"A bathing suit?"

She was wearing her usual look—a tank top and shorts—but I noticed then that orange strings rose from the top of her shirt to tie around her neck, and another set of orange ties poked out of her waistband.

She paused with a towel in hand. "You didn't bring one?"

"I don't own one. Besides, I'm not going to be in the water with you all. Right?"

Nya's dark brows raised in surprise. "No, but you may decide to take a dip at some point. Better safe than sorry. Especially since walking around in wet clothes will give you wicked chafing. But anyway, is that normal for someone from Cyllene? Is there seriously something that all of us out here own that you all don't?"

I shrugged. "Most of us don't really have a use for one. We may have access to more luxuries than you all do out here, but maintaining a swimming pool isn't one of them. I'm pretty sure the last person who managed to fill up one of the old concrete pools in the suburbs, without anything to properly clean or sanitize it, got really sick. And then the ocean's right over the wall, but we're not allowed to go outside the city under any circumstances."

The irony of my that last part wasn't lost on me.

"Wow," Nya drawled. She went to the closet—a space with missing doors, exposed drywall on the sides, and a back "wall" that was nothing more than a tarp—and began sifting through the clothes that hung there.

Meanwhile, in the crumbling hole that was once the doorway to the bedroom appeared a petite redhead with long lashes and a dusting of freckles across her cheeks.

"Oh, perfect!" she exclaimed in a voice that was like tinkling bells. "While you're over there, can you pass me my apron?"

"Sure thing," Nya tossed the words over her shoulder, right before she tossed a gray apron.

The woman caught it and pulled it over her head, smoothing the strands of her short hair in the process.

I gave her a small smile. "You must be Wren."

"That's me," she giggled. "And you're Maila. I hope you slept okay last night."

"I did. I'm sorry, I feel like I kicked you out of your own room."

"Oh, it was no problem at all!" Wren clasped her hands and leaned closer, her eyes wide with reassurance. She lowered her voice to a mock whisper. "Besides, absence makes the heart grow fonder, right?"

A trademark world-weary sigh sounded from the closet.

Wren giggled again and turned on her heel. "I've got breakfast to prep. See you two later."

As she pranced away, Nya turned around with a violet bikini top and bottoms in hand. "I know I'm taller than you are," she mused, examining her selection. "But you're curvier than I am, so hopefully it will all even out." She lobbed the bathing suit onto the bed next to me.

"Where did you get this?" I asked. Then, "Where do you get clothes in general, I mean?"

"Well, first off—bathing suits aren't exactly high on the list of priorities for anyone. Obviously. So they're easy to find." She tied her braids back into her usual thick ponytail. "As far as other clothes go, we get them the same way you do in Cyllene. Whenever you all are running low on clothes or other supplies, you either strike a deal with another city, or you send your Enforcers out on a supply run. Basically, you take what you need from somewhere else. That's what we do, too. Except for the striking deals with other cities part. I only know of a few that even exist anymore, and it would take days or maybe even weeks of travel to get there."

My knowledge about other surviving cities was limited, too. But I knew enough to know she was correct on the lengthy travel.

"And if we encounter another group like ours, which is rare, it usually doesn't end well. We're all just trying to survive out here, and no one's going to let some Stranger"— here she smirked at her own joke—"take clothes or food that they could be bringing home to their own children."

I let her words sink in. Then, beginning to undress, I asked, "How do you know so much about Cyllene?"

She pursed her full lips. "Because by default, anyone who finds out the truth of how Cyllene operates gets exiled. Some of us have been out here all our lives—like me, Kieran, Cecil, Rubi, and Xiomara—but we also take people in when Cyllene tosses them out and leaves them to die."

There was a lot to unpack in what she said. But a thought struck me. "By chance, is there someone here who was exiled recently? Like within the last week?"

Nya nodded. "You're talking about George. You'll see him at breakfast."

I suddenly couldn't wait to get to breakfast. I finished tying the bikini, then looked down at myself, twisting from side to side.

I frowned. "It doesn't fit."

Nya glanced up from where she was rolling up her sleeping bag and immediately burst into laughter.

"Oh, it fits!" she said after a moment, wiping her eyes. "Please, I have just one request. Actually, make that two. If you decide to strip down to your bikini, make sure Kieran is nearby. And make sure I'm there, too. So I can see his face."

I could feel my own face getting hot. There was no situation I could imagine where it would be appropriate for a Cyllene citizen to traipse around in something this provocative, just a few scraps of fabric away from being stark naked.

I almost took the suit off and insisted I wasn't wearing it.

Almost.

We ate breakfast around the bonfire, which I learned was the central meeting spot for the camp.

I hadn't been able to see the night before, but arranged in rings around the bonfire were chairs of all kinds, obtained during supply runs. Nya sat in a wooden chair that looked like it had once belonged to a dining room set. I sat in a blue and white beach chair, complete with an attached cup holder for my water bottle. There were several other groups scattered around the fire, but many still slept. Around and beyond the cul-de-sac, the dilapidated houses of Ersa Estates stood out in sharp relief against the lightening sky.

I couldn't recall ever sitting around a fire like this before, although I was familiar with the Pre-Awakening concept. Fire always posed a risk, and I considered myself lucky just to be allowed to use candles in my room. Now, basking in the warmth of the bonfire, I decided that the earthy, musky scent of burning brush might be my new favorite smell.

Breakfast consisted of eggs, fresh from the chicken coop that was maintained by the occupants of a house down the road, and jerky. I didn't ask what kind of animal—or other creature—the meat had come from. My gut told me it was best that I didn't know.

As we ate, Nya answered some of the questions I had about the Strangers' day-to-day life. I learned that not everyone in the camp gathered for meals and socialization. Some people preferred to keep themselves. So much so that rather than choose a house in the three main streets that made up the Ersa Estates camp, some people chose to live alone on unoccupied streets and only joined the rest of the group on important occasions. I also learned that when someone in the camp experienced hardship of any kind—illness, the loss of a family member, a curse from a magical creature, and so on—everyone else in the camp was expected to band together and help them in every way possible. The expectation made me think of Brielle and her joy in comforting the people she cared about with food.

Nya pontificated with her fork, a piece of egg speared on the end. She was explaining how the barbed wire fence around the camp was constructed, and how the Strangers hoped to be able to ward it one day, much like the walls of Cyllene.

As she was speaking, I caught sight of Kieran standing by the fire. And beside him, with tanned legs that seemed to go on for miles, was Xiomara. She put a hand on his arm, and he smiled in response. I couldn't discern from a distance if he was just being polite, or if the smile was genuine. Even if I were right next to him, did I know him well enough to tell?

Suddenly I didn't feel hungry anymore. I poked at my eggs.

"It's over, you know."

I didn't realize what Nya was referring to at first. Then I saw she was looking in the same direction.

"They used to date?" I asked, even though I knew it to be true. I had known it in my gut, my being, my very soul. There was no way two people that beautiful could live in close proximity to each other and be completely oblivious to one another.

I almost laughed at how my thoughts sounded like words straight out of Brielle's mouth. But even she would have to admit that Zander and I were completely average-looking if she ever had the opportunity to witness the genetic perfection that was Kieran and Xiomara.

Nya snorted. "They didn't date. They just hooked up for a while."

Wow. Casual hook-ups happened in Cyllene, sure, but I'd never heard it spoken about so plainly. I couldn't decide if it was a relief that they hadn't dated, or if that made it worse somehow—no real feelings for each other, yet a wild attraction that neither of them could resist.

I took a deep breath, inhaling that pungent scent of burning brush. "Is he dating someone else now, then?"

"You've heard me tease Kieran enough," she said, finally eating the piece of egg that dangled from her fork. "He's never 'dated' anyone. That would involve actually caring. Wanting to spend time with someone outside of fucking."

Clearly, if I wanted to fit in during my stay here, I was going to have to get used to speaking plainly about sex.

"I didn't realize he was so…" I searched for the right word. "Cold, I guess."

Nya shook her head vehemently as she finished chewing and swallowing. "You're not getting it. Kieran would do anything for the people he cares about. In Cyllene, do you only fuck if you're in a relationship?"

"No, people in Cyllene have casual sex sometimes, too."

So why was this bothering me so much?

Nya gave me a long look, and in it, I could hear her asking the same question. Finally, she gestured to my half-eaten breakfast. "Finish everything on your plate, or you're going to regret it later."

I did as she said. That was part of our agreement, after all. But my stomach still felt queasy.

Since Nya obviously wasn't going to say anything else about Kieran, I decided to change the subject. "So Wren seems really nice…" I let my voice trail off, the suggestion there in my tone.

Nya rolled her eyes, but also struggled to hide a smile. "Yes, Maila, Wren and I hook up every now and then. We agreed not to hook up with other people to keep things simple, but we're not in a relationship or anything. Maybe one day, when things aren't so crazy, I'll think about if I want something more with her or with someone else." Her voice became distant as she added, "Right now there's too much at stake."

"Morning," a familiar voice said from behind me, and I nearly fell out of my chair. Kieran and Xiomara slid into folding chairs in front of us, straddling the seats and resting their arms on the backs to face us.

"What are you two chatting about?" Xiomara asked innocently, tossing her dark curls over her shoulder.

I pressed my tongue to the back of my teeth. It was like she knew that we had been talking about them. And she was relishing it.

Nya's eyes narrowed. Then she flashed a smile that even I noticed was unusually large and toothy for her. "We were actually just talking about my dating life," she said dramatically, resting her cheek on her hand.

"What dating life?" Kieran's grin was as big as Nya's.

She socked him in the arm. "I was actually just asking Maila…"

Something in her voice made me set down my fork again.

"…about *her* dating life."

What the actual hell?

I instantly broke out in a sweat. Nya and Kieran were always making remarks about how naive they found me. Surely she knew my "dating life," at least at this stage of my life, was nonexistent.

When I didn't respond right away, Nya draped an arm over the back of her chair and continued. "Come on, Maila. Kieran and I observed you for *days* before you caught on to us and forced us to make our move. We saw you go to work every day at your 'Knowledge Center,' which was how we knew you'd be able to help us with the marsh wolves. And we also saw that hot Enforcer who can't go two seconds without eye-fucking you."

"Zander?" I choked out. I should have been concerned about all the possible implications of sharing his name. But that would've required a functioning brain.

"Mmm, he was gorgeous. I know your Enforcers despise us more than anyone, but that uniform did *wonderful* things for his ass. I would be down for some hate sex with him anytime." She shook her head appreciatively. "How long have you two been a thing?"

Xiomara's brows were furrowed slightly. She looked as confused as I was about where this conversation was going.

A creak and a flash of charcoal got my attention.

"I'm bored," Kieran declared. "I'll leave you all to your girl talk."

He sauntered off. After a moment, Xiomara excused herself as well.

I turned on Nya. "What was all that about?"

When Nya made eye contact with me, her smile was gone and one brow was raised. "If someone's going to come into my space and play games, they'll find another willing player. But they're going to lose."

"Are you talking about Xiomara?" I asked, struggling to keep up.

Nya gave me yet another meaningful look. Frankly, having someone constantly look at me like I was a moron was starting to get old. Finally, she said, "Come on. That man you wanted to talk to just sat down."

"Good morning, George!" Nya said brightly as we each dropped into a chair. "This is Maila. Believe it or not, she's here because she managed to sneak out of Cyllene for a few days. And she specifically asked to meet you."

I hadn't had an image in my head for this mysterious exile before meeting him. And yet somehow he looked exactly like I would've pictured. He appeared to be in his seventies. Slender, with a frail disposition. His white hair was both thin and full at the same time, resembling the top of a dandelion. His dark eyes were two beady dots in the center of his face, but they were magnified by glasses that looked much too big for him. He was dressed in a cobalt button-up shirt and rumpled khaki pants, and he was neatly cutting his scrambled eggs into bite-sized pieces.

"Ah, a citizen of Cyllene, escaped in the night!" His voice wavered with the weakness of age, but his enthusiasm made up for it. "How exciting!"

"It is," I agreed. "It's very nice to meet you."

He eyed me speculatively. "And why is it so nice to meet an old man like me?"

I swallowed. "My work assignment is in the Knowledge Center. Specifically in the Library. Along with Cato, I was responsible for…sorting your books. At least, I think it was you—"

George cut in with a barking laugh. "Deciding which ones to keep and which ones to burn, I suppose?"

I leaned forward in my seat. "To burn?"

He took a bite of egg. I tried to be patient as he chewed noisily. Finally, he finished swallowing and spoke, "I know who you are, Maila. I know you work in the Library. I've wanted desperately to meet you for some time now, but I was never allowed. I suppose if I had, my radical thinking might have corrupted yours, eh?"

He said the last part with emphasis, gesturing to the Strangers' camp around us. The camp where I had ended up anyway, without his influence. He laughed until he wheezed, holding his stomach.

"How do you know who I am?" I asked.

He set down his fork. When he made full, unwavering eye contact with me, I had the most overwhelming feeling of being seen. Truly seen. "How couldn't I know about the young woman who works in the Library, taking care of all our books?" he said softly. "Just because our paths were not allowed to cross, doesn't mean I couldn't recognize a kindred spirit from afar."

I don't know what I had expected him to say, but it wasn't that. We just stared at each other for a while in quiet understanding.

"I'm sorry about your collection," I finally said around the lump in my throat. "It must have been painful to have to leave it behind."

He nodded. "It was. So was leaving behind my friends and neighbors. Everyone I've ever known." He removed his glasses to wipe moisture from his eye.

I didn't know what to say to that. What I *could* say to that. So I asked instead, "What did you mean when you said some of your books might be burned?"

The chair creaked as he leaned against the backrest. "You're young, so the books you've seen and read are all you've ever known. But there used to be others." His gaze drifted above my head, as if he could see them just over my shoulder. "Books about anything and everything under the sun. Anything you've ever thought, anything you've ever wanted to learn…there was a book for it. Multiple books, even."

"What happened to all of them?"

He sighed. "Anything that could incite rebellion… anything that could give citizens 'ideas' of any sort… those were all burned. Except for a few that some of us stubborn old people have held onto over the years." He resumed eating. Yellow pieces of egg were visible in his mouth as he spoke again. "I bet Cato made certain you didn't come across any books like that."

Apparently. I certainly hadn't seen any.

"The piles we separated the books into," I explained, "were books to add to the Knowledge Center and books to share with the public." This had him pausing mid-bite. I continued, "Cato said there's no point in going to all this effort to preserve the books in the Library if we're not raising another generation to take over for us when we're gone."

George's eyes became glassy again. "I agree wholeheartedly."

I felt a gentle touch on my arm. I had nearly forgotten that Nya was sitting beside me. Now she was beginning to stand.

"We have to go," she said, her voice low and apologetic.

I followed her gaze beyond the bonfire, where a group of around twenty people had gathered, all young and able-bodied. I spotted Kieran, Cecil, and Xiomara among them.

George followed our eyes, too, then smiled kindly. "You kids have fun. If you two join me for breakfast again sometime, I'll tell you all about what it was like before The Awakening." He added with a snort, "From a child's perspective, anyway! But then, what better perspective is there?"

As we made our way through the sea of chairs to the rest of the group, two images kept circling through my mind.

A room full of books.

And an old man, alone by the fire.

CHAPTER NINE

According to Nya, the hike to the beach would take several hours. Even though it felt like we were backtracking the same way we had come the previous night, we eventually turned to head further south.

The landscape was much the same as what we had traversed before, but seeing everything during the day was a whole new experience. Thick forest surrounded us in every shade of green. We shouldered through fields of giant foxtail, pushed through clusters of palm fronds, and passed through clearings where the surrounding trees were so tall, they blocked out the sunlight. The hum of cicadas sounded all around us.

Cecil and Kieran led the pack, with me, Nya, and Xiomara trailing close behind. There didn't seem to be any rhyme or reason to the order the rest of the group walked in.

Besides taking in the beauty of the plant life, I kept my eyes peeled for any other creatures that dared make an appearance. So far on our journey, I had seen a swarm of gnats, a warty toad, a single ladybug, and about a million mosquitoes. But as we reached the peak of a hill dense with scrub, I spotted something in a clearing to our right that made me gasp.

Cecil and Kieran whipped around, on high alert.

"A hamina!"

Cecil roared with laughter, and Kieran's eyes softened.

"You all go on ahead," Kieran said, falling out of step with Cecil and motioning for me to follow him. "We'll catch up."

Nya waved as I passed by her. When I crossed in front of Xiomara, I caught her sneering.

I trailed Kieran through the foliage, mimicking his movements. When he crouched low to the ground, I crouched also. We moved slowly through the tall grass and weeds, trying to make our footsteps noiseless.

When we were within a few feet of the hamina, Kieran held up a hand.

I sat back on my heels.

Ahead of us waddled a pale yellow ball of fluff, roughly a foot tall and a foot wide. With each step, its tufts of fur shifted from side to side.

I was just lamenting that I couldn't see its face when it turned. Its small, round ears perked at some noise that was too faint for us to hear. Its large eyes were heart-meltingly cute, and its nose was a pink speck that barely stood out against all its fur. With a twitch of the fluff that must have been its snout, it returned to snuffling through the grass.

I watched its retreat, my heart swelling.

This was what I came here for. To see. To learn. To just... experience. The hamina were harmless, which meant that the Library was full of information about them, dating back to the earliest days of The Awakening. It was one of the few magical creatures that we even possessed photographs of.

But what was a photograph compared to the real thing?

After some time, I became aware of how close Kieran was beside me. The sleeve of his shirt was barely brushing my arm, his cheek just inches from mine. With his eyes trained on the hamina, I could take in his profile. Notice how the view highlighted his sharp features. The fullness of his lips. The definition of the muscles of his neck.

His eyes cut to mine, startling me. "What do you think?"

It took me a moment to realize he was talking about the hamina.

A moment too long, because a slow smile spread across his face. "Now," he said, his voice low. "What would your Enforcer friend think of you looking at me like that?"

"I think he'd say it's time to catch up with the others," I replied. My face was on fire, and I couldn't decide if I was more annoyed with him or with myself.

I stood. And when I did, I surprised myself by shoving him. Hard enough to tip him over, I hoped, as he was resting on the balls of his feet.

Instead, he whipped out his hand and grabbed my upper arm, using my own momentum to pull me down with him. We were facing one another when we flopped on the grass, the crunch of our fall sending the hamina scampering away with a squeal.

"It's like we've been here before," he said, his silver eyes twinkling. "Except last time, you almost puked on me." I tried to jerk my arm away, but he tightened his grip. "Did you seriously just try to push me over? You're like half my size."

"I am not!" I cried indignantly.

He raised his brows and frowned, full of sympathy. "You're not much bigger than that hamina."

I grunted in frustration. I was trying to come up with something clever to say back, but I was drawing a blank. Why did this always happen with him?

I sighed, deciding to speak honestly instead. "Thank you for stopping with me. I know you all probably see creatures like this all the time, so it's nothing to you. But it's a big deal for me."

"Anytime." After a moment, he added, "Did you know the hamina are good for the forest?"

"I did," I replied. "The aura they give off is like a fertilizer for plants, helping them to grow. And for plants that are already full height, it still encourages them to become healthier and flourish."

"Of course," he laughed. "I forgot the whole reason we met is because you're the expert on all things magical. On the whole world, probably." He idly picked at a few blades of grass.

I scoffed. "I highly doubt that."

"Come on, don't be modest. Name one thing that I know more about than you do."

More than a few things came to mind. But I wasn't about to mention any of those. I propped my head on my hand and took a deep breath. "Well…for starters, I can't swim."

He flung a piece of grass at me. We both watched it flutter uselessly through the air and land between us, nowhere near hitting me. "That's nothing. I can teach you to swim."

"Really?" The thought of knowing how to swim was exciting. The thought of what all him teaching me would entail was nerve-wracking.

"Sure," he said. "Some other time, when we're not about to potentially be swallowed whole by a sea monster."

"Right." His words filled me with a cold, creeping dread. But I tried not to let it show on my face.

Eventually, we tramped back through the underbrush in the direction the group had been headed in. There wasn't a moment of silence as we walked. We drew comparisons between daily life in Cyllene and daily life in Ersa Estates. We lamented that neither of us had much in the way of "free" or "leisure" time, but shared the things we enjoyed on the rare occasion that we did get a moment to ourselves. He educated me on the adrenaline rush of sparring and surprised me by looking genuinely interested when I talked about my world of books.

We were walking slowly. Taking our time. We both knew it. And we both feigned obliviousness.

When we finally caught up with everyone and Kieran resumed his position beside Cecil, I felt a strange mixture of heaviness and restlessness. Like there was somewhere else I needed to be, but I had no way to get there.

Then I understood.

It was longing. For the first time, I was experiencing what it felt to long for someone.

I knew we were getting close when the forest gave way to a field, which then faded into dirt that was ever so slightly grittier.

The sand dunes were dotted with clusters of sea oats, which dipped rhythmically in the salty ocean breeze.

Beyond the dunes, I could hear the steady rhythm of waves lapping at the shore. The sound sent a thrill through me.

By the time my feet were sinking in powdery sand, I was grinning from ear to ear. Back in Cyllene, I never would have thought that I'd actually see the beach. It felt like at any moment, I was going to wake up and find that this was just another vivid dream.

Then it was there.

The ocean.

A turquoise blanket extending all the way to the horizon.

Kieran teasing that I was small was one thing, but this made me feel small in the best possible way. And arcing over that vast expanse of water was the backdrop of an equally clear blue sky.

"Let's set up here," Cecil announced, stopping where the dunes leveled off and transitioned to flat beach.

He and the others had brought large hiking backpacks, the kind that made my shoulders ache just to look at. Without a word, everyone began unloading and organizing the supplies in their respective packs. I tried to help Nya where I could, but it was hard not to feel like I was just getting in the way. After twenty minutes of setting up, they had a ten-by-ten canopy erected with bags of food and water arranged neatly underneath.

Also under the canopy was a pile of spears of various sizes and designs. Nya confirmed that the spears were part of what was looted from the cave devils. Not one of the blades were dull. All were sharpened to a perfect, menacing point.

"Okay, listen up!" Cecil said. His voice was so loud naturally that he barely had to raise it to get everyone's attention. "I know we've already been over the plan for today. Let's take some time to eat, rest, and rehydrate. And if a beautiful woman with a fish tail sings you a song, and you swim out to try and fuck her, you get what you deserve. Sound good to everyone?"

Nineteen voices at once gave their assent, and the group began to disperse.

I turned to where Nya and Kieran were standing nearby. And froze.

Nya had stripped off her tank top and shorts in an attempt to cool down, and she was stunning, to say the least. The bright orange of her bikini top was set off by her dark skin. And the solid muscles of her abdomen, shoulders, and thighs were on full display.

Then there was Kieran.

My mouth went dry as I took in the sculpted form of his body, his muscles rivaling Nya's in their definition. My eyes followed his carved abdominal muscles downward, lingering on the V-shape that disappeared beneath the waistline of his black swim shorts.

I was immensely grateful when my eyes darted up to his face and found him looking away, listening to something Cecil had said. I didn't need him to catch me checking him out twice in one day.

"Don't you need to cool off, Maila?" Nya asked. Her brown eyes were sparkling, and I had to resist the urge to roll my own as I remembered her request from earlier.

Anxious to get whatever this was over with, I yanked off my shirt and shorts in the least artful way possible and tossed them in the sand. I had never worn so little clothing in public before, but I braced my shoulders and hoped beyond hope that my posture made me look more relaxed than I actually felt.

Nya fluttered her lashes at Kieran, waiting for him to turn around.

When he did, I got to witness firsthand what I must have looked like when I saw him a few moments before. He stilled, and his eyes widened almost imperceptibly as they skimmed down my body.

What he was seeing was Nya's violet bikini bottoms, which had a ruffle across the top that accentuated how low they hung on my hips. And the matching violet bikini top, thin straps resting on my shoulders and wrapping around my rib cage to clasp at the back, with pads that were also trimmed in ruffles.

And barely contained my breasts.

Kieran's eyes lingered there for a fraction of a second. Then he was shoving his hands in the pockets of his trunks and flashing his signature smirk. "Look at you!" he said brightly. "If only your Enforcer friend could see you now."

Nya was biting her lip, holding back laughter.

While everyone else busied themselves with preparations for the confrontation ahead, I continued to take in the view, watching the bright turquoise of the water dissipate into white foam at the sand. Before I even realized what I was doing, I was standing right in front of it. When the water drifted upward again and caressed my toes, I smiled. The crisp coolness of it felt incredible against my hot skin.

For the briefest of moments, I felt something that I think was peace.

There was no past, with memories that wouldn't leave me alone.

There was no present, with confusing feelings about Kieran.

There was no future, where maybe these people I was becoming so attached to didn't survive the next few hours. Where maybe I didn't survive, if Cato or Brielle or literally anyone else figured out the truth of where I was. What I had done.

There was just me and the ocean.

"Wow!" Cecil exclaimed, absently stroking his beard. "You must have been just minutes away from melting."

"I'm glad you can see the humor in it," I said dryly, sipping from my water bottle.

The sun was low in the sky and a slight chill was forming in the air, but my skin was practically pulsing with heat. I stretched my legs out in the sand in the shadow of the canopy. I could swear that I was watching my skin get pinker with each passing moment.

"I really am sorry, Maila," Nya said from where she stood beside Cecil, a hand on her hip. "We're all so used to being out in the sun every day, we didn't even think about how it would affect you."

"It's okay, I should've known better."

It was true. I'd read plenty on sunburns. I'd even watched Zander cope with one several years ago, after his first day patrolling the city streets from sunrise to sunset. But I guess it was one thing to have knowledge, another to actually put it to use.

Kieran passed by us with an armful of spears. He was distributing weapons to the group.

And he was still shirtless. The muscles of his back rippled as he wore a path in the sand between the pile of weapons and the waiting semi-circle of Strangers.

"Why doesn't Kieran burn?" I lamented. "He's almost as pale as I am."

Nya snorted. "Kieran's only half human, remember? Who knows what kind of crazy sun-resistant genetics are floating around in there."

After a moment, she and Cecil stepped out from under the canopy and took up spots with the rest of the group.

"That must hurt," a voice behind me exclaimed.

I turned to see Xiomara stepping around me to grab a hunk of jerky from one of the supply bags. The steady misting of saltwater on the breeze had turned her already-curly hair into a voluminous mass.

A force to be reckoned with. Which I had a feeling was not so different from the rest of her.

"It's going to hurt a lot worse later," I sighed. I poked my arm and watched the white imprint of my fingertip fade back to pink.

"True," she agreed with a wince.

I racked my brain, trying to think of something I could say. Literally anything at all. Where was Brielle when you needed her?

Right, she was back in Cyllene. Not being a liar and a traitor to her entire city.

Xiomara stepped closer, snapping me out of my thoughts. She crouched down so we were at eye level with one another, hugging her bronzed knees against her chest. "Look, I don't want there to be any tension between us," she began. "I'm sure you know about my history with Kieran, but I just want you to know I'm cool with whatever's going on between the two of you."

I could feel the surprise register on my face. "That's kind of a relief to hear," I said. "I feel like we got off on the wrong foot somehow? Even though there's nothing going on between me and Kieran."

It was the truth, wasn't it? Sure, he liked to mess with me. We flirted with each other, and Nya cracked jokes about how one or both of us were grossing her out. But it was harmless.

Granted, I was pretty sure I didn't want it to be harmless anymore. But she didn't need to know that.

"Right," Xiomara drawled, her voice somewhere between true agreement and sarcasm. "Well, I just thought you should know I'm used to this sort of thing. It's part of the package with Kieran. Maybe even like a rite of passage, you know?" Here she laughed, a throaty sound that even I had to admit was sexy. "He's always moving from one woman to the next, so you can't get too attached."

A knot formed in my stomach.

"I mean, I remember when we first started sleeping together." She shrugged her shoulders and bared her teeth in a mock cringe. "There were a lot of women back at camp who had a tough time with it. But Kieran and I have known each other forever. He and Cecil are very close. So it was just natural that our friendship would turn into something more." She leaned in again, adding conspiratorially, "I remember the girl he was with before me tried to confront me one night at camp, and it was *so* uncomfortable. I told her, look, you just can't beat a history like ours, you know? Friends turned lovers?"

I forced my face to remain impassive.

She stood then. She was already on the taller side, like Nya, but in this moment, she somehow seemed even taller. "You might get confronted while you're at camp, too," she warned. "But just let it roll off your back. The thing is, Kieran gets bored quickly, but he's also worth the trouble. I mean, look at him. Right? And he's a great lay."

I swallowed. Xiomara's blows were landing just the way she wanted, and we both knew it. I wanted to say something back, but I wasn't used to this. This verbal sparring. Cutting someone down with a smile plastered on my face.

"If you decide to take it to the next level with him while you're here, just let me know. I might be willing to share a few secrets on what really gets him going." She sighed wistfully, as if reflecting on fond memories. "And remember what I said. Don't get too attached, and enjoy the ride."

With a wink and a wave, she sauntered out to join the rest of the group.

It was time.

Shimmering gold filtered through the trees behind us, while the sky above the ocean was a muted blue. Soon, the sun would meet the horizon.

But not before the Strangers confronted the Leviathan.

When we had first arrived at the beach, Cecil had promised the group a second run-through of the plan. But he covered it a third and even a fourth time before everyone readied themselves and moved into position. And he did it all in front of me, which I guess was to be expected. But it was nice, being included. Being treated as someone they could trust.

The Strangers waded out until the water was chest-deep, forming a line that ran parallel to the beach. All of them were standing tall, shoulders braced.

What would they have done if the water was rough today? If the waves were crashing against them, threatening to knock them off their feet?

As soon as the question formed in mind, I already knew the answer. They would have done the same thing they were doing now. Because they didn't have a choice.

Just like with the marsh wolves and the cave devils, there was a goal for this venture beyond just capturing or outsmarting a terrifying beast.

The marsh wolves had provided the Strangers with pelts that were not only waterproof, but that were imbued with magic that gave them enhanced strength, speed, and endurance while swimming. Each member of the group had donned one of the slick, gray-brown, wet suit-like outfits.

The cave devils had, of course, provided the Strangers with an abundance of weapons. It was decided that spears were the best fit for this particular quest, but Nya mentioned that there were a variety of other weapons back at camp.

Then there was the Leviathan. Once defeated, its enormous scales—each one was nearly as tall as Cecil— would act as shields. Whether it was during a conflict with a predator, arranged in a wall formation around the camp, or something else, the uses for the impenetrable barriers were endless.

That is, if the Strangers made it out of this alive.

The plan, informed by my research, was to wrench the spears up and under those scales to pierce the tender flesh beneath. An action that was far from intuitive, according to the fishermen who once confronted the Leviathan several decades prior. Their captain noted that the scales gave the appearance of stiff, immovable armor covering the surface of the sea monster's body. It was only up close, fighting for their lives, that his crew found where the scales flared slightly, like feathers on a bird, creating inconspicuous openings between them.

Even with that discovery, everyone except the captain and one other man were slaughtered and swallowed whole. If the Strangers couldn't find an opening to land a blow, the same fate probably awaited them.

Not for the first time, I wished I could do something more useful than standing on the beach. Watching it all play out.

Once everyone was lined up, Kieran stepped forward.

My breath caught in my throat as I waited for what would come next.

Slowly, he extended his javelin, gripping it near the steel head. Then he slid the diamond across his palm.

From where I stood, I couldn't see the blood. But I cringed.

His hand still extended, Kieran submerged it, letting the blood mingle with the seawater.

There was a chance that it could attract some other carnivorous beast. A shark certainly wasn't out of the question. But if my research was correct, most creatures in the ocean would steer clear while the Leviathan was nearby.

A few in the group began to shift in the water, full of anticipation.

I could relate. A sickening feeling of dread washed over me, and it took everything in me not to scream at the Strangers to come back to shore. To go out there and drag them all, one by one, back to the beach. I wasn't strong enough to force any of them to do anything, though.

But suddenly, I desperately wanted to try.

I was walking, then jogging. The waves seemed to be picking up, reaching farther and farther up the beach. I followed their lead, gaining speed until I was at a full sprint. The soles of my feet pounded against the tightly packed sand, still damp from where the tide had been moving out.

It was rising now. The waves were climbing to meet me.

Maybe I was physically weaker than the Strangers, but my mind was sharp. I could convince them to come back. I could find another way to get them what they needed. After all, I had the entire Library at my disposal, not just the basement. Once I got back to Cyllene, I would make it my mission to find an alternative to the Leviathan's scales. No one needed to die today.

Now my feet were slapping against the line where the sand became slick and spotted with foam. And then they were splashing through the water itself, until I was knee-deep.

I stopped cold.

Ahead of the Strangers, water was erupting as if from a massive geyser, showering their faces. The waves were no longer just climbing back toward the shore. They were wild, directionless. Several people lost their footing and disappeared under the surf.

Then, through the spray, it emerged.

Towering over the Strangers was something like the head of a snake. Three stories tall. Maybe more. Fins protruded from the sides of its massive jaw and the top of its head. The surface area of each of them was larger than the canopy back on shore. The beast's eyes were an opaque black. Its scales—those impermeable scales—were iridescent even in the fading light.

It dropped its jaw. The fangs it revealed could've pierced through an entire person, head to toe, and still kept going.

Then it roared. And it was the first time a sound caused me physical pain.

My knees buckled under me. My ears were ringing so loudly, I couldn't hear the splash as I fell, could only feel the water close over my legs as they sank into the sand. Once down, I could feel a release. Although I was sitting waist-deep in water, I was certain I had wet myself.

I had just enough awareness to note that Nya and Kieran were still standing.

And then it was chaos.

A wave knocked me over, and at the same time knocked me out of my stupor. Another wave was right behind, and I braced against it. Out of my left peripheral, I saw a giant curving shape arcing through the air.

The Leviathan's tail. It was churning the water. In part because of how close it had come to shore, beaching itself. But maybe on purpose, too.

It was effective. In the distance, more heads dipped beneath the surface.

Cecil's face contorted as though he were shouting something down the line, but even his voice wasn't loud enough for me to make out over the commotion. Somehow, the rest of the group must have heard him, because they jumped into action. Cecil and Kieran charged straight at the Leviathan, while Nya, Xiomara, and the others seemingly rushed away from it. They were flanking it, as planned.

Kieran leapt into the air, using the force behind the Springing Spell to bring him even with the Leviathan's face. He thrust the javelin straight at one of its obsidian eyes—an attack, and also a distraction.

The Leviathan tossed its head like it was shaking off a gnat, the scales of its cheek connecting with Kieran's body with a sickening smack that sent him careening through the air.

Only moments after he landed, he was resurfacing and using the Springing Spell to bring him to stand near Cecil once again. The two of them aimed their spears at the sea monster's neck, in that bend just below its jaw.

At the same time, the Leviathan lunged. I held my breath.

Then a wave knocked me off my feet again, dropping me straight down on my tailbone. Pain rocketed up my spine, and for a second, my vision became dark at the edges.

I staggered to my feet again. But I couldn't make sense of the chaos before me—flailing arms and legs and the blunt ends of spears. Where was Kieran? Where was Cecil? Had they dodged the attack?

The Leviathan's head was still above water, but it was moving faster than my eyes could track. Waterfalls of spray crashed down in every direction.

The monster roared again, and the sound mixed with the screams and shouts of the Strangers as they struggled. Then I spotted Xiomara and noticed she was braced against something, the butt of her spear sticking straight up as though it were embedded in something.

Please, please let that roar have been a roar of pain. Please tell me she had managed to wedge her spear between its scales.

What happened next, I couldn't process.

I watched dumbly, motionless, as something shot up in the air. Spinning, turning, twisting.

A person.

The Leviathan had tossed one of the Strangers in the air. I watched numbly as it caught the body in its mouth, clamping its jaws shut with a clack that echoed across the beach.

A person.

It had eaten a person.

It had eaten a person whole.

Was that Kieran? Nya? Cecil? Even Xiomara, I wouldn't wish such a fate on.

I was crying then, in a way I hadn't cried since I was a child. I was crying for someone. For Irene, or maybe even my parents. I couldn't explain who I was crying for.

"*Help!*"

The scream came from nearby.

I whipped my head back and forth, scanning the waves until I caught sight of a dark shape. Then a wildly gesticulating hand. One of the Strangers, a teenage boy whose name I never caught.

Instinctively, I headed for him.

The ebbing of the ocean must have sucked me deeper, because I was now submerged up to my thighs. As I smashed through the onslaught, waves breaking against my face, it was only moments before I was in water up to my waist. Then my ribs.

A wave lifted me, and for the first time in my life, I knew what it was to be weightless. I kicked as hard as I could, trying to stay upright. As soon as the soles of my feet connected with the sand again, I continued on.

"Please! Help me!"

As I neared, I saw that the boy was screaming at me and also screaming at the world, eyes terror-stricken and unfocused. His blood clouded the water around him.

"I'm here!" I called back.

His curly head kept bobbing out of sight. Each time, I feared that he was gone. Then he would pop up in a slightly different spot than before, choking and sputtering. Behind him, the Leviathan was still swinging its mighty head and tail, teeth bared. Who knew how much more of it there was beneath the surface?

Then I had him. I grabbed the boy under one arm, my head over his shoulder, trying to pull him to shore.

"I've got you," I repeated over and over, through his screams.

But he wasn't calming down. The harder I pulled, the more he thrashed. Hysterical.

"Please!" I shouted. "I've got you!"

I could feel my feet slipping. A wave sailed over us, submerging us completely. When we resurfaced, we were both choking and sputtering.

"Please, I—"

And then I was down. Not just below the surface, but really down.

In his desperation, the boy had shoved me beneath him until my knees hit the bottom. I tried to resurface, but his arm smacked my face as it floundered. There was a tangle of limbs and the whirring of bloody water swirling around me, and then I was completely disoriented.

My brain blitzed through everything I'd ever read on swimming.

I kicked my feet again, trying to pull myself through the liquid, cupping my hands. But I wasn't breaking the surface. I didn't even know where the surface was anymore. I had swallowed saltwater on the way down, and my lungs burned with a pain I'd never experienced before. I wasn't getting enough air.

Fuck, fuck, fuck.

I was drowning.

This was it. I was going to die.

For an uncertain amount of time, I thrashed there. The pain bordered on unbearable. The edges of my vision darkened.

And then there was a light.

Was I at the surface?

No. The light was underwater, illuminating the sand and shells and everything above me. Above me, because I was upside down.

Someone grabbed me. Spun me until I was upright. Then we were ascending at a speed that felt impossible.

Finally, the warm evening air hit my face.

Someone continued to hold me as I choked and gagged, salty sea water spewing from my throat. I coughed and gulped air, coughed and gulped air. Over and over until the coughing slowly subsided, my breathing becoming more regular.

My breathing. My lungs still ached, and my throat felt raw, as if pure flame and singed it, but I could *breathe*.

Then the air left me again. For a different reason.

The waters were still. The Leviathan's tail, half a mile away now, was dipping under. Retreating into the distance.

And the arms that held me, like the eyes that stared back at me, were not human.

CHAPTER TEN

The face was oblong, with the barest hint of a nose and mouth. Like the Leviathan, it had large opaque eyes and fins protruding from its head and jawline. But unlike the Leviathan, its eyes were centered on its face, giving it a less fish-like appearance, and its translucent fins appeared delicate rather than intimidating.

It was clearly an aquatic being of some kind, but there was also something human about the way its head sat atop a graceful neck, which swooped into the smooth shoulders and arms that held me.

What entranced me the most, though, was its magnificent skin. Like the luminous surface of an opal, it glowed in overtones of turquoise and lilac, mint and watermelon. With even the subtlest movement, the colors would shift into an entirely new palette.

I couldn't say if it was fear or wonder that kept me from screaming.

The creature opened what looked to be a small mouth. "This is the tongue in which you speak, yes?"

Their voice was masculine and feminine, thunderous and soft, gravelly and musical. It was as if the moment they finished speaking, I had already forgotten what their voice sounded like.

After a beat, I remembered they had asked a question. "Yes," I answered hoarsely.

Their face was devoid of expression. "Are you sufficiently recovered?"

"Yes," I repeated. Then added, "Thank you for rescuing me."

There was a subtle sensation of movement, and I became aware that we were gliding along the surface, toward the shore. It was only then that I saw just how far out the current had carried me.

And that the ocean was as still as a pond. No waves in sight. Not even a ripple.

I felt the slightest drag against the hands that held me upright. Then I realized they were not hands at all, but some sort of fin-like protrusions, as delicate as the fins encircling the being's face.

"You are the leader of your group, yes?"

If I weren't still recovering from a brush with death, I would have laughed. "No, not at all. The leader is—" I paused. Who was the leader? Cecil? Kieran? Did the

Strangers even have a leader? I said finally, "The leader is someone else."

"I see."

As we drifted soundlessly inland, another realization hit me. Where was everyone?

I wanted to twist to look behind me. But even though I felt confident that this being wouldn't have saved my life if they had wanted me dead, something told me I should keep my eyes trained on their face.

They spoke again. "You must communicate to the rest of your group that my 'Leviathan,' as you have named it, is to be left alone."

At least a dozen questions began to form in my mind. But since I still had no idea what sort of being I was speaking to, I said simply, "I apologize that we disturbed the—I mean, *your* Leviathan. I'll share your message with the others."

"The misstep is understandable," the being replied. "You may fish from my waters. You may take what you need to sustain yourselves. But you are not to involve the inhabitants of my waters in your human conflicts, indirectly or otherwise."

Something struck me as odd about that phrasing, "indirectly or otherwise." I couldn't imagine anything more patently direct than attacking something with a spear. But my head was a muddled, murky mess. How many times could I escape death in this life before it finally claimed me?

"You may stand."

Up until that point, my legs had been raised, my kneecaps almost grazing the surface. Now I lowered them and felt the cushiony feel of sand against my feet. The sensation was comforting. Yet my legs instantly gave out beneath me. The water was only chest-deep, but I almost slipped under again.

The being's head tilted slightly to look over my shoulder.

At the same time, a different pair of arms caught me from behind, warm and strong.

When looked up, I could've cried with relief to see Kieran staring back at me.

His features were weighed down by fatigue, his breathing heavy. Rather than the silver that I had become accustomed to, his eyes were dark. The color of the sky on a dreary day. After he took in the sight of me, assessing, his gaze drifted up to the being who hovered next to me.

"You will relay my message," the being said. It was a statement, not a question.

"Yes," I confirmed. Then added, "I can't thank you enough for saving my life. Would it be alright for me to ask for your name?"

The being remained unblinking. Expressionless. "You would not be able to pronounce my name in your tongue.

Please give me a name that you find suitable, and that is what your kind shall call me."

Wait. What?

I asked for a name, and the response was to *name this magical being myself?*

I couldn't have imagined a task that came with more pressure. As spent as I was, my body still found the means to bring a flush of color to my cheeks.

"Um…okay," I began, stalling for time. Then, "Your skin reminds me of an opal. But there's also something in it that reminds me of the surface of the ocean, particularly with all the shades of turquoise. How about Larimar? After the stone?"

The being was silent.

Then they lifted one of those fin-like protrusions, the movement so abrupt that I would've jumped if I could have. Sitting in the center of their outstretched fin was a larimar stone, its veined surface a near replica of how the ocean had looked when we first arrived at the beach, while the sun was high. "This is the stone you speak of?"

I should have been more surprised that the being summoned a stone out of thin air. But they had magic, after all. And considering the way this day had gone, it only made sense that they would do something fantastical.

I nodded.

"Then that is what you shall call me." The being extended their fin further. "Take this. If there is a discussion to be had or a conflict to be settled, you will use it to summon me. The events of this evening will not be repeated."

With effort, I extended my own hand and grasped the stone.

Then I blinked, and Larimar was gone. In the same moment, the waters subtly began to shift again.

Kieran hoisted me up, cradling me in his arms, and began carrying me back to shore.

As soon as he turned, I saw Nya, Cecil, Xiomara, and the rest of the Strangers standing in the shallows. Including the boy I had tried to save, I noted with enormous relief. All of them were standing with arms at their sides, mouths hanging open, wide eyes fixed on me.

Feeling self-conscious, I turned into Kieran's chest. The warmth of his skin radiated through me. My self-consciousness increased tenfold, and I was thankful he couldn't see my face.

"What was that?" he asked, his tone even. Almost forcibly so.

"I don't know. My only guess is some kind of water spirit—"

"I'm not talking about the being," he interrupted, each word clipped. "Why were you out that deep? Or in the water at all?"

I swallowed. "I was trying to rescue someone. The boy with the curly hair. He was hurt and screaming for me to help him. He was going to drown."

My head rose and fell with Kieran's chest as he took a deep breath and let it out slowly.

"Right. You can't swim, so you try to save someone who's drowning. Makes perfect fucking sense."

As we approached, the others gathered around us.

I relayed Larimar's message, and none of them seemed surprised. Apparently, around the same time I saw the light beneath the surface, the group was abruptly pulled back to shore by an unseen force. And the Leviathan, in all its mammoth glory, seemed to be jerked by some unseen force back out to sea.

The message was expected. And yet, as we trooped the rest of the way back to the beach, Kieran still carrying me in his arms, I couldn't shake the feeling that they were all eyeing me warily.

We made camp for the night amid the sand dunes. The beach would have been a more convenient spot, but after the events of the evening, everyone wanted to put at least a little distance between us and the water.

A few suggested we just go ahead and make the hike back to Ersa Estates. But Nya declared that the injured would benefit from at least one night of rest, and soon everyone agreed.

Only one man had died. The one whose death I had witnessed. Nya explained that the Leviathan had plucked the man, who had been standing to her left, out of the water with its fangs. I had obviously seen the rest for myself.

I had expected a bigger reaction from the group to the loss of their comrade, but they were all surprisingly stoic. When you lived Outside, Nya had explained, the loss of companions, and even close friends and family, came with the territory.

"If you cried for everyone who died," she had said. "You would never stop crying."

However, everyone was quiet the rest of the evening. Somber.

The only outburst of emotion was from the boy I had tried to save. His injures—a broken leg and a slew of bloody friction burns—were from getting slammed by the tip of the monster's tail. He was lucky to be alive, and he knew it. He gave me a giant bear hug and wept as he alternated between apologizing and thanking me.

That night, we settled onto blankets and sleeping bags. Spaced out enough to give each other room to breathe, but close enough to provide a sense of security.

I was thankful that Nya had reminded me to pack a change of clothes. The feeling of my dry cotton shirt and shorts against my skin was a comfort, helping to distance me from all that I had endured that day. I couldn't even imagine how the others felt.

But long after the rest of the group fell asleep—or at least laid still and silent, trying for sleep—I found myself wide awake, staring at the stars. As utterly exhausted as my body was, my mind was overwhelmed. I ruminated on all the events of the day. I combed through the conversation with Larimar. Why would they think I, of all people, was the leader of the group?

The more my brain tried to make sense of what my life had become, the more I ached for my safe space. But where was that, anymore? The Library? My apartment?

The moon was high in the sky when I gave up on sleep. I tiptoed around Nya and the other women sleeping beside me. I couldn't quite believe that my feet were carrying me back toward the ocean, but I let them.

When I reached the beach, I lowered myself to the ground in front of a dune. I ran my hands through the sand, letting it slip through my fingers. The sound of the waves breaking against the shore was rhythmic, soothing. It was hard to believe what all had transpired just a few short hours ago.

I closed my eyes. Focusing on that sound. Trying to clear my jumbled mind.

"There you are."

My eyes flew open.

Kieran was standing in front of me. He had also changed into dry clothes, a black T-shirt and shorts.

"What is it?" I asked, starting to stand. I paused as he sat down beside me instead.

"Just making sure you're not off trying to get yourself killed again," he said, resting his forearms on his thighs. His tone had a slight lilt to it, as if he were trying to sound lighthearted but couldn't summon the energy. "How are you doing?"

"I'm okay."

It seemed like the right thing to say. I wasn't sure if it was true.

I let my eyes travel then from the ocean, up to the stars, marveling once again at how different the view was outside of Cyllene. How could the same sky appear so changed just by me being in another location?

I remembered reading an old book years ago, from Pre-Awakening times, that explained the concept of light pollution. But that didn't exist in a city with no electricity. When I looked at the sky Outside, I felt a sense of wonder, and a sense of…was it freedom?

It took a minute for me to realize that Kieran hadn't responded. I glanced over and found him staring intently at me. As they so often did under the moon and stars, his eyes were shining silver. Framed by his long, dark lashes, their glow felt timeless. Ageless. Like the family he had inherited them from had lived long before humankind existed, and would live on long after we were gone.

"I'm glad you're handling this okay," he said finally. "Today was a lot. Even for us."

We sat in companionable silence for a while, him gazing out to sea and me gazing at the stars. But as the silence dragged on, a knot began to form in the pit of my stomach. Before I could stop myself, I said, "Xiomara was really impressive today. During the battle. She's so strong and agile."

"She is," he agreed.

The knot twisted, growing in size. That strange irritation that I sometimes felt toward Kieran resurfaced, with more intensity than usual. I wasn't sure if it was the events of the day or something else, but I suddenly wished he would just go away.

"Maila," he asked. He sounded like he was choosing his words carefully. "Have you ever been...intimate with someone?"

The knot clenched.

"That's kind of a personal question."

"So 'no,' then," he said decidedly.

I opened my mouth, but he cut in, "Have you ever kissed someone?"

"I've had sex before, you asshole!" I spat at him, sounding much more defensive than I had intended.

Kieran's eyes were truly sparkling now, and it wasn't just from the reflected light from the moon and stars. He was enjoying watching me squirm, as usual.

"What does it matter to you?" I demanded. The knot had expanded until it reached my chest, making it hard to breathe. "Maybe I don't have a harem like you do"—I remembered his reaction when Nya had said this and hoped it had the same effect now—"but some people only want to be intimate with someone when it means something. And I don't think there's anything wrong with that."

It took an immense amount of willpower to look back up at the sky and not watch for his reaction.

"Interesting," he said. I could still feel his stare fixed on my profile. "And what makes it 'mean something?'"

I couldn't help it. My eyes snapped back to his.

His smile was gone, but there was still amusement dancing in his eyes.

"What?" I asked, dumbfounded.

He stretched out his legs and shifted closer to me, turning away fully from the view of the ocean. "Does it 'mean something' only if you care deeply about the person? Or is it enough just to enjoy yourself? Does it have to be someone who you're having romantic encounters with on a regular basis? Someone who's chosen to take no other romantic partners?"

"I don't know."

I really didn't, I realized with dismay. I couldn't say what my past experiences meant to me now that they were over, and those men were gone from my life.

"I think you do."

My temper flared at the challenge. "Look, Kieran. Last night, I went outside the walls of Cyllene for the first time. I slept outside the walls. Today, I saw the most terrifying creature I have ever seen, almost drowned, and came face-to-face with a being the likes of which I wasn't even sure existed. Every single second I'm out here, I'm risking my life in more ways than one. I could get back to Cyllene tomorrow night and have Enforcers waiting at my door, ready to put a bullet in my head for sneaking out of the city and helping the people who, in their minds, are a bunch of wild, lawless, deviant criminals."

Wow. The more I spelled it out, I really was fucked.

"There are so many things weighing on me, so many things I'm trying to think about, to understand, to get a handle on…I'm sorry if I don't feel like explaining my romantic preferences right now."

I forced myself to hold his silver gaze, refusing to look away this time.

Now both the smile and all traces of amusement were gone, replaced by something I didn't recognize. He sighed. "I know you've got more important things to worry about, Maila. Believe me, I know. It's just…you said there's a lot you're trying to understand." He paused for a moment, throat bobbing. "I guess I'm just trying to understand *you*."

When I didn't respond right away, he continued, "I know Nya has you convinced that I've fucked around a lot with women who don't mean anything to me. And I guess if your definition of 'meaning something' involves wanting a committed relationship or wanting to get married, then that's true. But all the women I've been with knew that and accepted it."

When I still didn't respond, he exhaled in an exasperated way through his nose.

What the hell did he have to be exasperated about?

I almost asked him outright. But I said instead, "I don't think Xiomara 'accepted that.' She seemed to *really* enjoy telling me about your time together."

"And that bothered you?"

"What bothers me is why she felt the need to tell me at all. Why she keeps glaring at me and trying to make me feel like I'm an intruder." Which in a sense, I was. I wasn't one of them. But that was beside the point.

Kieran flexed his jaw. "You really don't know why?"

The knot was no longer a knot. It was acid, and it was spreading through me. It boiled up in me, along with an avalanche of words that some sensible part of my brain was trying to keep at bay.

"Okay, fine," I said. "Because you want to fuck me? Because you want to add 'sheltered city girl from Cyllene' to your list of conquests?"

The silver in Kieran's eyes flashed, becoming an icy white. "Wrong."

It should have been the right answer, but it was like a physical blow.

Was he lying to save face? Or in all the moments we had shared where it felt like there was this spark, was that only on my end? Was I fooling myself into thinking he even found me attractive to begin with?

The avalanche gave way then, and there was no clawing back the words as they spilled from me.

"You know what I don't get then? Why you always mess with me. One minute you're nice to me, the next minute it's like there's some inside joke that I'm not in on. I don't know if I'm just a source of entertainment to you, or if you really were hoping I could be another one of your conquests and you're just covering your ass now. But I don't think it's funny. I don't like being toyed with, and I don't want to be just another woman you've slept with. Honestly, I wish you would just leave me the fuck alone."

The only sound then was the lapping waves.

I kept my eyes trained on one random star, steeling myself against the lump in my throat. There was a shuffling sound next to me, and my heart sank. I waited to hear his footfalls receding in the sand.

"Maila."

I turned. His face was inches from mine.

"Is that how you really feel? Everything you just said. Is that what you really think of me?" His expression was unreadable. Then just for a moment, so quick that I almost missed it, something like hurt flashed across his features. It was there and gone in an instant.

"I don't know," I said softly. Then, "No."

The breeze ruffled Kieran's hair and blew a few loose strands of my own across my cheek. I couldn't have said how or why, but there was a sudden weight to the space between us. A charge to the air like just before a storm. His eyes darkened, and the intensity in them made my body burn again. But not from anger or the sunburn or even that sickly knot in my gut. It was something uncomfortable and pleasurable all at once.

Time seemed to slow.

Kieran gently placed his fingers on my face, tilting my chin upward. And then everything around us—the lapping of the waves, the mild breeze, even the stunning night sky—seemed to cease to be, as he pressed his lips to mine.

His lips were warm and soft. He brushed his thumb across my cheek gently, as if testing my reaction. I found myself extending my own hand, placing it on his arm. I ran my fingertips along the curve of his bicep, then his shoulder over his shirt, traveling upwards. My hand finally came to rest on the back of his neck, and when it did, he slipped his tongue into my mouth.

He tasted like the salt from the ocean, and like something unplaceable but distinctly him.

Somewhere in my mind, I questioned if I was kissing him the way he liked. If he was feeling everything that I was feeling. But my worries floated away as something stronger took their place. Something that felt like the moment when Larimar had pulled me above the surface, and I took that first lungful of air that I had so desperately needed.

My hand still on Kieran's neck, I brushed my fingertips up and down, feeling the warmth of his skin and then the softness of his hair. I lightly twisted a few strands around my fingers.

At the movement, Kieran shifted so that his body was against mine, making my mind turn hazy. With some effort, he extracted his lips from mine. But only to press them against my neck, trailing his tongue from my clavicle up to my jawline.

The sensation was overwhelming.

My head rolled against his, my lips grazing his cheek. Some part of me was vaguely aware that I was breathing hard in his ear. Kieran made a rumbling noise in his throat. Feeling encouraged by the sound, I pressed my lips to the spot just behind his ear.

He stilled. Then in one swift movement, he rolled and lowered us, so we were laying in the sand, his weight on me fully. "Maila," he breathed, his fingers skimming the curve of my breast. It took me a second to realize he was asking for permission, practically vibrating with restraint.

"Yes," I murmured, and no sooner were the words out of my mouth than he was cupping my breasts, feeling me with his hands and then with his mouth. There was something practiced and skilled in each movement, but also something messy and desperate and even a little greedy.

"I've been wanting to do this since you walked out in that fucking see-through nightgown," he growled against my skin. Then, almost involuntarily, he ground his hips against mine.

In that moment, three things happened.

The first was that when his hips rolled into mine, I got physical confirmation that he was enjoying this as much as I was.

The second was that the friction of him against me, even with several layers of clothing between us, sent a spear of pleasure through me that had every nerve standing on end.

And then the third.

"Kieran." His name escaped my lips before I could stop it. It was a moan, soft and low and a harbinger of what lay ahead of us. What I suddenly needed from him more than I needed air.

Abruptly, he sat up.

It happened so fast that it took me a second to open my eyes. I blinked at him as if waking from sleep.

His breaths were still coming hard and fast. His eyes were glazed but also looked strangely conflicted. They searched mine. For what, I wasn't certain.

"Did I do something wrong?" I asked, not sure I wanted to hear the answer.

"No." His voice was strained. "But I think this is a good place to stop."

"To stop?" The words were a physical blow. "You want to stop?"

His jaw shifted, as though he were grinding his teeth. "No," he said. He attempted to adjust the fabric of his shorts where it strained, but there seemed to be no give. He hissed as if in pain. "That's the problem. I don't want to stop. And you deserve a hell of a lot better than getting fucked thirty feet from camp after almost dying."

I gaped at him. "And what exactly is the alternative? I mean, this is probably how it's gone down with all the other women you've been with, right?"

"More or less."

"But not with me?"

"Correct."

Before I could respond, he stood and stalked away.

I stood, too, and watched him walk not toward where the others slept, but in the opposite direction. He cut across the mounds of sand toward the woods, away from the beach entirely. Still dazed, and now completely bewildered, I stared after him until he disappeared behind a cluster of dunes.

Everything that had faded away during the kiss now came back into focus. And the cool breeze carried away the remaining warmth that lingered on my body from his.

CHAPTER ELEVEN

Our hike back to Ersa Estates was subdued. Even the sky was overcast, matching the mood. After the injuries that some in the group sustained, the loss of a man's life, and the fact that the Strangers were walking away from it all empty-handed, nothing felt worth saying.

Which was probably for the best because my head was still a mess of ruminating thoughts. I had gone to sit on the beach in hopes that it would give me some clarity, but instead, the encounter with Kieran had only left me with more unanswered questions.

We walked in the same formation as we had the previous day. Which put me behind him, staring at his back as he walked.

After our kiss, I had crawled back into my sleeping bag, heart pounding. It was some time before I heard the shuffle of fabric a few sleeping bags away, letting me know that he had also returned.

What had he been doing? Why did he go into the woods alone? My mind kept running through the possibilities. Then I considered his visible pain as he denied us something that I thought we both wanted. Suddenly, it seemed pretty clear what he had disappeared to do.

My feet were moving automatically as my imagination ran with that idea. Picturing how he must have looked, relieving that tension. The sounds he might have made. If he continued thinking of me during. The expression on his face when he finally found release.

An ache formed in me that was almost unbearable.

I blinked several times, then forced my gaze beyond Kieran to the trail ahead of us.

Regardless of what he had been doing, he had barely spoken to me that morning as we packed up camp. Now, as we hiked back through the forest, I wished he would say something. Even him poking fun at me or making a sarcastic comment would've been better than silence.

We arrived back at Ersa Estates while Nya's roommate, Wren, and the other cooks were still dishing out breakfast. Eggs and jerky again.

Rubi was sitting at the edge of the circle of chairs, bouncing Filimena on her leg. The second she caught sight of us, she grabbed the baby and ran to Cecil. The two of them almost disappeared in Cecil's giant hug. Then Xiomara joined them.

Nya had already agreed to take the difficult job to break the news to the family of the man who wasn't coming home. She turned onto a side street before the cul-de-sac and headed toward a house where a woman and teenage girl were already waiting in the yard.

I averted my gaze and focused on the bonfire ahead. I knew what it was like to get that news, to know that someone you loved was never coming back. I tried to tune in to the conversations around the fire. Tried not to hear the piercing wail that carried from that yard.

The group continued to splinter off, including Kieran. Eventually it was just me.

I understood. After what was essentially a defeat, everyone needed some time with family. With friends. Alone, even. Their lives were here, and they couldn't be expected to babysit me all hours of the day.

I chose one of the chairs closest to the fire, then instantly regretted it when the heat rubbed up against the heat from my sunburn. I moved to an old lawn chair a few rows back.

I was going home tonight. Returning to Cyllene.

I couldn't decide how I felt about that.

I stared into the flames, listening to the crackle and breathing in that musky scent that had already become a comfort.

The day passed quietly. The clouds remained gray and heavy overhead, but no rain fell. Eventually, Nya found me where I sat by the fire and let me know she was going to her room to rest. Her eyes were weary, and I knew it wasn't just from the battle with the Leviathan. After I reassured her that I would be fine on my own for a while, she headed to the house.

For lunch, the cooks served plates of summer vegetables, fresh from the camp's garden. Juicy red tomatoes joined yellow squash, purple eggplant, and bright green cucumber in a mixture that was surprisingly delicious. Even without a protein, the cooks had prepared the meal in a way I imagined even Brielle would appreciate.

"We have more to work with when hunting's good," Wren had explained as she handed me my plate and cutlery, a bandana tying back her auburn hair. The large folding table she reached over was tidy, the platters of vegetables neatly arranged, still keeping with that theme I was noticing, that what the Strangers did have, they tried their best to maintain. "But everyone's been busy with other things lately. As you know."

While walking back to my spot by the fire, my gaze snagged on another girl around my age, whose almond eyes were fixed on me. Even though my stomach clenched,

I forced myself to look straight ahead and pushed a breath in and out my nose.

I was a visitor here. An anomaly. There were multiple reasons why the girl may have been staring at me, including something as simple as that I had something on my face. I refused to let Xiomara get in my head even more than she already had.

I was still eating, lost again in my thoughts while the fire danced before my eyes, when I heard the chair next to me creak. I turned, expecting to find Nya or Kieran.

It was Cecil.

He gestured to my plate with his own. "It's not much, but we're running low on meat right now."

I wished they would stop explaining why they couldn't serve me a more impressive meal. Like I was there to cast judgment.

"It's really good," I said, and meant it. There was a question that had been tugging at my brain, though, and I decided this was as good an opportunity as any to ask it. "If you don't mind me asking…how do you, Nya, Kieran, and some of the others maintain being so muscular?"

Cecil swallowed more than just his food, his eyes downcast. "The cooks usually insist on giving us extra rations, even when we try to refuse. They say it benefits everyone because we need the calories to hunt and to protect the camp. But it still feels wrong, you know?"

The cooks' logic made perfect sense, but I imagined I would feel the same way if I were him. Not wanting to take more than my equal share, no matter the reason.

We sat in silence for a while. Mostly companionable silence, although I was becoming curious why he had chosen to join me. Where were Rubi and Filimena?

His blond hair curled around his shoulders at the ends, blending with his fair beard. Once his plate was empty, he crossed his arms over his rumpled shirt and stretched his legs toward the fire.

"You know," he said. "Rubi is the love of my life."

I smiled politely. "I can see that. You two seem to love each other very much."

"We do."

Some time passed, and I assumed he was done speaking.

Then he said, still staring at the fire, "I want you to know, though. There was a time when I would have said the great love of my life was your sister."

At first, the words didn't process. I set my fork down. "My sister?"

"Yep," he said, popping the *p*-sound. His eyes were trained on the fire, but they had a faraway look to them. As if he was seeing something else instead. "I was crazy in love with Irene."

I should have been incredulous. I should have bombarded him with questions. I should have unloaded on him for not telling me sooner that he knew my sister. But instead, I sat there. Plate on my lap. Still.

Waiting.

"Part of Irene's job was coming Outside to do supply runs. You know that."

I did.

"We crossed paths one day when she got separated from her troop or squadron or whatever the hell the Enforcers call their little groups. She practically chased me down. Wouldn't leave me alone until I stopped to talk to her." He chuckled. "She said she had always wanted to know what it was like Outside, how we all lived. And this was her chance! I needed to man up and have a conversation with her! Whatever I was doing could wait!"

I could practically hear Irene's voice telling him all of that. Scolding some random passerby and railroading him into talking to her. It was so typical of her.

"Well, after that, I guess you could say we became friends. She told me what the Enforcers' schedule was for making supply runs. And she told me where on their journey home they would usually stop to take a breather. So I would wait for her around that spot, hiding in the trees. Sometimes I'd bring others from the group with me. And she'd always sneak off somehow, with some 'lost' supplies for us."

I could barely breathe.

"I still don't know how she pulled it off," he mused, shaking his head. He bounced his leg anxiously, as if the answer still ate at him. "But she did, and I can't tell you how grateful we were for it. Food, clothes, you name it. I could sit here for hours telling you about the difference it made for us. And do you know she never asked for anything in return? I mean, I guess you probably would've figured. You know your sister's heart. The only thing I could think to do to make it up to her was give her something I knew she wanted, that we didn't have much use for in our day-to-day—books."

My heart stopped. Just for a moment, I was certain, it had stopped. Skipped a beat, then found its rhythm again.

This was all too much. And yet not enough.

A family of four scooted past us, plates of food in hand, and Cecil gave them a friendly wave. Then he continued, "Every now and then, our meetings wouldn't go to plan. Sometimes she got pulled for a different assignment. And obviously she couldn't insist on going on the supply run instead, or her boss would get curious."

I stifled a humorless laugh. "Get curious" was an interesting way to put it. Irene's Mentor was never simply "curious" about the things she did, in that simple, removed way that one would expect from his role. He was always deeply invested in whatever she was doing, in her success, in her well-being.

In mine, too.

But having worked side-by-side with my parents for years and being one of my father's closest friends, I suppose that came with the territory. We lost our dad, so he stepped up to fill that fatherly role in our lives.

Until he didn't.

"The last time I saw Irene" Cecil said, oblivious to my spiraling thoughts. "She was worried that they were on to her. She said someone had finally started asking questions, really digging into why certain things weren't making it back to Cyllene." He turned to look at me then, raw pain in his eyes. "We had talked about her coming here, to Ersa Estates. With you. Maybe on the next supply run, maybe sooner if she could swing it. We don't have much here, but we have each other. I told her if the two of you could get out, if you could get away, I would make sure you had a home waiting for you here. I told her…" He cleared his throat. "I told her that we couldn't provide you two with those big city conveniences, but there is one thing we would give you, always. A family."

Tears were sliding down my cheeks. I didn't try to stop them.

When he spoke again, his voice was just above a whisper. "I kept coming back to our spot. Waiting for her. Hoping every time that I'd see her there, bags packed, with a ten-year-old girl in tow. After several months passed, and she never showed, I figured what that meant. But I never stopped holding out hope. I told myself maybe she changed her mind. Maybe she settled down eventually, too, and had a husband and some kids on the other side of that wall."

The hand he put on my shoulder was so large, it encompassed my shoulder and then some.

"When Nya and Kieran came back after that second trip and told me what you'd said, about her being executed—" He stopped abruptly. Swallowed. "I'm happy that you're here. But I wish I never had to find out the truth."

A sob escaped me, and he looked away. If it was to give me space or because his own eyes were glistening, I wasn't certain.

"The thing is," he said after a while. "I never knew if she felt the same about me. If she saw me as anything more than a really good friend. But I didn't care. She was the most beautiful woman I'd ever seen. And smart and kind and funny and…I don't have to tell you this."

I shook my head. Beyond words.

"When Nya and Kieran were gearing up to go find you that first time, I had a good laugh." He smiled at the memory. "Kieran and these other young bucks, they don't listen to me. I'm only thirty-six, but to them I'm just some old married guy. I remember I said to Kieran,

'You may think you're hot shit here at camp, but let me tell you—if Maila is anything like her sister, you're in for it.'" He was laughing now, a deep rumbling in his chest. "I said to him, 'You just wait. You're gonna be trailing after that girl like a sick pup.'"

In spite of my tears, I smiled, too.

"Anyway, I know there's a lot to talk about still. A lot that you don't know about us, and things for us to learn about you. But I just wanted you to know that." He pressed his palms to his knees and began to rise. "I was waiting for you to ask how we knew who you were and why we sought you out, and then I was going to tell you. But you never did ask."

Our eyes met again as he stood. When I spoke, my voice was thick. "I didn't care what the reason was. Not anymore."

His expression had more warmth in it than the fire before us. "I know," he said. After one more long look, in which it felt like we said a thousand things while saying nothing at all, he added, "By the way, I'm the one who made all those maps. If there's anything you remember about me when you leave here, besides all that I just told you, I want it to be my incredible artistic ability."

I wanted to laugh. But when he walked away, it was more tears that came.

"Ready?"

I turned away from Nya and Kieran to look back at the camp one last time. I took in the dilapidated homes, the cul-de-sac, the fire. The people passing by, some of whom I hadn't had an opportunity to talk to, but who still gave me a friendly wave goodbye. I tried to memorize the faces of Cecil and Rubi and little Filimena, who were there to see me off.

Even Xiomara was there. To her credit, she waved. But maybe she was just glad to see me go.

"Wait!"

In the open doorway of a house to our left, George had appeared and was stepping gingerly across the crumbling front walk. Cecil moved to offer him a hand, but George stubbornly waved him away.

He came to stand in front of me, adjusting his glasses and smoothing the wrinkles out of his pants. Then he stuck out his hand. "It was wonderful to finally meet you, Maila."

I accepted his hand, and he clasped his other over top of it.

"It took a lot of bravery to come here," he said. "And it will take a lot of bravery to return."

His words contained more than one meaning, and we both knew it.

"It was wonderful to meet you, too," I replied. There was so much more I wanted to say, but the words stuck in my throat.

As if he could sense the emotion that was rising in me, George patted my hand. Like he was assuring me that he had seen it all, lived it all, and that everything would be okay somehow. Then he leaned in, so only I could hear.

"I do see what would make a bookworm from Cyllene so brave."

I could feel my eyes narrow slightly as I tried to grasp his meaning.

"Being kicked out of the city by The Council is one thing. But we should all be so lucky to have a dashing young man steal us from our bed in the night."

I followed his appreciative gaze to where Kieran stood. It was an effort to hide my smile.

"Be safe," George said finally, stepping back to the others.

"I will."

Finally, I turned to Nya. "I'm ready," I said. Even though, inexplicably, it felt like my heart was breaking.

We headed back toward Cyllene the same way we had come, and we walked mostly in silence. Reality was lurking on the horizon, about to come crashing down, breaking the spell of this trip. And maybe breaking me, in general, if anyone had realized I was gone. The realer it all felt, the more I began to wonder which was the worse decision—leaving Cyllene in the first place or returning there now. At one point, I had the overwhelming urge to beg Nya not to take me back. But I stifled it and continued putting one foot in front of the other.

Nya's subdued demeanor, on the other hand, seemed to be because her heart was heavy. Her thoughts were still with the family from this afternoon.

As for Kieran…I still didn't understand why he was being so standoffish. Multiple times, I gathered the courage to say something to him. But each time I opened my mouth, the fear of his reaction kept me silent. I decided it was better not to know what he was thinking, than to have him confirm something I didn't want to hear.

When we were halfway across the field that led to the walls, Nya twisted her backpack around so she could dig in the front pocket. She pulled out a glass vial filled with some sort of dark liquid. With the skies cloudy and starless, I couldn't make out the color of it.

"This is for when we cross the wall," she said. "And the trip through the city."

"What is it?"

"It's a potion. Before you ask, yes, it employs magic. It will make you drowsy and relaxed." She tilted it back and forth, watching the liquid slosh around. "I know last time was rough for you, and we're not going to have the option to stop and let you puke your guts out this time. We have to be quiet. And more importantly, we have to be quick."

She wordlessly handed me the vial.

Maybe I should have been more hesitant. But she had trusted me not to poison her that time—it felt like ages ago now—when I offered her dinner, and I owed her that same trust. Not to mention that she had already had just about every opportunity under the sun to kill me, if that's what she had wanted.

I popped the cork and downed the contents in two sips. To my surprise, it was tasteless.

When I was finished, I handed the empty vial back to Nya to stow away, then glanced at Kieran. His face was unreadable.

"Where do you all get this stuff?" I asked. I kept waiting for my throat to burn or my stomach to gurgle. Something to indicate that I had just ingested a magic potion. But it was no different than if I had sipped water.

"Sigrid," Nya responded. "She's an enchantress who took pity on us years ago and decided to join us. We would be lost without her."

My mouth fell open. "You actually have an enchantress who lives with you all? In Ersa Estates?"

"We do." Nya sounded uneasy. As if she already knew what I was going to ask next. "We would've taken you to see her, but she's wary of strangers."

I nearly laughed aloud at the irony in her words. But something told me it wasn't just strangers in general, but me specifically that their enchantress didn't want to meet. And that was deeply disappointing.

The Strangers had been so welcoming overall, I couldn't believe it had never occurred to me that some of them may have purposely kept their distance during my visit. Why would everyone be so quick to trust a woman from Cyllene?

As we crunched through the grass, the edges of my vision began to soften. By the time we reached the foot of the wall, I could barely stand. My mind slowed, then was quiet.

I felt Kieran lift me and hold me against his chest, positioning my legs around his waist and draping my arms over his shoulders. "I know it might be difficult, but still try to hold on to me if you can. Okay?"

It was the first thing he had said to me in hours. Maybe all day. But all I could say through the cloud of the potion was, "Okay."

From there, everything was a blur. Flashes of the wall, of buildings, of the streets. Things I thought I was seeing, but could have been dreams. Then I was in my apartment. In my bed. Someone was pulling the covers up to my neck. I said, "Wait." In my mind or out loud, I wasn't certain. But they needed to wait. Because somewhere in the far reaches of my mind, where some semblance of thought was trying to fight its way to the surface, I realized that we had never discussed when I would see them again.

If I would see them again.

There were silver eyes. Silver that I could see somehow, even in the dark. I felt something soft brush against my forehead. Like Irene's lips when she would kiss me goodnight each night. But this was different. It was sweet, gentle, but not the kiss of a sister. I would decide later that that part, definitely, was a dream.

I don't know how long I was asleep for. Only that when I woke up, it was still the middle of the night.

And I was alone.

CHAPTER TWELVE

It was happening again. I could taste the smoke…feel it burning my nostrils…enveloping me. Panic was a lightning strike through my veins.

Everything around me snapped into focus. I saw the shadows of the flames, which I knew were billowing just behind me, flickering across the faces of the Enforcers. I saw those mysterious white guns, which I knew they had every intention of using, drawn and aimed at us. And I saw Irene, gripping her injured shoulder, standing in front of me. Shielding me with her body. I knew the words that were about to come out of her mouth before she uttered them.

"She doesn't know anything."

What didn't I know?

Leon would speak next. Leon, the Mentor of the Enforcers. Leon, Irene's personal mentor. Leon, the only person left in this entire city, in this entire world, who gave a shit about the two of us. Whatever was happening, whatever this was, he would make it right.

That's what I thought the first time. But I had lived this too many times. I knew better now.

We needed to run.

Run. Run. Run. Fucking run.

"I mean it," Irene said, a note of desperation creeping into her voice. "Maila's just a child. She doesn't know anything."

"That seems unlikely," he said flatly, in that gravelly voice that will haunt me forever.

"You have my word."

Irene was back to being calm, strong, unfazed. Or at least she had mustered everything in her to appear that way. Inside, I wondered if she was terrified, like I was. I could feel the tears burning my eyes, but I was too scared to release them.

This time, I would get out. This time, I would make it stop.

I squeezed my eyes shut. I opened them. The scene before me was the same.

"Your word doesn't mean much, now does it?" Leon sighed, pulling me back to the conversation and back to what I knew was going to happen next.

At this, all the men shifted on their feet, eyes darting around uncomfortably.

Leon could feel their unease. He looked each of them in the face, one by one, ten in total. He saw them staring at my sister with pain in their eyes and knew he was losing them. She was their fellow Enforcer. Their friend. How many times had one of her comrades told me Irene was "the best of them?"

Leon needed to act fast. I saw this now as I saw it then, and I knew what was coming. He stalked over to my sister and jerked her down to her knees.

Now came my part in this.

In the blink of an eye, I was jumping to my feet and sprinting toward him. My brain was running through every weak spot that existed on his body. Should I kick? Punch? Claw?

All I knew in that moment was that I was going to kill him.

But like always, I suddenly jerked backwards. Someone was behind me, holding me. One of Leon's men. I could see the hands on my arms, feel the leather of his gloves. Hear him grunting as I thrashed against him.

It all happened quickly from there. It always did.

Leon removed a pistol from the holster at his side. It was smaller than the large white guns that the other Enforcers were carrying. But the moment he aimed it at Irene's head, it became the single most terrifying thing I had ever seen.

A scream erupted from me. The men averted their eyes.

My sister, despite being on her knees in the dirt, completely disheveled, arm hanging at an unnatural angle, skin damp from our proximity to the fire…she held her head high.

Leon fired.

I watched Irene slump to the ground, never to move again.

But I was certain it was me who had died.

I don't know which was worse—waking up in the middle of the night and realizing Nya and Kieran were gone, or jolting awake again from my nightmare a few hours later and realizing that I was back. Back to my usual. Back to my day-to-day.

My time outside the walls was over.

The return to my routine felt like a physical force weighing on me, tugging me down. A force that I had no choice but to succumb to, because what else was I going to do?

"I'm glad you made a lot of progress on your project," Brielle exclaimed as we walked to our work assignments. She had baked blueberry muffins as if me going back to work was something to celebrate. "But I missed you!"

"I missed you, too." I set a muffin carefully inside my book bag. If there was anything worth celebrating, it was that she bought it. She thought I had truly been holed up in my apartment, sitting in the middle of a sea of books and hand-scribbled notes, working on a project.

Brielle eyed my bag. "Aren't you going to eat it now?"

"Oh, I wish I could," I said. "But my stomach's been acting up this morning. I don't think I could eat anything right now, no matter how amazing it tastes."

Brielle frowned. Her hazel eyes flitted over me, assessing. "Maybe you overdid it. Working day and night on that project. Did you even sleep?"

I shrugged and flashed a smile that I hoped looked reassuring. "I'll be fine. Really."

The walk to the Knowledge Center was the same as always. Eventually, I got Brielle talking about a shipment of food items that Culinary Preservation was going to be getting soon, and what they would be able to make from some of the delicacies it contained. When I arrived in the Library, Cato seemed pleased to see me. I assured him that the past few days had been relaxing and much-needed, and I thanked him for allowing me to take that time. When he heard that, he had such a self-satisfied look on his face. Like he had made some breakthrough as my Mentor. It made the guilt curdle in my stomach. Thankfully, he had a stack of research assignments for me that had piled up while I was gone, and I threw myself straight into them. I worked on them diligently throughout the morning and into the afternoon.

Doing what was expected. What was required.

At lunch, Brielle chattered on about the happenings in Culinary Preservation. Then, once she had exhausted that topic, she shared the latest gossip that was floating around the Knowledge Center.

It was innocent, I knew. Brielle kept me informed on these things because she felt like it was her job to do so. Her role as my more extroverted friend. And it was something to fill the silence on days like today, when my mind was so clearly elsewhere.

But today, more than ever, the stories about the couple who had started seeing each other while I was gone and the once-friends who had had a screaming match in the middle of the courtyard reminded me of a swarm of gnats that we had encountered on our hike to the beach a few days ago. Buzzing around my ears, attempting to fly in my eyes and nostrils. An intolerable nuisance.

"Hey, there!"

Zander sat down next to me with his tray of food. His plate was piled high with pasta, bread, and a fresh side salad. He dug in right away. "I didn't think I was going to make it in time to have lunch with you two," he said between mouthfuls. "We've been so busy today!"

"Well, we're glad you could make it," Brielle chirped. "Now we're all reunited!"

I just smiled politely.

With Zander joining us, Brielle naturally had to repeat all the same stories to bring him up to speed. He nodded along, occasionally chiming in with a "Wow!" or a "No kidding!" I stared at my own plate. It was just as filled as Zander's, also with pasta, bread, and salad. Our assigned lunch. I stared at it until I was certain my eyes would bore holes in the buttered top layer of the bread.

It wasn't fair that we were so limited in what we were permitted to eat, was it? That's what I had always believed, if I was being honest. There were loopholes, like the ones Brielle took advantage of, to getting more exotic food. To getting the food you wanted. If you worked in the right department or knew the right people.

But then, weren't we also lucky to have what we had? Maybe pasta wasn't what I felt like eating today, but it was something substantial. It was calories. It was something to fill me up, make me feel satisfied. Something to give me the energy I needed to get through the rest of the work day.

"What are you thinking about?" Zander's voice snapped me out of my thoughts.

I met his amber gaze.

He was different somehow. Still handsome, but different.

I waited for that usual flush to creep up my cheeks. For that simple, biological reaction to having an attractive man stare at me like he was struggling not to picture me naked. Instead, a melancholy feeling drifted over me.

What had changed about him in the few days that I was gone?

"I'm not really thinking about anything in particular," I said with a dismissive wave of my hand. "Just got lost in thought, I guess."

Zander continued to look at me for a moment, refusing to avert his eyes.

Something in his expression made me feel tense. Like he thought if he stared at me long enough, I would reveal what was truly on my mind. Or maybe it was more than that. It was like he was studying me. Trying to make sense of me.

When he finally turned back to Brielle, asking a follow-up question about whatever it was she had last said, I was relieved.

I shifted my focus back to my food. My untouched food.

After lunch, I was passing through the main atrium of the Knowledge Center, headed back to the Library, when someone caught my arm.

Even though he had made to head back in the direction of the city, I somehow wasn't surprised when I turned to find Zander standing there.

"Hey, Maila."

No nickname. I don't think that had happened since we first met years ago.

"Are you sure everything's alright?"

My immediate reaction was to insist that it was and then regurgitate one of my go-to lies about a project from Cato or getting lost in a daydream or some other dismissive shit that frankly, I was getting tired of myself. But the sincerity in his eyes had me giving as honest an answer as I felt comfortable giving.

"Some of the projects I've been working on lately have had me thinking about Outside," I began slowly. "About the people trying to survive out there. About the people who *don't* survive. It's really…weighing on me, I guess."

Zander seemed to realize then that he was still gripping my arm because he abruptly let it drop. "I know what you mean," he said, running a hand through his cropped hair. "Even though they're out there for a reason, you still feel bad for them, you know?"

Something flickered in me. "They're not all out there 'for a reason.' There are several generations of people out there who didn't have the luxury of living in a city like Cyllene when The Awakening hit. There are also generations of people descended from the citizens we've exiled, who themselves have done nothing wrong."

Zander was studying me again. There was something in his face, a slight shifting, that signaled that he had shifted from concerned-friend mode to Enforcer-assessing-a-situation mode.

"That's true," he said finally. His words were an agreement. But something in his tone wasn't. Not quite.

I should've just accepted his polite acknowledgement and moved on. Yet I couldn't let that note in his voice go. "I'm sure as an Enforcer, you probably feel differently about them."

"No, I agree," he said quickly. "It's just...it's complicated, you know?"

"In what way?"

Now Zander didn't look like he was trying to understand me. He looked like he was openly wary of me. He shifted on his feet, his tell when he was uneasy. "Sometimes we have to make hard decisions to keep Cyllene safe. If there were no rules, where would we be? If we let in every person who wandered up to the gates, where would we be?"

"It's not that simple, though." Why was I pushing this? Why did I care what he thought? But I couldn't stop myself. "You can have rules without kicking out every person who doesn't agree with you and leaving them to die. You can have restrictions on who can come and go without keeping literally everyone out. You can choose to care about other people, instead of always putting yourself—your needs, your safety, your well-being—first."

If Zander was wary before, he looked flat out horrified now. His amber eyes were wide, his mouth hanging open slightly.

"You're an Enforcer. You're aware, I'm guessing, of the man that The Council exiled last week?"

I was met with silence. It was my cue to shut up. At least, it should have been.

"I had to help Cato sort and catalogue his books. He said that Enforcers were coming the next day to move everything out of his house. Were you one of them?"

The question was so beyond inappropriate that Zander would have been justified in turning on his heel and walking away. I was the one who had asked the question, and still I could barely believe it when he actually answered it.

"Yes, I was."

"Did you know that he's an elderly man?" Somehow it was crucial to me, in this moment, if he did. "Do you know if anyone even tried to give him other options? An alternative to being thrown out of the city and left to die?"

"I don't know details," Zander said flatly, fully in his Enforcer role now. "Only The Council knows, which is how it should be. For all our sakes."

"Should it, though?" I challenged. A group of people passed on our left, clearly oblivious to the traitorous, blasphemous words that were being uttered only a few feet away.

Zander shifted his weight again. "How did you know he was elderly?"

Shit. Shit, shit, shit.

"Cato told me," I said quickly. I may have been willing to risk my own well-being with this conversation, but I sure as hell was not willing to risk the Strangers'.

I visualized the heat that had risen in me dissipating, schooling my features into a nonchalant expression. "Speaking of Cato, I'd better get to work."

"Hold on."

My legs were practically twitching to walk away. But I paused.

"Maila." He was still saying my name in full. "There was another reason I wanted to catch up with you."

I waited.

"Are you seeing anyone?"

The question should have shocked me. Especially considering what we had just talked about. The deeply concerning things I had just said, out loud, in the middle of the Knowledge Center atrium. But it didn't. In fact, for some unexplainable reason, it felt like the most predictable thing he could have asked in that moment.

What did surprise me, though, was the sickening pang that I felt in my chest when I answered honestly, "No."

"Got it." He looked over my head for a moment. When his eyes snapped back to mine, they were full of resolve. "You're not seeing anyone. But you don't see me that way, do you?"

I forced myself to do him the courtesy of looking him in the eye when I answered, "I'm sorry, Zander. There's nothing about you that I would change. And I'm sure any woman in Cyllene who could hear our conversation right now would think I'd lost my mind. But I've… honestly, I've tried to see you as more than a friend. And for whatever reason, I just don't."

"Got it," he repeated. His eyes flashed with something like anger, and for a split second, I thought he would ease the guilt in my chest by lashing out to protect his pride. But the expression was only there for a moment, and then he was smiling that easy smile of his. "Well, I guess we'd both better get back to it, huh?"

"I guess so."

As I headed in the direction of the Library again, listening to his footsteps recede in the opposite direction, I knew.

At lunch, I had been trying to assess what felt different about Zander. But he wasn't the one who was different.

It was me.

CHAPTER THIRTEEN

I moved through the rest of the day robotically. When the sun finally set and I had nothing else to do except climb into bed, it wasn't a moment too soon. I was just pulling back the comforter when I heard a thud out on the balcony, followed by a whispered "Damnit!"

I hurried to the sliding glass door and slid it open to find Kieran hunched over on the concrete in front of me. He was rubbing his left calf muscle. Even in the darkness, I could see the rectangular shapes of blades of grass clinging to his clothes and sticking out of his hair.

He finally looked at me. "Consider this a heads-up that you're going to have increased security throughout the city tomorrow."

I would've felt his smirk even if my eyes were closed. That expression was so normal, so typical of him, that it made my heart swell to see it.

"Do I even want to know?" I asked, stepping aside so that he could enter.

"Hmmm…probably not." He limped past me and over to my desk, where he half sat, half fell down into the chair. He took off a bandolier and slung it on the desk. Another prize from the cave devils' collection, I was sure. "Unless the story of me taking down four Enforcers would make you swoon."

I shot him a look, which I knew he and his enhanced vision would be able to see clearly in the dark. How could he joke about something so serious?

"Thought not," he chuckled, then added, "There were four Enforcers hiding near our usual spot on the inside of the wall. Obviously, they figured us out somehow. The Enforcers are…let's just say they're incapacitated."

I felt a chill run down my spine. My eyes landed on the dagger that was poking out of the bandolier. "Did you…?"

"Did I stab them to death? No, I knocked them out with a powder from Sigrid." He shook his head. "For fuck's sake."

I wanted to ask just why exactly he was armed then. But one thing at a time. I needed to see the extent of his injuries. I reached over him and struck a match, then began lighting the candles. As soon as the candlelight illuminated him, I let out an involuntary gasp.

Besides the leaves and grass sticking to him and whatever had happened to his leg, Kieran's face, neck, and arms were covered in cuts and gashes of varying severity. His shirt was torn at the top, between the collar and right sleeve, as if someone had yanked on the bottom of the shirt and ripped it in a desperate attempt to restrain him. At first glance, his pants and boots appeared normal at least. Then I noticed the strange way that the light was reflecting off his left leg, and realized there was more to his leg injury than I had thought. The black jean material was soaked in blood.

"What in the actual fuck, Kieran?"

He looked genuinely confused by my reaction. "I just told you what happened."

"Right, but it looks like it was a really serious fight."

He barked out a laugh. "What part of 'four Enforcers' didn't sound serious to begin with? I'm not immortal, you know."

I actually didn't know that. Not for sure. I tucked that bit of information away for future reference, then began rifling through my cabinets. I gathered antiseptic, bandages, a jug of water, towels, and…food? Was he hungry?

Of course he was.

I hurried back to where he sat, my arms full. But before I did anything else, I found myself voicing the question that was on the tip of my tongue.

"Why are you here?" I tried to make my tone as even and non-accusatory as possible. But a little bit of hurt may have snuck through.

Kieran's expression was unreadable. When he spoke, it was in that tone that grated on me, the one that made me feel like he was trying to be patient with me. "You *named a water spirit*," he said slowly. "And *received a gift from a water spirit*. You really think we were just going to say, 'Thanks, see you later!' and never seek you out again?"

I had already forgotten about the larimar stone that was tucked in the underside of my mattress. "I don't know what any of that means, though."

"Neither do we."

After an uncomfortable moment, I set the jug of water down in front of him, along with a drinking glass and one of the blueberry muffins that Brielle had baked. I filled his glass with water and pushed it toward him meaningfully, then went to work cleaning his cuts and gashes, one at a time. I wet the towels and used them to carefully dab away the dirt and dried blood from each laceration, then followed with Medical division-issued antiseptic and a bandage.

Even with the state Kieran was in, I couldn't ignore the warmth of his skin and the solid curves of the muscles of his arms as I applied each bandage. There was still tension fizzing in the air between us. Tension after how he had acted the day after we kissed. Tension that seemed to come from words unspoken on both ends.

I was already looking ahead to the cuts on his face with dread. I wasn't sure if I could bear to be that close to him.

Kieran was quiet while I did all of this. If the antiseptic burned as I applied it to each open wound—which I was certain that it did—he didn't show it. I had started at his wrists, traveled up his forearms, across his biceps, and was finishing bandaging his shoulders when I realized that the fabric of his shirt was glistening with the same blood-soaked sheen as his jeans.

Before I had time to feel nervous, I ordered, "Take off your shirt."

Still without a word, he complied. I wasn't sure if it was the uneasy energy between us that kept him from making one of his usual suggestive remarks, or something else. But I decided not to push my luck by questioning it. As he dragged his shirt over his head, I allowed myself exactly one second to marvel at the sight of him. And then I forced my brain to return to the task at hand.

He had a slash along his left pectoral muscle, the shape of which told me that it was from an Enforcer's dagger or sword. And he had a gash between his right hip and his abdominal muscles, which was still bleeding and had tiny rocks embedded in it, as if from a bad fall. The hip appeared to be the worse of the two, so I started there. When my fingertips grazed over his lower abdominal muscles, he inhaled sharply.

I jerked my hands away and looked up at him.

"I'm sorry. Did that hurt?"

He blinked a few times. Then turned and grabbed the untouched muffin and the glass of water. "You're fine," he mumbled around a bite, not making eye contact. He chased it down with a quick swig of the water. "Just took a hard fall on that side. As you can see."

"Yeah, I can."

Something flitted across his face. Was it…humor? Disappointment? Both?

I felt like I had said the wrong thing somehow, so I lowered my head and returned to bandaging the wound. When I was finished with his hip, I moved on to the slash across his chest. Afterwards, I sat back on my heels to survey what was remaining.

The cuts on his face and the wound on his leg.

In retrospect, I should have started with his leg. That was probably going to end up being the worst of his injuries. But somewhere in the back of my mind, I had known from the way the shine of the blood traveled up his pant leg that he was going to need to take off his pants. Between that and tending to the wounds on his face, I didn't know which made me more anxious. I wouldn't have given it a second thought if it were anyone else. But not knowing where we stood with one another, it all felt too intimate.

Even though these thoughts flashed through my mind in a matter of seconds, that was apparently enough time for Kieran to pick up on my hesitation. He swallowed the last bite of muffin and drained what was left of the water from the glass.

"Don't you have a shower?"

Fuck.

If I could have burrowed through the floor of my apartment, and the floor below that, all the way until I was burrowing deep into the ground, I would have done it.

"Uh, yeah," I stammered, my face blazing with humiliation. I forced out a laugh. "That probably would have been the more efficient thing, huh? Rinsing off in the shower instead of me wiping you down one cut at a time?"

My self-deprecating humor fell flat. I didn't even have to look up at him to know it.

Just fucking great. He probably thought I wanted to sit in the candlelight and tend to him like we were in one of those romance novels on the eighth floor of the Library. Actually…he had grown up Outside and had probably never seen those kinds of books before. Or had he? Cecil had said he brought Irene books because the Strangers didn't have much use for them, as in they weren't necessary to survival. It didn't mean that people outside the walls didn't read for fun.

It didn't matter. There was no denying how it looked, and he wasn't about to let me off easy.

"I can't say what the smart thing would have been." He started to stand, then leaned over at the last second so his lips were an inch from my ear. "But I did enjoy this."

Pre-Awakening or Post-Awakening, there was no bigger idiot than me.

Kieran limped in the direction of the shower. The limp kind of detracted from the effect of his words, but I was too frazzled to even begin to think of how to point that out. I grabbed a towel from one of the cabinets and thrust it into his arms, not meeting his eyes or even checking to make sure he had a grip on it before I hurried back to my desk. I grabbed the empty glass and saucer and deposited them in the sink.

On the other side of the bathroom door, I heard the shower turn on.

I couldn't think of anything else to do with myself at that point other than climb into bed and pull the comforter over my head.

I lost track of how long Kieran spent in the shower. It felt like a while, but I couldn't blame him—living Outside, how many opportunities had he had to use a working shower? The cool water probably felt refreshing after being out in the humid night. Running around. Almost getting himself captured or killed.

He was so fucked. And I might be, too.

The reality of our situation was finally starting to creep over me like threads of ice. But then I heard the click of the bathroom door, and my heart jumped into my throat.

Kieran emerged wearing nothing but a pair of boxers, scrubbing his hair with a towel. Even looking like he had taken a tumble off the edge of a cliff, his body still made my breath catch in my throat. The candlelight flickered off every pane of muscle, lighting him up in an almost otherworldly glow.

No one in Cyllene looked quite like that. Even Zander. There was no substitution for a life spent literally fighting and clawing for survival.

"How was your shower?" I asked lamely.

"Great." His smile was neither amused nor smug. He seemed genuinely happy and relaxed, and seeing that brought a smile to my face as well.

"I see you finished bandaging your leg."

I waited for him to jump at the opportunity to embarrass me some more, but his mind seemed like it was somewhere else as he stood in the middle of the room, flexing his leg beneath the bandage.

"Yeah, I have to say…I'm not used to walking away from a fight with injuries like this. One of the Enforcers shot at me when I was coming over the wall, and I guess my head was somewhere else because really, what a fucking horrible landing. It's not broken or anything, but I'm probably not going to be able to put much weight on it for a while."

I considered what he had said. And realized he had never actually answered my question from earlier. I smoothed the comforter with my hands. "You never did say why you're here. Do you all need me for something else?"

Kieran was silent for a moment. He was no longer examining his leg but still seemed distracted. Suddenly, as if making up his mind about something, he strode over to the bed and sat down on the edge. "Give me the larimar stone."

A beat passed.

"Damnit, not like that," he huffed, rising again and disappearing back into the bathroom. I heard the rustling of fabric, then he returned with a chain of some sort, dangling from his fingers. It was silver. Pretty, actually. "I brought this for you, for the stone. So you don't lose it."

I retrieved the stone from under my mattress. There was a clump of some sort of silvery wire on the center of the chain, and he manipulated it with careful fingers, clamping it around the stone until it was perfectly caged in. A necklace.

When he handed it back to me, a lump formed in my throat. "I can't wear this around Cyllene," I said, trying to force my emotional mind to be rational.

"Not every day," he conceded. "But it's better for it to be portable."

"True," I said quietly. Then, "Thank you."

"There are a couple other things that I wanted to run past you," he said with a heavy sigh. "But it's been a hell of a night."

I nodded. An incident like the one he had caused tonight had never happened before in the time that I had been alive. At least as far as I knew. I wondered what The Council's reaction would be. What it would mean for the city.

"I'm not really in any shape to make the trip back tonight," Kieran continued. Suddenly he wasn't meeting my eyes again. "And if anyone has come across those Enforcers at the wall, they'll be looking for me. Would you mind if I slept here tonight?"

There was nothing suggestive in his tone. And nothing pleading, either. I could tell that if I said I wasn't comfortable with it, he would turn and head right back out the glass door, onto the balcony, and into the night. To face whatever might be waiting for him out there.

"Of course I don't mind. You're more than welcome," I said. "I don't know what's going to happen once they find those Enforcers. But with your injuries, you need to rest and recover before you try to take off again. I just hope they don't know it's me that you've been visiting."

We both sighed at the same time. We really were fucked.

I flattened imaginary wrinkles in the comforter again. "You can rest here tomorrow while I'm at my work assignment. There's bread and some other stuff in the cabinets. The good stuff—like the blueberry muffin, or the chicken that one night—I usually get from a friend. But I also get an assigned lunch at the cafeteria in the Knowledge Center. I can just pack it up and bring it to you."

There was something like true gratitude in Kieran's expression as he smiled at me again. And there was also something else that, like so many of the looks that Kieran gave me, I couldn't quite place.

I returned the smile. Then I realized there was one tiny problem with him spending the night.

Where was he going to spend the night?

The thought must have been showing on my face, because he stood from the bed and walked over to my desk. "If you have a spare pillow and blanket, I can make myself comfortable here. I sleep sitting up all the time during scouting missions, so I'll be fine."

"Absolutely not!" I said so vehemently that his head snapped back to me, eyes wide. "That's ridiculous for you to sleep in a chair when there's a bed right here."

I said this even as I knew what it would mean.

"You're fine with us sharing a bed?" he asked. His amused smile was back, and I instantly wondered if he was going to make me regret this decision.

"Yes. I think we're both mature enough." There was an unspoken "I hope" at the end.

"I don't know. Speak for yourself, Maila."

"It's either that or you can take the bed, and I'll take the chair or the floor. I'm not making a guest—and an injured one at that—sleep in a hard wooden chair."

"If you say so," he said. His grin was huge now. "Want me to blow out these candles?"

"Sure." I scooted over toward the wall to make room for him. Thankfully, I already had a second pillow on the bed. I scanned it quickly for stray hairs or anything else embarrassing. Then the candles were out, and we were submerged in darkness.

Or at least, I was. I remembered once again with annoyance that he could see me just fine.

I felt the mattress dip as he sat down, then the full weight of him lying down beside me. The comforter tugged a bit as he pulled it up and over himself.

This was fine. No big deal.

I laid down next to him. Our hands brushed and I jerked mine back, folding it over my stomach instead. Even without touching, I could feel the heat radiating from his body.

He just had a cold shower—how was he still that warm?

The clean, fresh scent of my soap and shampoo filled my nose. Both were standard issue, nothing like the exotically scented bubble bath and perfumes that Brielle always managed to get her hands on. But the scent of *my* soap and *my* shampoo mingling with the scent of his skin…it was the most intoxicating thing I had ever smelled.

It was going to be a long night.

We laid there in the dark. I was so lost in my own thoughts that I couldn't have begun to guess how much time passed. Hours? Minutes? Seconds? It felt like an eternity.

Even without night vision of my own, I could feel that he was still awake. In fact, my intuition told me that he was staring up at the ceiling as well.

That lump returned to my throat, and before I even fully understood what was happening, my eyes began to sting.

"Hey, Kieran," I said, so softly it was almost a whisper.

"Yeah?"

"Do you regret kissing me?"

For a beat there was nothing but silence.

Then there was a shuffling of blankets and a shifting of the mattress, and I realized he had turned to face me. He was raised up on one arm, leaning over me.

"Are you serious?" His tone was even. I wished that I could see his expression, even if that was often just as hard to read.

"You took off so abruptly." The words kept coming. Why did I always seem to do this with him? "And then you barely spoke to me the rest of the time I was outside the walls. Barely looked at me. And left me here without even saying goodbye. Now you're in my apartment, without Nya...in my *bed*, even...and I don't understand why."

He exhaled. "Maila," he said in as serious of a tone as I had ever heard from him. "I came here because I wanted to see you."

I rolled over to face him.

"You're right," he continued. "I was being distant. And I'm sorry for that. I just had a lot on my mind. I didn't know what to expect that night on the beach. I thought maybe we'd make out for a while, and it wouldn't be all I had built it up to be."

"Ouch."

He let out something between a sigh and a laugh. "That's not what I meant. What I'm trying to say is...I just thought..." He trailed off.

I had never heard him at a loss for words before. I stayed quiet, giving him time to gather his thoughts.

After a moment, he laid his head back down on the pillow. Our faces were inches away from each other. When he spoke, his voice was soft. "Look, what matters is I'm here because I couldn't stand not knowing when I was going to get to see you again."

I felt a few of the tears that had been burning my eyes slip down my face. I lifted my hand to wipe them away, but instead I felt his fingers brush my cheek, wiping them for me. There was something so tender in it, I didn't care that he knew I was crying.

Afterward, his hand drifted to my hair. The gentle tugging sensation as he trailed his fingers through the unbound strands was so soothing, I found myself closing my eyes.

His voice was just above a whisper. "It's late, I look like I've been beaten to hell, and you have your—what do you all call it? 'Work assignment?' You have your work assignment to go to in the morning. Let's get some sleep."

Then he grabbed me, gently but firmly, and pressed me against his chest.

It was so unexpected that whatever response was forming on my lips completely dissipated. The feeling of being held by him, his arm draped over me and his chin resting on the top of my head, was pure bliss. Despite him saying we should both get some sleep, I could still feel him idly playing with my hair. Summoning some courage, I scooted my legs closer, so that they were touching his. He let out a hiss and I realized I had bumped his left leg.

"Sorry. I didn't mean to hurt you."

"No worries. But wow, that actually did hurt this time."

I furrowed my brow against his chest. "What do you mean 'this time?'"

He chuckled softly, shaking us both. "You're always surprising me with the things you choose to be oblivious about."

I opened my mouth to respond, but he let my hair go and gave me a playful squeeze, pressing my face against his chest too tightly for me to get the words out. "Go to sleep, Maila."

He didn't have to tell me a third time. In his arms, in the bubble of heat that we had created, I was already drifting off.

CHAPTER FOURTEEN

That night, I dreamt of Irene. But for the first time in a very long time, it was not a bad dream.

Irene and ten-year-old me were snuggled up in the bed we had always shared, and she was gently ruffling my hair as she told me the story of Larimar the water spirit. When she finished, I leapt from the bed, reached under the frame, and pulled out the necklace with the larimar stone. The moonlight streaming through our bedroom window glinted off it, making it look especially spectacular.

And then I was my present day, twenty-year-old self, telling her all about my encounter with the water spirit. How I had given them their name.

Irene was amazed. She hugged me closer and exclaimed, "Look at the adventures you're having! You have no idea how proud I am of you."

Then I woke up.

The first thing I felt when I opened my eyes was that all-consuming grief. The raw kind that only hits first thing upon waking, too quick to steel your mind against. When you remember that your reality is that that special person is gone. I threw up those familiar mental walls against the storm of sorrow, stamping it down until it was this manageable thing that I could shove back behind its designated door.

As my eyes adjusted to the gray glow of morning, still hours before I needed to meet Brielle to walk to work, I reflected on the dream. I started to feel a new emotion, one that took me by surprise.

Gratitude.

Then I remembered who was sleeping next to me.

Sometime in the night, I had rolled back to my own pillow and was facing the wall. I wondered if Kieran was awake.

I didn't have to wonder for long. Suddenly his arm snaked around my front, pulling me back into his warmth.

"How'd you sleep?" His voice was a lazy rumble in his throat.

"I slept great." I couldn't remember the last time I had slept so soundly. "How about you?"

"Same," he said with a yawn. His exhale tickled my ear.

I remembered a time, a few years ago, when Brielle overslept and I had to hurry upstairs to her floor and wake her for her work assignment. She had opened the door groggy and confused. But the braid that she wore to bed was mussed in the most flattering way, with a few stray wisps here and there that looked like they had been deliberately styled that way. Her cheeks had an equally flattering flush from waking from a deep sleep.

I was wishing with everything I had that when Kieran had a chance to see me full-on, that that was how I looked this morning.

"I'm glad you slept well," Kieran said. He sounded more awake now, and a bit like he was looking for something to say.

"I dreamt about my sister," I replied, surprising myself with the fact that I wanted to share that with him. "I dream about her often, but usually not in a good way. I have nightmares where I replay the day she died over and over. But last night was different. It was a happy dream."

Kieran was quiet. Listening.

"I think the reason I dreamt about her was because you're here. Which sounds weird, but we used to share a bed when I was growing up. I haven't felt this close to someone since she died."

Kieran was still silent.

Suddenly feeling nervous about everything I had shared, I rolled over to face him.

His eyes were luminous in the morning light. Was there any lighting that didn't make his eyes look absolutely spectacular? His dark hair had the Brielle muss—gently tousled bedhead— that only made him look sexier. The cuts and scratches on his face from the previous night did nothing to detract from how handsome he was.

"I dream about my family sometimes, too," he said quietly. "I promise I'll tell you more about them one day. I just…" He trailed off, then let out a frustrated breath. "I just really fucking hate talking about them."

"It's okay." I wanted to touch his face, but my nerves got the better of me and I touched his arm instead. "You can tell me whenever you're ready. No rush."

He watched me for a moment, then inhaled deeply. "They're from Oryx. My father's people."

I stilled. "Where is Oryx?"

"It doesn't have a physical location." He looked up as if searching for the right words. "I mean, it does, but it doesn't. It's hard to explain."

It was my turn to be quiet now, waiting patiently for whatever he felt comfortable sharing with me.

"The Oryxians are protectors, in a sense." He twirled a strand of my hair as he spoke. "The world that merged with the human world has its own circle of life. But it's more fragile. More volatile. The Oryxians keep everything in balance. And now that 'everything' includes the human world, too. So they not only maintain the balance in their own world, but have to maintain it between the two merged worlds as well."

"That's what The Awakening was, then? Two worlds merging?" I could barely keep the excitement out of my voice.

He chuckled softly. "I'm not an expert on this stuff. You know more about magic than I do. I just know a few things from my parents."

My excitement twisted into something more akin to dread, as further implications of what he had said dawned on me. "That explorer, Matthew. If an Oryxian interfered… if they killed him and his group…his intentions weren't good, were they? That's what you were hinting at before?"

"It was." He smiled grimly. "It's probably hard for you to understand, since you're one of the only people in Cyllene who is allowed to really know details about magic beyond just 'It's out there and it's scary.' But your Council pretty much hates magic. They use it when they have to, like with the wards, but they're always searching for a way to shift things back to how they were before, Pre-Awakening."

"I do understand that," I said quietly. Like so many things, The Council didn't state that outright, but they didn't exactly hide their intentions either. It's not like magic was ever talked about in a positive light. "Magic is a threat to humanity. You know that better than anyone, living Outside."

"Sure," Kieran agreed. "But we lose just as many people to starvation and untreated illnesses and injuries as we do to magic-related incidents. Don't think for a second that all of us in Ersa Estates have something against magic. Our problem is not being given a fair shot at survival, magic or no magic."

A long silence followed. After what he had just said, nothing else felt worth saying. I was imagining he must be feeling the same, when he suddenly spoke again.

"I want you to know that I haven't been this close to anyone, either." Then, "I mean, I guess you could say that I've been close to women, in a sense…in other ways."

The reminder that he had had many romantic partners was a physical sting. It was hypocritical, I knew. But I couldn't help the emotion that swelled in me. Images flashed through my mind of the faceless, nameless women who had come before. Of Xiomara. Of him kissing them. Holding them. Doing things with them that I probably couldn't even imagine.

"But not like this," he said sharply. His fingertips grazed my cheek, my chin, my mouth. "I've never shared a bed with someone all night, same as you. Or had these kinds of conversations. Told someone about my family beyond what they figured out on their own. Or… everything else. It's different."

"Why is that?" I asked softly. "Why are things different with me?"

His stare took on an intensity then that made me wonder if I had asked something I shouldn't have.

Then he leaned in and touched his lips to mine.

I didn't hesitate. I kissed him back. And it was like a hunger that had been building in me since the first night we kissed was finally being satisfied. At the same time, a new and different one was forming.

My palm pressed against his bare chest as his hand caught my leg, pulling me further against him. Only moments later, he was on top of me. His lips, hands, body were everywhere at once.

Last time, there had been a sense of urgency, like we couldn't wait a single second longer to give in to our feelings for each other. But this time it was almost frantic. As if one or both of us were about to disappear into thin air, and we were trying desperately to memorize every single thing about each other.

Just like before, he ran his hands over me, exploring, grinding his hips against mine. And just like before, his name escaped my lips. But this time, he didn't stop. He ground his hips against me again. And again. Over and over until my body was trembling.

"Maila," he murmured against my lips. "I really don't think you understand how sexy you are."

Before I could even think of what to say to that, his tongue was pressing against mine again, hot and full of that taste that was purely him. Then his tongue found my jaw. My neck. His mouth continued to travel down, trailing soft licks. It found my breasts over the thin fabric of my nightgown, and I gasped when I felt the graze of his teeth. Then he was trailing kisses across my stomach, leaving heat and gentle tingling in their wake.

Before I knew it, he was crouched in front of me, hands resting on my thighs, fingertips brushing the edge of my nightgown. He was still, looking up at me expectantly from under hooded eyes.

I realized after a beat that he was seeking permission.

I gave him a quick nod.

Then I raised onto my elbows, lifting my arms overhead. In one movement, he had my nightgown off. I heard the soft swish as it sailed through the air and hit the floor.

Another soft sound of fabric hitting the floor. This time it was my underwear.

Then Kieran backed off the bed, standing to remove his boxers.

I marveled for what had to be the millionth time at the structure of his body, the definition in each muscle. But I couldn't help but wince several times as my eyes landed on his wounds, some bandaged and some too large to be covered fully. Particularly the one on his leg.

"I'm fine," he said quietly as if reading my thoughts.

Then his boxers slipped past his thighs.

My breath caught in my throat.

With that last barrier gone, I could now confirm that every single inch of him was perfect. And seeing the effect that I had on him, how he was visibly aching for me…it made me ache in turn. With an intensity I had never felt before.

Eventually my gaze drifted back up to his. As our eyes locked, I imagined that the glazed look in his must have been mirrored in my own. He climbed back onto the bed, and I raised up to kiss him. But he resumed the same position, kneeling between my legs. The corner of his mouth turned up in a slight smile. Then he lowered his head.

What happened next was something I had fantasized about endlessly but had never experienced. Which probably said a lot about the two men I had chosen to share my body with in the past. But all thoughts of them were long gone at the first touch of Kieran's lips. His tongue. Touches that consumed every thought, every nerve, every part of me. There was no room in my mind for self-consciousness. There was no room in my mind for anything.

Anything except Kieran.

The waves of sensation came in all different forms— fast and slow, rough and gentle, abrupt and lingering.

Meanwhile, his fingertips grazed the outside of my thighs. Gripped my hips. Slid between my legs to caress me in the same way his mouth did.

Soon it was difficult to be still. My legs trembled. I was grasping the bedsheets. Grasping for something. Anything.

I had found release on my own before, but that's all that it was—release. Like scratching an itch or eating when hungry. What was building in me now was something else. Something sweet and deep and all-consuming.

"Kieran." I didn't know what I wanted, what I needed. But I pleaded all the same.

I felt his body tense against me, his grip on my hips tightening. "I love the way you say my name," he murmured, the words and the shuddering breath that followed vibrating against my skin.

"Kieran." I was desperate now. The pressure almost unbearable.

"Fuck," he whispered. "Yeah, Maila, just like that."

Our eyes met, and his were wide. Watching me unflinchingly. Expectantly.

Then I understood why, as he used his mouth and fingers to apply the perfect amount of pressure. My whole body spasmed. Seized. Ignited.

The tidal wave of pleasure that tore through me was something I couldn't have dreamed of. Couldn't have known my body was even capable of. Far away, I heard a cry erupt from me. Something primal. It must have echoed through the room. Through the living quarters. Through all of Cyllene.

But I was somewhere else. In another world.

After some time, my mind drifted back. My senses slowly awakened. Aftershocks of pleasure radiated through me.

I realized my eyes were closed, and with an immense amount of effort, I opened them.

Kieran was still kneeling there, sitting back on his heels, his mouth hanging open. He dragged the back of his arm across it. The light in the room had increased only slightly with the rising sun, but there was no mistaking the look in his eyes.

They were wild. And molten silver.

"So that's what that's like then," I said to fill the silence. The intensity of his stare was making me feel bare in a different way, beyond the physical.

"What do you mean?" His voice sound strangled.

"I mean…" I don't know why I let the words fall away. There was nothing to be ashamed about. I swallowed. "That's the first time someone's ever done that for me."

Kieran's eyes slammed shut, and his hand dropped to grip himself. A minute passed in which his body remained absolutely rigid. When he finally spoke, it was with a shuddering breath. "I don't get this effect you have on me. You tell me something like that, all shy and embarrassed-looking, and how do I react? I almost blow my load like a damn teenager."

I grinned. "I would've loved to watch that."

He hissed, but there was a smile playing at his lips, too. "Stop saying shit like that so I can calm down."

Eventually, he moved back up the bed, lowering himself onto me.

When he kissed me, I expected it to be frantic again. But instead, it was painfully tender. He pressed a kiss to my chin, my cheek, my eye. He kissed me on the nose, and I was so surprised that I couldn't hold back a quiet chuckle. Then he moved to the other side of my face to repeat the kisses again.

He raised up on his elbows then, gazing down at me. A flurry of emotions crossed his face, too fast for me to pinpoint. I stared back at him, relishing the feeling of being skin-to-skin. Everything still. Like we were the only two people in the world.

Something bloomed in me then.

No, it had always been there. Waiting patiently for me to figure it out.

I wanted Kieran.

Not just his body. I wanted all of him. Every part of him. The good and the bad.

I was already floating through a haze of euphoria, but my acknowledgment and acceptance of this settled over me like a warm blanket on a cold day, bringing its own brand of elation.

I ran my fingertips gently down his back. Beginning with his neck, feeling the muscles of his shoulders flex beneath my hands, trailing down his spine. When I moved to do the same to his front, he closed his eyes. I moved so just my fingernails grazed his chest, his abdomen. I let them trail lower.

When the skin of my fingertips finally drifted over the length of him, he inhaled sharply.

I began to move rhythmically, letting his face, his breaths, the very feel of him in my hand guide me in what he liked. It wasn't long before every stroke was drawing a low groan from his throat.

I tightened my grip.

"*Fuck*," he choked out. I felt it like a physical touch, reverberating through my body.

It was an intoxicating cycle—the more I massaged him, the louder he groaned, and the more it felt like those temporarily stilled waters were beginning to thrash again. Building momentum. Readying to come crashing through me once more.

Gently, he caught my wrist in his hand. When he opened his eyes, they were the color of smoke.

"Did that not feel good?" I asked.

"It felt too good," he breathed.

I didn't understand what he meant at first. But then he shifted his body, moving so that we were perfectly parallel to one another. He ground his hips against mine. Except this time, there was nothing between us. Just the friction of skin against skin. A preview of what was to come.

"You sure you want to do this?" he asked hoarsely.

"Yes," I replied without hesitation. "I trust you."

His eyes widened, and he blinked several times as if waking from sleep. Then he lifted his body, creating space between us. Something had changed in his face, enough that I raised up on my elbows.

"Maila," he whispered between shaky breaths. His voice was so soft that it took me a moment to realize he had spoken. "Before we do this, there's something else we need to talk about."

I blinked, too. My logical mind taking the reins again. "Right," I said. "Um…I don't take anything."

He tilted his head. "What?"

"Contraception," I said, wincing. "We have to jump through a lot of hoops to get it here, because The Council wants us to reproduce. They don't say that that's the reason, but it obviously is. And I haven't gone through that whole process because…well…I haven't had a need for it in a long time." One of these days, I was going to stop giving him ammunition to say that I was naive. But apparently today wasn't that day.

He chuckled, gently shaking the both of us in the areas where our bodies still touched. "You're fine, Maila. I have a brew from Sigrid that I drink."

"Oh, good." I reached for his face, letting my fingertips graze the edge of his cheekbone, beside those eyes. Those beautiful silver eyes.

Kieran shook his head, as if clearing it. "Sorry, that's not what I was referring to. There's something else that I need to tell you."

"Can it wait?" It was a joke. Sort of.

Maybe it was the raw need in my voice, or maybe it was something else. But I watched the silver of his eyes liquify in front of me, melting me along with it. "Yes." His voice was rough as he lowered his face back to mine. "It can wait."

Everything was still. Silent. His lips softly grazed mine again. And in that same moment, there was sudden pressure and a hint of pain as he began to move into me slowly, giving my body time to adjust. Taking me inch by inch, until he was sheathed to the hilt.

The fullness of him was overwhelming.

"Doing okay?" His voice was strained.

"Better than okay," I breathed, the corner of my mouth turning up at his concern for me.

"Perfect." His words were an exhale. The tension dissipated from his shoulders as he began to move.

The first thrust pulled a gasp from me. And then I was meeting each roll of his hips, the two of us moving at a rhythm that was slow and steady and forced me to languish in every burst of pleasure that he coaxed out of me.

"You feel so fucking good," he murmured between kisses that were as agonizingly and gloriously slow as our pace. He lowered his lips to my neck, and my head lolled, eyes slipping closed.

Every part of me was sensitive from my climax, every nerve standing on edge. It wasn't long before I was about to break again. My nails dug into his back, causing him to groan against my neck. My hips ground urgently against his, trying to go faster, desperate for that pleasure he had given me before.

"You want it harder?" The challenge in his voice had me opening my eyes, meeting his gaze.

Suddenly, it wasn't about my own release anymore. I wanted to see him lose himself fully, like he had seen from me.

"Yes, please," I said sweetly and raised up. He let me roll him over, and then I was astride him. The angle allowed me to feel him even more deeply than before. I moved harder, faster, and he met me at each crest with a force that took my breath away. I wanted more of him. All of him. And I knew he was willing to give it to me.

The skin of my palms tingled against the muscles of his neck, and a strange sensation snaked through my veins. I felt…invigorated.

I felt powerful.

His hands disappeared from my hips, reaching instead to unlace my fingers and cradle them gently between us. "Easy," he breathed, pressing a kiss to my clasped hands.

"What was –" I couldn't get the words out. They were erased. Obliterated. Along with all other semblance of thought as my body launched without preamble into another shattering release. The cry that tore out of my body was his name, and all I could do was hold onto him as sharp waves of pleasure ripped through me.

His answering groan was something I wanted to capture and replay over and over again, the sound thick with need, with pleasure, and with the sound of my name.

Then he was bucking wildly, frantically. Ravenously.

Seeing him like that pulled me out of the limp haze of my orgasm. I started matching him thrust for thrust, riding him with an urgency that had us both gasping for breath. My hands untangled from his, and they joined my mouth in exploring every part of him, every surface of his skin within reach. I let my teeth graze the rounded muscle of his trap, and he cursed under his breath.

I barely recognized my own voice when I ordered, "Let go, Kieran. Let go for me."

As if on command, I felt him thicken inside me. Then my name tore from his throat in a roar.

For a split second, as I felt him throbbing with release, it was like a hurricane was unleashed in my bedroom. Through the ecstasy of watching him, I was vaguely aware of my hair whipping against the both of us. The candles on my desk tipping. The glass of my window and balcony door rattling.

And then we were collapsed in a heap on the bed, me still straddling him. My head bouncing with the heaving rise and fall of his chest. My own breaths still coming just as fast.

"You're incredible," he whispered against my hair.

There was so much that I wanted to say to him.

But I didn't have time to respond. Because in the next moment, there was a deafening crash. Kieran and I leapt from the bed at the same time, feet slamming the floor as we readied for fight or flight.

Then the fight left me just as quickly as it had appeared, replaced by a familiar sense of terror as once again, there were Enforcers in my home. Five of them, to be exact.

Leading the pack was Zander.

CHAPTER FIFTEEN

Zander's expression, which had initially held that dutiful impassiveness of an Enforcer, contorted in shock and hurt as he took in the sight of us. I tried to cover my upper half with an arm and my lower half with my hand, but even I felt the uselessness of it.

All five Enforcers had guns drawn, and the bulky, white-barreled monstrosities looked exactly as I remembered. The whole situation was so familiar, I had never been more certain that everybody was right about me.

I was fucking cursed.

"Sorry to interrupt," the Enforcer to Zander's right said with a hearty laugh, grabbing Kieran's bandolier off my desk and slinging it over an arm. He had a round face and mild blue eyes. Under normal circumstances, he would have given the impression of being friendly and agreeable.

"Don't feel too bad," the Enforcer to Zander's left chimed in. He was tall and relatively thinner than the others. I recognized him as the man who had interrupted me and Zander when we were talking that rainy morning before work. "Looks like they're already finished."

The fact that they had seen evidence of that on the both of us went so far beyond humiliation, I wouldn't have known what to call the emotion. I had watched my home burn to the ground, had seen my sister murdered right in front of my eyes, but this was a whole new way to feel utterly violated.

"Both of you shut the fuck up," Zander commanded. "Right now."

It was the most unkind thing I had ever heard come out of his mouth. And it was well-deserved. He shook his head as if clearing it, as if trying to make the scene before him disappear. Then he said, "You've both been summoned to meet with The Council. I suggest you put some clothes on."

He must have seen Kieran's eyes dart to the balcony because he added, "We have you surrounded. If you choose to leave from the balcony, then there will be another escort waiting for you where you land."

Kieran's laugh was full of mirth. "And if I don't want to meet with your 'Council?'" His tone was as casual as if we were discussing what to eat for breakfast.

"The meeting isn't optional."

Kieran laughed again, and I could sense his movement beside me. He thrust my nightgown and underwear into my hands, then moved with exaggeratedly slow steps, hands raised in mock surrender, over to my desk. He dragged on his jeans.

"I like your euphemisms." He finished buttoning his pants and strode back to where I stood, still clutching my nightgown. "Almost makes you feel like you're not about to be captured and held hostage against your will by a bunch of grown men that feel the need to point their big, bad guns at one of their own defenseless citizens."

At his words, Zander quickly scanned his fellow Enforcers then locked eyes with the two who were bringing up the rear. Their guns were, in fact, pointed at me. Without a word, they shifted so they were trained on Kieran instead.

"You don't want to put on a shirt?" Zander asked flatly.

The tall Enforcer snorted. "I'm sure she"—he pointed in my direction—"would rather he didn't."

Zander's answering expression had enough venom in it that the Enforcer clamped his mouth shut. Out of the corner of my eye, I saw Kieran tense slightly. Zander's protective attitude toward me wasn't lost on him.

"My shirt is in the bathroom hanging over the edge of the tub," Kieran said. He added, his tone saccharine, "If one of you would be so kind as to grab it for me."

After a moment of hesitation, one of the Enforcers toward the back rolled his eyes and stomped into the bathroom, returning with Kieran's blood-stained shirt.

He tossed it at his feet and seemed miffed when Kieran actually caught it.

Kieran shrugged the shirt over his head then slipped on his boots. "I think the lady would like some privacy," he said without looking up.

I was still frozen in place.

"I think 'the lady' forfeited her right to privacy when she decided to harbor a Stranger in her home," the round-faced Enforcer fired back. Zander glared at him, but unlike his comrades, the Enforcer pretended not to see it. He gestured to my clothes with his gun. "Hurry up."

My body felt like it was moving of its own accord as I turned away from them. I slipped on my underwear and pulled my nightgown over my head. Pins and needles were making their way up my arms and legs.

I was going to pass out.

But before I had time even to faint, our wrists were bound with thick pieces of plastic, tight enough that it hurt. Zander refused to look at me as he tied mine.

We were ushered out of the apartment and into the hall. As we crossed through the open doorway, I realized we were stepping on my door. The crash from earlier had been the Enforcers breaking it down.

Thankfully, none of my neighbors were gathered to witness the spectacle. I wondered if they had actually managed to sleep through my door being kicked in. More likely, they were pressed against the inside of their doors, watching through the peephole.

We went in the opposite direction of the main staircase, which I assumed was an attempt at discretion. The main staircase had multiple landings and was visible from different vantage points on all floors. We walked instead toward the less grandiose stairs at the other end of the hall which were intended to be an emergency exit. The tall Enforcer held the door to the stairwell as we all passed through. We walked down the concrete stairs in silence, our footsteps echoing. When we reached the landing, the round-faced Enforcer held the door this time. Then we were headed down the hall on the ground floor.

As we approached the foot of the main staircase, I wondered vaguely what the purpose was of bypassing it to begin with, if we were just going to circle back to it. Obviously, we were about to leave out the main entrance and head to the Enforcers' headquarters in the city.

But right before we reached the landing, the Enforcers came to a halt, stopping us with them. We were standing in front of an inconspicuous wooden door in a series of doors that led to rooms I had never been in before.

Zander ushered us inside, still refusing to make eye contact with me.

The room we entered was spacious, with plain white walls and diamond-patterned carpet. It was mostly empty, save for more Enforcers. They were standing in a semicircle around a long table where five people sat. Kieran and I were led to folding chairs in front of the table, with Zander and his four colleagues taking positions behind us.

Once seated, I finally took in the faces across the table from me.

On the far left was a middle-aged woman with meticulously coiffed black hair, tawny skin, and a smile that didn't quite meet her green eyes.

Next to her was a slight man of indeterminate age, with pale skin and equally pale eyes. His voluminous red hair was half-heartedly styled, with tufts sticking out in odd places.

Then came a man who appeared to be in his late fifties or early sixties, with white hair and kind brown eyes. He was handsome and polished, and something about his placement in the center of the group seemed to signal his importance.

Next to him was Cato. His dark eyes, always expressive, looked deeply pained.

And finally, seated at the end of the line, was another familiar face.

The person who used to cook us dinner several times a week after our parents died.

The man who patched our roof after a particularly bad storm, showed me how to play chess, and taught Irene how to do pull-ups.

The Enforcers' Mentor.

Leon.

The man who killed Irene.

At the sight of Leon, the feeling that I was going to lose consciousness came back with a vengeance. I shifted in my seat. Although I desperately wanted to be strong, my body began to shudder with chills. In just a few short moments, I was fully trembling.

The corner of Leon's mouth turned up ever so slightly. For some morbid and unfathomable reason, my discomfort pleased him.

Fuck, I hated him. I hated him so much that the hate was a tangible thing, boiling and bubbling and *burning* in my veins. I hated him, I hated him, I hated him.

Kieran exhaled steadily beside me. I stole a glance at him and noticed his eyes were trained on me, studying my face, traveling down my body. For the briefest of moments, his cold, irreverent expression was replaced by one of deep concern. Then his gaze flicked to Leon and narrowed in a way I had never seen before. The silver of his eyes had liquified, but the heat in them wasn't sensual. It was the opposite. It was…terrifying.

The man seated in the center of the table spoke.

"Hello, Maila." His voice was soft and soothing. "Kieran," he added with a nod in Kieran's direction. He spoke with amiable familiarity, as if we were all old friends reunited. "I'm so glad you two could join us. I do apologize for the nature of our summoning you here and the security presence. But it was crucial that we meet with you. And I'm afraid we couldn't take a chance on you saying no."

Kieran was silent, but I could feel that he was eyeing each one of them with quiet defiance. I, on the other hand, was blacking out in earnest now.

"Can someone get her some water?" the woman with the shiny hair asked irritably, her question directed to no one in particular. Fading in and out, I didn't register right away that she was talking about me. "She looks like she's about to be sick."

A few moments later, a glass of water was being pressed against my clammy palm. But I my fingers wouldn't cooperate when I tried to grip it. I had a vague awareness of the glass slipping out of my hand and heard someone's fumbling steps, their mumbled curse, but no crash. Someone must have caught it in time. Then what felt like a cool towel was being pressed against my forehead.

"Just take deep breaths," a voice said. I recognized it as Zander's.

The towel disappeared from my forehead, and I felt it reappear against my face, neck, and arms, gently patting away the sweat that coated my skin.

"What's wrong with her?" The woman's bark sounded close, yet far away at the same time. Other voices were murmuring as well, but I couldn't make out the words or who was talking.

"Maybe…" It was Kieran speaking now. "And this is just a guess. But maybe she's reacting to the fact that you dragged her into a room against her will to sit across from the piece of shit who murdered her older sister."

Even as I faded in and out of awareness, I wanted to weep at hearing that he had put the pieces together. Wanted to weep at hearing him use that word—"murdered." Wanted to weep at the barely restrained rage in his voice, the indignance on my behalf, the protectiveness.

For the first time in ten years…for the first time since I lost Irene…I knew what it was to have someone on my side.

At his rebuke, the voices around me stopped, as did the sensation of someone patting me with the towel. I was still floating through darkness, but I slowly started to find my way out of it. The room and the faces across from me fizzled back into focus as if emerging from beneath grains of sand.

Zander was standing to the right of me, holding a damp towel. On the other side of the table, the five seated people were whispering amongst themselves. There was a humorless snort of a laugh from Leon. Then he was pushing his chair back from the table and striding across the room.

He exited out a side door.

"We apologize for the faux pas," the man seated in the center said. "Leon"—I flinched at hearing his name spoken out loud, a cruelty that Zander had unknowingly spared me from all these years in by referring to him only as *my Mentor*—"has certainly been tasked with doing some difficult things for the greater good of our city. I commend him for doing what is necessary even when it involves taking actions that would be hard for the rest of us to stomach." At this, he glanced to either side of him at the remaining group, and they each nodded their agreement in turn. "But I can certainly see how Leon's role in protecting our city could cause him to represent feelings of hurt, anger, and resentment for some. And so, I apologize, again for our insensitivity in including him in the discussion today."

I should have been appalled at how every sentence contained a clear defense of the man who killed my sister. Burned down our home. But by now I couldn't feel anything except a deep-seated fatigue and relief at the implication that he would not be returning.

"Although we certainly know the two of you," the man seated in the center continued, and it finally clicked that he had greeted Kieran by name earlier. He knew Kieran? How? "I recognize that you may not know us. My name is Addis, and although we all work as a team, as we do on a larger scale in our great city, I suppose you could say I am the leader of The Council."

Wow. I couldn't decide which surprised me more—the fact that after all these years, I was face-to-face with the head of The Council, or his use of the word "leader." It was common knowledge that The Council didn't approve of words like that, hence the term "Mentor." But apparently, an exception could be made to use a word that signaled power and authority as long as it applied to himself.

Addis paused here, giving the others the opportunity to introduce themselves.

The woman introduced herself as Quinn, the Mentor of Education. She oversaw the training and development of Cyllene's children until age thirteen, when they were old enough to receive their work assignments. Unless, of course, you were forced to begin working at ten because your whole family was dead.

Her attempt at a smile was haughty and laced with that same irritation that had been on her face since we walked in. How ironic that someone so sour-looking would work with children. She couldn't have been that involved in the day-to-day of the Education division, because I had certainly never met her or even heard her name as a child.

Next came the red-haired hair man next to her who introduced himself as Westley. He was the Mentor of the

Medical division of Cyllene, which, although it worked closely with the Knowledge Center on numerous projects, was headquartered in a different part of the city. Westley had an unsteadiness to his voice, and he fidgeted in his seat. He said we were welcome to call him "Wes," which earned a snort from Kieran.

Cato gave his name for Kieran's benefit and didn't say anything else. His elbows were resting on the table, hands clasped in front of his face.

Once everyone had finished introducing themselves, Addis resumed speaking.

"It was important that we meet with the two of you today to make sure we're all on the same page about some things," he said. "Kieran, I understand that you managed to break into our city last night from Outside, and that in the process, you left four Enforcers unconscious. Those are some truly admirable men who have dedicated their lives to protecting Cyllene. Each of them have families who are anxious to see them fully recovered. With these men's spouses and children in mind, can you share with us how our medical team should go about waking them up?"

Kieran snorted again. I allowed myself a sideways glance and saw that he was shaking his head. "They should wake up soon enough. In the meantime," he said, looking pointedly at the Enforcers stationed around the room. "It looks like you're getting by just fine."

"I think their spouses and children would disagree," Addis replied evenly.

"Right, yeah. The spouses and children."

There was a pause as Addis waited for him to continue.

Kieran sat back in his chair and crossed his arms.

"Well," Addis finally said into the uncomfortable silence. "I suppose we can come back to that later."

"That was the plan anyway, right? We've gotta save something to talk about when you torture me. Otherwise, how will you justify it?"

Addis grimaced. "We don't use torture as a method of gathering information here in Cyllene."

"Of course not."

I scanned the faces of the other Council members and found them all to be impassive. All except Cato. He was no longer leaning his face on his hands, and I could see that his mouth was twisted slightly. He looked uncomfortable.

Was Kieran right, then? Did The Council really torture people? How often, and for what reasons? Kieran was always saying that I was naive. After the past few days, I was starting to think he was right. How had I gone all these years believing that the same people who were capable of executing my sister were above other forms of violence?

Maybe I didn't believe it, though. Maybe I just chose not to think about the possibility.

"Our primary concern here," Addis said, turning his attention to me. "Is this young woman here. Maila, you are such a valuable asset to Cyllene. Despite a difficult upbringing, with family members making poor decisions, you have earned our trust through years of devotion to the betterment of our community. The work you do in the Library is crucial to our continued success in this world of…magic."

I watched his lips move without hearing. My brain was stuck on "difficult upbringing."

I saw Irene's reflection in the mirror as she stood behind me, teaching me how to braid my hair. I saw her making me a pot of soup when I came down with a cold, and us both laughing—me until I was wheezing and coughing—because it tasted like seasoned water. I saw fuzzy memories of my mother and father. A smiling face here, a warm hug there.

"It's not enough that you killed my sister." Somewhere far away, I realized it was my voice that was speaking. "And that my parents gave their lives for this city. You also have to assassinate their character and tarnish their memory?"

The silence that followed was deafening.

Now I was the one whose stare was boring into Addis. And what I felt blazing inside me wasn't humiliation, or anxiety, or the pleasant burn that I felt when I looked into Kieran's eyes.

It was rage.

"I said earlier that we think it's important," Addis began carefully. "To get on the same page about some things. There have certainly been some misunderstandings here, and I think Kieran and the others in his group have…stoked the flames a bit." Here he gave Kieran a sympathetic smile. "Your family was on a dangerous path, Maila. One not only of self-destruction, but one that had the potential to take all of us down with them. Beginning with your mother."

At his words, everything in me became still.

"She realized her own abilities purely by accident. Abilities your father didn't have, of course. But it didn't take long for it to become apparent that those abilities were passed on to Irene."

I blinked at him. Everything felt like it was happening in slow motion.

"The benefits of those abilities were…immeasurable. The possibilities for how they could have been used to help the citizens of Cyllene—to help us not only survive, but *thrive* in a world full of magic—were simply endless. But your mother had other ideas." He paused here, seemingly for dramatic effect. "Obviously, we have a duty to protect Cyllene's citizens, above all else. And so that was the first time Leon had to step in and…handle things."

Deep in my soul, behind that door that I kept locked at all times, I had suspected the truth. How could I not, after what happened to Irene? Yet his words made me feel like my insides were clawing their way out of my body.

"We had hoped that all these wild ideas, these threats to our citizens' safety and security and well-being, belonged to your mother and your mother alone. But unfortunately, your father supported her in her beliefs. They were misguided, Maila. I need you to understand that. They weren't evil people or bad-intentioned. They were just very misguided. And none of that is your fault or your burden to bear."

I was shutting down. This was something I could not handle. I needed Addis to stop talking.

"Your parents and sister couldn't let go of these idealistic notions of letting Strangers—outcasts and criminals—into our city. They couldn't let go of this idea that everyone should have an equal say in what happens in Cyllene, that everyday citizens should get to know the details of its inner workings." Addis laughed. "Maila, no one else *wants* that. No one wants to open their home up to dangerous people and wait for that inevitable day when they hurt us, take advantage of us, or worse. People don't *want* the burden of the responsibilities The Council bears. Maila, our citizens want simplicity, they want safety, and they want contentment. And we give them that."

He sighed here. Something about it felt rehearsed. "The decision we were forced to make regarding your mother, and your father, and later Irene, was a difficult one."

Stop. Stop. Stop.

"I hope you don't think we took those decisions lightly, or that they don't haunt us every day. But we are tasked with preserving what is in the best interest of our citizens. Which brings us to you." Another sympathetic smile. "We want to see you take a different path than the one your family took. We want to see you use your abilities—no, let's call them your *gifts*, because that is what they are—for the betterment of our people."

My brain was in a tailspin. Abilities? Gifts?

I stared at him blankly.

He leaned back a bit, brows furrowing, pressing his fingers to his lips.

"Kieran did explain this to you already, didn't he? Your gifts? Why he and his group sought you out? Took an interest in you?"

Addis's eyes drifted to Kieran. And behind the calm demeanor, the soothing tone, the nonthreatening brown eyes, I saw it. A twinkle in his eye. A slight relaxing of his facial muscles. A twitch in his lips.

Addis had won. I didn't know what, and I didn't know how, but he had won.

Kieran's voice beside me was a low growl. "Fuck you, you self-righteous prick."

I turned to Kieran and was startled to find that his face was frozen in fury, eyes blazing.

"Ah," Addis said knowingly. I could see him nodding in my peripheral, but I was still looking at Kieran, willing him to look back at me. "So there's even more to discuss than I had thought."

Another voice sounded next to Addis. "Why don't we take a break? This would be a lot for anyone to process."

Cato. The sincerity in his tone made my eyes burn.

"Yes, yes, this is certainly a lot," Addis agreed. "But I imagine Maila's exceedingly confused and doesn't want to be left hanging."

What "Maila wanted" was to not be here. For him to fucking stop talking. Stop saying things that made my head ache. But more than anything, I just wanted Kieran to look at me.

"Maila," Addis said, pulling my attention back to him. "I want you to know that we are here to help you through all of this." Quinn and Westley, who had been silent up until that point, nodded their agreement. Cato's hands were clenched into fists on the table in front of him. "We've been willing to make accommodations for you all these years, to work with you and support you and keep an eye on you, because you have a special gift. You are what we call a Conductor."

Next to me, I heard Kieran take a steadying breath.

"With the right input and control, you can wield magic."

CHAPTER SIXTEEN

"Wield magic?" I repeated.

Over my shoulder, I was pretty sure I heard Zander stifle a gasp with a cough. But if his shock mirrored my own, it must have been a hallucination. Because clearly, I had suffered some kind of a psychological break. The real Council, the real Zander, they must have been standing over my catatonic body, trying to figure out what to do with me.

A few short minutes ago, I had been holding back tears. Now I was holding back hysterical laughter. My cheeks strained with the effort.

"I know! Crazy, right?" Addis threw his hands up in the air.

"It's a truly fascinating phenomenon," Westley chimed in. His uneasy demeanor was gone. Now he was leaning forward, eyes bright with enthusiasm.

"What does that even mean?" I asked, a few chuckles escaping.

"To put it in simple terms," Westley began. His role as Mentor of Medical was an almost tangible aura around him. "You don't have magic of your own. But when granted access to magic through a magical object, a location that is particularly ripe in magic, or a being that does have magic of their own, you can harness and use it." He tapped his chin. "I suppose you could say that you have the ability to borrow it, temporarily. You make physical contact, siphon their magic, and it's yours to use for a period of time. Obviously, we haven't had many opportunities to study exactly how long it lasts each time, the limitations on how much magic you can hold at a given time, and how the capability is affected by changes in variables. But what we do know from tests we ran on your mother and Irene is truly remarkable."

I tried to let his words sink in.

I could wield magic.

I could wield magic.

I could wield *magic*.

The Council watched me carefully, their expressions near-perfect mirrors of one another.

"How?" It seemed like the logical thing to ask.

Maybe the question indicated some kind of acceptance because Westley's toothy smile brightened even more. "That's something we're eager to learn ourselves. Your mother and Irene both had similar experiences, although separate from one another, where they accidentally siphoned outside the walls. That's when they learned of their abilities."

Oh, no.

A stomach-twisting dread washed over me. The kind that only comes when you realize something that you very much do not want to be true is, in fact, true.

When we were crossing the wall. Kieran jerked my hands away from his arms. Away from the tattoo that contained the magic of the Springing Spell.

And earlier. In bed. The surge of…strength that I felt. The way he lifted my hands from his shoulders. Breaking the connection.

Bile rose in my throat, and I clamped my hand to my mouth. As if that would stop it.

I turned to Kieran. I could feel by the subtle shifting of The Council members in their seats that it was right on cue, exactly what they wanted. But I didn't care. "You knew about this?"

Finally, he twisted to face me. His jaw was set. "Yes."

"You and—you knew that I could wield magic?" I had started to say Nya's name, but somehow, even in the midst of the storm of chaos that was thundering in my head, I had the presence of mind not to mention her name in front of The Council. Just in case.

"Yes," he repeated.

"So you didn't—when you first—I mean, you knew from the beginning?" There was so much that I was afraid to say.

"Yes."

Somewhere far away, I mused that this was much like the first time that Nya and Kieran had visited me. When all I could say, as Nya spelled out how the interaction was going to play out, was "Yes."

"How?" I demanded.

"I can't answer that." There was an unspoken *right now* at the end of his sentence.

Fine. He didn't have to answer now. Or at all. Because even as I asked the question, I was already remembering everything that Cecil had shared with me.

Irene had obviously told him about her abilities. Maybe even demonstrated them.

Not with me, her sister. Her sister who had those same abilities and could have used her guidance. Used her fucking trust and transparency. But with Cecil, some man she had met in the woods.

Cecil knew. Nya and Kieran knew. All of the Strangers knew.

"When were you going to tell me?" I pressed.

"Today."

I heard a scoff across the table. It sounded like it came from Quinn.

"So all this time, you knew that I was a…a Conductor. And that's why you sought me out. And you didn't want me to know at first." My thoughts were picking up speed. Piling on, one after the other. Piecing it together. Then it snapped into place.

"Everything you all were doing," I whispered. At the change in my tone, Kieran's eyes softened. As if he knew the conclusion I had just reached. "You all aren't just trying to survive out there. Outside. You're trying to get inside. Inside the walls."

I didn't wait for him to answer. To deny it.

"You're trying to infiltrate Cyllene. And you were using me to help you do it."

Even though we had the eyes of The Council and all the Enforcers on us, including Zander, it suddenly felt like we were the only two people in the room.

"You said you needed me for…unrelated things. For an unrelated purpose. But you knew I had this ability. And you thought…what? That you could get me on your side, convince me of how evil Cyllene was? And then I would use my abilities to help you destroy The Council? Destroy the whole city and everyone in it?"

"None of what I told you was a lie," he cut in. He put an ever so slight emphasis on "I," as if pointing out in a way that only I could understand that he was speaking for Nya and the others as well. "Everything that I asked for your help with was legitimate. You knew that I was trailing you for a while. And yeah, I made sure the things you were helping me with were things you would know about. But I still used your advice. I followed through on your suggestions. None of that was a lie."

The marsh wolves. I was researching the marsh wolves, and then—it wasn't a coincidence. But he was right, they did still track the marsh wolves afterward. I saw the pelts myself. And yet…this was too much. This was all so, so much for one person to bear.

"Maila," Kieran said, and it was physically painful to hear him say my name. "You know I don't want to destroy this city or its people. You know the truth about Cyllene, about The Council"—he shot a look at the four people across the table—"and how they're hurting people both inside and outside Cyllene. Don't let them get in your head and make you forget the things you know."

The Council had been observing quietly, but Quinn spoke up now. "That's big talk coming from someone who's attacked Cyllene many times before." She tilted her head, in a way that was almost predatory. "If we hadn't prevented those attacks from making it past the walls, how exactly would the people of Cyllene have fared, do you think?"

Kieran grinned. "No better than they do on any other day. Having their every move monitored, controlled.

Decided for them. Provided with the basic necessities for survival so long as they fall in line. And if not, well…we all know how that goes, right?"

"Ah, Kieran." Addis clucked his tongue. "It's a shame you're so misguided. I get it, though. We've built something wonderful here in Cyllene. A safe haven for our people. And I understand why you and the Strangers envy it."

He cast a sidelong glance at Quinn and Westley, who both nodded. It was as if they had practiced that routine—a knowing look from Addis is met with a nod. Addis tried to repeat the routine with Cato, but Cato refused to make eye contact.

Addis continued on, "Unfortunately, regardless of the empathy we have for the men and women outside the walls, we must protect what we've built here. And that means protecting our citizens—protecting people like Maila—from people like you."

"And who's going to protect her from people like *you*?"

Addis's brow twitched, but his pleasant smile remained. He turned to Westley.

It must have been yet another of their rehearsed signals because Westley leaned forward again, clasping his hands. "Maila, I know you must have a bunch more questions about what it means to be a Conductor. This probably isn't the time or the place, but later, I'd be happy to sit down and have a conversation about what we know.

And discuss how we can partner on learning even more. We've been waiting for the right time to sit down with you and talk about this, and"—here he mirrored Addis, looking around at the rest of The Council members and urging them to join in on his beaming smile—"now that the time has come, we can't wait to find out all there is to know about your special gifts."

Kieran leaned forward, too, making Westley flinch. "Will you also explain how she's going to be your magic-wielding slave? That's how it works, right? Agree to do The Council's bidding or meet an untimely demise?"

Addis shot a meaningful look over his head. The gloved hand of an Enforcer appeared in my periphery, jerking Kieran back against his chair.

Addis sat back in his own chair and exhaled in a way that signaled that the conversation was coming to a close. "As Cato said, you have a lot to process, Maila. I think a pause in this discussion would do everyone some good. Before we break—Maila, do you have anything else you'd like to say to Kieran? Or to ask him?"

Something in his words set off warning bells. But I didn't know what else to do, except to ask the question that had been sitting on the tip of my tongue as everyone else was speaking.

"What about the other things?" I asked softly, searching Kieran's face.

His eyes were roaming my face in turn, trying to understand my meaning.

"Everything else," I prompted. "Was everything else real?"

His eyes narrowed then. In hurt or in anger, I couldn't tell. When he spoke, his voice was cold. "Yes, Maila. You shouldn't have to ask me that."

I wanted to believe him. I really did.

But suddenly all the adrenaline, all the rage that had been building earlier, the desire to make sense of all of this…it all melted away. I felt an exhaustion the likes of which I have never felt before, even the day that I lost Irene and my father.

There was nothing for me. There was no one for me. I couldn't trust Cato. I couldn't trust Zander. Most painfully of all, I couldn't trust Kieran.

I was completely, utterly defeated.

Kieran's eyes widened in alarm. His gaze trailed downward, and I realized tears were dripping down my cheeks. I didn't try to stop them. Didn't care to stop them.

"Maila." His voice cracked on my name. "I need you to trust me. They're trying to turn you against me, but I've never given you a reason not to trust me."

He had to be joking. Wasn't this about as big a reason not to trust someone as you could have?

My hands were still tightly bound, as were his, but he reached for them. The Enforcer yanked him back into his chair again.

A different hand rested on my shoulder, and a voice sounded from behind me.

"I think you've done enough damage here," Zander said. He was speaking in that commanding tone again, the one that left no room for questions. "Stop trying to justify what you've done and just let it be. Let her process and heal from this."

Kieran smirked. I knew him well enough to brace for whatever was about to come out of his mouth. "Why, so you can move in?" he asked with a wink. "You *are* in love with her, aren't you?"

"I do care about Maila," Zander said carefully but also confidently. "I'm not ashamed to say it. Unlike you, I see the wonderful woman that she is and how much she has to offer. I would never dream of hurting her. Using her the way you have." As he said the last part, he rubbed his thumb against my shoulder. Affectionately. Possessively.

A beat passed.

Everything happened at once.

A flurry of movement. Kieran was no longer across from me. There was shouting all around. I twisted to look behind me and saw Enforcers from both sides of the table converging on one spot. In the breaks between them, I caught flashes of fabric and of limbs. I heard a series of thuds, a zapping noise, something slamming against the carpeted floor, a shuffling of fabric, a zapping noise again, and various other sounds that I couldn't place. And grunting and Enforcers giving commands overlapping with one another.

Then there was quiet.

When the knot of Enforcers thinned, I saw Zander sitting with his head in hands. Blood poured between his fingertips, gushing down his arms in rivulets. There was so much that it was impossible to locate the source. His eyes were squeezed shut. He was panting heavily.

Next to him, Kieran lay prone on the ground, hands bound behind his back this time instead of in front of him. His ankles were bound as well. He was unconscious.

"Well," Addis said from his spot at the table. "Things have certainly taken a turn. I was hoping we could all remain civilized, but we are dealing with a Stranger here. Maila?" At my name, I tore my eyes away from the scene behind me. Addis was standing, as were Quinn, Westley, and Cato. "Rest up, and we'll chat more later." Then over my shoulder, "Bergam, why don't you take Maila home?"

Before I could respond, the round-faced Enforcer with the blue eyes was standing in front of me, offering a hand to help me rise. I took it and was immediately grateful for the support, my legs wobbling. He was directing me toward the door we had entered through when I paused, turning back around.

"What about Kieran?" I asked. Several Enforcers had positioned themselves around his limp body and were beginning to lift him.

"Don't worry," Addis replied warmly. "He has a lot to answer for, but we'll be taking him somewhere safe and secure in the meantime."

The word "secure" set off those warning bells again, but Bergam had a hand on my back and was gently but swiftly guiding me forward. My head still turned, I heard the click of the door opening behind me. Meanwhile, the Enforcers back at the table, with a suspended Kieran between them, were starting to move toward the alternate exit that Leon had left through earlier.

Even after everything, I made a move to go back. Back to Kieran.

But Bergam pushed me—hard this time—out the door and pulled it shut behind us.

"Here's you," Bergam said cheerfully, holding my apartment door open for me.

My new door, I observed. Someone had replaced it while we were gone.

I stepped inside and noticed immediately that all remnants of my old door had been cleared away. It even looked like someone had gone the extra step to clean my carpet.

I moved deeper into the room.

The counter above my cabinets was the cleanest I had ever seen it. Practically shining. The saucer and glass that Kieran had used were no longer in the sink. The desk also had the gleam of being freshly wiped down. My candles, which had been stumpy and dripping from use, had been replaced with new ones. The bed was made. I could only assume that my comforter had been replaced, as the one in its place was nearly identical but missing a few rips and permanent stains that had accrued over the years.

I turned on my heel and hurried to my bathroom to find a similar scene—everything fresh, clean, sparkling. The towels and bandages and other items that Kieran had used the night before were gone.

I knew, intuitively, that the items Kieran had used, the traces of him left here, were not simply put away. I went to the kitchen cabinet where I kept cups and plates.

Three glasses and three saucers. I was missing one of each.

"Who cleaned my apartment?" I turned back to Bergam, who was still standing in the doorway. "And why?"

"You've been through a lot," he replied, scratching the back of his neck. "And we kicked down your door. The Council thought it was the least we could do for you."

The answer only raised additional questions. Had someone literally been standing around the corner with a fresh comforter and a caddy of cleaners, waiting for the Enforcers to usher Kieran and I out so they could get to work?

Instead, the question I asked was, "When can I see Kieran?"

Bergam gave me a smile that didn't quite meet his eyes. "Kieran doesn't seem to play well with others," he said, as if that were an answer. "Why don't you just focus on getting some rest, and I'll be out here if you need me."

We shared a long look as his meaning sunk in. He wasn't going anywhere.

And neither was I.

Bergam stepped out into the hall and closed the door behind him. I continued to stand there motionless, staring after him.

Eventually something in me urged me to move, at least enough to go sit down. I passed my desk and my bed. I thought about opening the glass door and going to my balcony, my usual spot. But something told me there was an Enforcer posted just out of view, eyes trained on the balcony. Partnered with Bergam to make sure I stayed put.

I sat down in the middle of the floor. I considered myself to be a clean person, but my carpet truly hadn't been this clean since I first moved in ten years ago. I ran my hand across the fibers.

Slowly, a rumbling began to build in me. It rose up like a tsunami.

I curled into a ball, pulling my legs into me. Wrapping my arms around them. Holding on so tightly that my knuckles turned white. My breaths came fast and hard as I squeezed my eyes shut, willing someone, anyone, to rescue me from what was coming. But the wave was rolling in and there was no stopping it.

The sound that erupted from me was somewhere between a scream and a wail.

No one was coming to save me. No one cared enough.

In every aspect of life, I was just a means to an end. Something to be manipulated. Something to be used. Something to be lied to and taken from and ripped to pieces until there was nothing left of me.

And I felt it again. Rushing through me, filling every part of me. The same feeling that consumed me after I watched the light go out in Irene's eyes. Smothering the sobs that wracked my whole body. Smothering my sense of self. Smothering any flicker of anything that was left in me. That creeping numbness. That living death.

It was all that I could feel. All that I was.

I felt nothing.

Absolutely nothing.

CHAPTER SEVENTEEN

The sun finished its ascent. It dipped below the horizon again. I was there and not there. Asleep and awake.

I saw Irene. What I could remember of my parents. Brielle and Zander. I saw all the members of The Council, including Cato. I saw Nya, and the faces of the people I had met Outside.

I saw Kieran.

I also heard something like a giant bang and a rumble somewhere nearby. I'm not sure if what I saw were dreams or visions. Or a mixture of both.

At some point, I realized vaguely that I needed to go to the bathroom. I wasn't sure if it was that sensation that pulled me out of my trance, or if it was the fact that I was already coming out of it that allowed me to recognize the sensation. Either way, I raised slowly up onto my hands and knees. My limbs trembled with the effort, and I realized I hadn't eaten since dinner the night Kieran arrived.

Was that only yesterday?

As soon as the realization hit me, sickening, gut-wrenching hunger exploded through my stomach and burned my throat.

I hurried to the bathroom and emptied my bladder, then tore through my cabinets, consuming anything edible I could get my hands on. Bread, a stray apple, a jar of peanuts, a quarter of a bag of sugar…I shoveled it all down, too ravenous to even try to throw together something that resembled a meal. When I was finished, I filled a glass to the brim with water and downed it, then repeated the motions twice more.

I leaned against the sink, breathing heavily. Water dripped from my lips. My hands were sticky from where I had been grabbing sugar out of the bag by the fistful. When my breathing steadied and the feeling of hunger was sated, the sensation of pain rose to the surface. My muscles and joints ached.

I crossed to the bathroom, carefully avoiding looking in the mirror. This time, it had nothing to do with not wanting to see my resemblance to Irene. It was because I knew I would be horrified to see how the mess inside of me was manifesting on the outside.

I rinsed the sugar off my hands, then stripped off my nightgown. Once in the shower, I let the cold water wash over me. Over and over and over. Relishing how it made me feel as numb on the outside as I still felt on the inside. Afterward, I brushed my teeth then ran a comb through my wet hair and braided it.

When I emerged from the bathroom, I went straight to my bed. With all my basic needs met, I felt the gentle brush of a thought, which was equal parts tentative and urgent.

What the fuck was I going to do?

I ran through all the events of the past twenty-four hours Then I ran through them again. And again. There were so many things that had been kept from me for so long…I needed to replay every conversation, every interaction, every subtle change in expression and body language that had caught my attention, to make sure there was nothing left that I was missing.

In spite of myself, I found a fresh wave of tears spilling over as I replayed the night and morning that Kieran and I spent together before the Enforcers showed up. Each memory brought fresh pain. He had said that he had something to tell me. Now I understood it was the truth about me being a Conductor. But the memory that stuck in my mind the most at this moment, making my chest ache, was not that revelation. It was not the Enforcers breaking down my door, or even when Kieran and I were moving against each other, as close as two people could physically be.

It was that moment, after he pleasured me, and before we both found our pleasure again in each other, when he pressed gentle kisses across my face.

The feeling of his lips against my skin was arousing under any circumstance. But those kisses, soft and gentle, hadn't been meant to arouse me. They were communicating something else. Something he was struggling against his pride, or maybe even his nerves, to say.

In that moment, I had known, somewhere in the depths of my soul, what he felt for me. Yes, he was feeling attraction and lust and all the things that went along with what we had done. What we had been about to do. All things that I was feeling too, toward him. But in that moment, I had also felt something else from him.

I had felt cherished.

A feeling I hadn't experienced since Irene was alive. And, if I was being honest, a feeling that I hadn't thought I would ever experience again. I thought it had died along with my family.

My mother. My father. My sister.

What must they have gone through when I was still too small to understand? What was so compelling that my mother and father were willing to risk death? Risk leaving their young daughters behind? Was it truly just compassion for the people outside the walls? Wanting more for the citizens of Cyllene?

Then there was Irene. A big sister, a caretaker, an Enforcer. And yet, so much more. Hiding so much more. Protecting me from so much more. I could recite her final conversation with Leon word for word, but this time it held new meaning. "Your word doesn't mean much, now does it?" Leon had said. Her betrayal wasn't just the betrayal of an Enforcer, sneaking supplies to the Strangers and smuggling books into the city.

It was the betrayal of Cyllene's most valuable asset. Greatest weapon to greatest threat.

And when I thought now of Irene's refusal to cry or beg for her own life…the way she held her head high in the face of certain death…

She knew she was right. She knew she was about to die, but she also knew that she was right. That death was a more acceptable fate than succumbing to what was wrong. She must have believed with all her heart in the cause that the Strangers were pursuing now. In making the city a *real* safe haven—a place where everyone would be fed, clothed, sheltered. A place where people could have agency in their own lives, make informed decisions. Be themselves, without fear of retribution.

As much as it pained me, I would never know all the details of what Irene did, what she thought, what she endured. But that was okay. There were countless things in life that I didn't know, and the past few days had only expanded that list further.

I still knew Irene. I knew her heart.

I was surprisingly calm as I realized what I had to do.

I jumped over the side of the bed, flipped onto my back, and pushed myself into the space between the floor and the mattress. I knew my room had been searched top to bottom, so the chances were slim that it was still there...

It was.

I crawled out from under the bed and hurried to the bathroom. Once there, I put the stopper in the drain and turned the shower on full blast. Carefully, I set the silver chain and the attached larimar stone in the tub.

It was a ridiculous idea. It might have even bordered on insane to think that such a thing could work. But it was all I had.

I stared at the stone. Holding my breath. Kneading my hands. Watching it get pelted by the spray. I willed everything in me to focus on this one thing, this one request. I willed it so hard that a lump rose in my throat.

Come on, come on, come on, come on...

I blinked and there was just the stone.

I blinked again and there was Larimar.

As hard as I had been wishing for it, I still startled.

Larimar was standing over the stone in the shower spray. Seeing them in full, above the surface of the water, confirmed a theory I had had. Rather than the fish tail I associated with sirens, their body dipped smoothly into two defined legs, each of which ended in the same fin-like protrusions that took the place of hands.

Their opalescent skin was just as I remembered, somehow no less magnificent in the dim light of the bathroom.

Their expressionless face was also just as I remembered.

"You have summoned me…" they began, voice echoing.

I felt heat rush to my cheeks.

"…to a bathroom."

They inclined their head slightly. As if trying to make sense of the idiocy that they were being asked to endure.

I thought back on all the humiliating moments of my life, including some recent ones with Kieran. This one topped the list. By a long shot.

"I'm so sorry, Larimar," I blurted out. "I really didn't want to disturb you. But this is an emergency, and I don't have anyone else to call on. I need your help."

Larimar stared at me wordlessly.

"I promise I'll make it up to you somehow," I rambled on. "Anything that you need from me, I'll do. Not that there's much that you'd need me for, I'm sure. Being a water spirit and everything. That is what you are, right? But if there's something you need, something I can do for you as a lowly human, I'd be more than happy to do it. I would never ask for your help without offering something in return."

I realized with horror that I was still standing. I dropped to the tile in a low bow. The movement was so abrupt that I slammed both knees harder than I had intended, and I bit my lip against the pain.

Larimar's opaque eyes beheld me. Suddenly even Kieran felt wildly expressive and easy to read by comparison. "I told you when we met by the shore," they said. "I cannot interfere in conflicts between humans."

"I completely understand," I said. "I'm not asking for you to interfere in a human conflict necessarily. The thing is, I learned that I'm a Conductor. Which I guess is what my people are calling it when a human can borrow magic temporarily." Wait a second. "You already knew that, though, didn't you?"

Larimar nodded once in affirmation.

"Then I guess maybe you already know where I'm going with this," I mumbled, looking down at the side of the porcelain tub. I didn't have it in me to continue looking them in the eye.

"Correct," Larimar said simply. "You want me to lend you my powers so that you can assist the, as the citizens of your city refer to them, 'Strangers,' in their present siege of your city."

My eyes snapped back up, my embarrassment temporarily forgotten. "What do you mean by 'present siege?'"

There was a pause. "You are unaware, then, of the battle that is taking place on the eastern shore of Cyllene."

I swallowed. "Yes, completely unaware. Please tell me, what battle?"

"The 'Strangers' are attempting to enter Cyllene from the water. Their understanding is that this is the weakest point of entry. The citizens that your city calls 'Enforcers' are defending Cyllene against the attack."

I thought I had experienced enough shocking revelations to last a lifetime. Yet here was another one.

The marsh wolf skins. The cave devil weapons. The Leviathan scales that would have made impenetrable, waterproof shields. All things that would allow the Strangers to approach and invade, undetected until the last minute, from the ocean.

I dropped my head into my hands and let out a sigh of frustration.

As expected, Larimar remained silent. Then, unexpectedly, "What is that liquid?"

Larimar was pointing their fin at the small jar sitting on the edge of the tub.

I stood immediately and grabbed it. Turning the shower head away from us, I held the container out in both hands for Larimar to inspect.

"This is bubble bath," I explained. "It's meant to have a pleasant scent. This one is lavender."

Larimar tilted their head to the side. Waiting. For what? Oh. A demonstration.

Without another word, I unscrewed the lid and dumped some of the contents of the bottle just below the spray from the shower. It didn't take long for thick, purplish foam to begin forming.

The bubble bath, yet another rare luxury that Brielle had gifted me, had only been used once or twice. Luxuriating in a bath wasn't really my thing. As I breathed in the sweet scent of lavender, I tried to imagine what Brielle's reaction would be if she knew it had been used in the presence of an ancient, intimidating, and apparently curious water spirit.

Larimar knelt and cupped a mound of light purple bubbles in their fin-like hands. As they stood, some of the bubbles floated into the air. Larimar's gaze followed the bubbles' path.

I hadn't thought it was possible for this encounter to become more absurd. Yet here we were.

"You can have it if you want," I said lamely, holding out the still half-full jar.

"I have no use for bubble bath," Larimar said, even as they examined the bubbles again. While Larimar did what I could only describe as poking a few bubbles with their pearly fins, I shut off the shower to keep the tub from overflowing. The quiet that followed only added to the awkwardness.

After a moment, Larimar stood up straight and directed their full attention toward me again. "You were not aware of the conflict taking place. What, then, do you need my magic for?"

"The Enforcers have detained both me and Kieran. My room is being guarded as we speak. And I know it's worse for Kieran. They're probably..." I struggled to finish the sentence. "They're probably torturing him."

If Larimar knew anything about that, they did not let on. "What is it that you wish to do?" they asked.

"I wish," I began. "To have enough magic that I can disarm the Enforcers. Not kill them or seriously hurt them, but just temporarily disarm and disable them. And then I need to break Kieran out of wherever they're holding him and get him to safety."

Although Larimar wore no expression, they tilted their head again. I was beginning to understand that they did this in the same manner that humans did, when considering. "Kieran's companions are currently engaged in conflict. What of that?"

What of that was right. "I'm not sure what to do about that yet. I just need to get Kieran out of Cyllene."

The water spirit studied me carefully. When they spoke, it was with a slight sense of accomplishment, as though they had figured out the answer to a puzzle. "You are, to again use a phrase invented by your kind, in love with this Kieran."

Hearing the words spoken aloud should have alarmed me. It had been driven into me over and over again, all my life, that having something to love was having something to lose. But instead of feeling panicked, I felt a strange sense of peace.

"Yes," I whispered. Then I added, "Larimar, I can't lose anyone else. I had a family who loved me, and they were taken from me. Ripped away from me. I thought I would die from the pain of losing them. And in some ways, I think I did. But now I have someone in my life who I love…and not just Kieran. I have multiple people in my life who I care about, who mean something to me. And I can't let them be taken from me, too." My voice had gained strength as I went on. "I *won't* let them be taken from me. Especially not Kieran."

The smooth skin of Larimar's face adjusted slightly, a minor shifting. I couldn't quite say what had changed. They still lacked any particular expression, but something about them seemed…softened. "You are aware," they said. "That Kieran is not of your kind. He is descended from the Oryxians on his father's side. He is living alongside humans now, as one of you, but that cannot last forever. It is not the way of things."

The words were not said harshly. They were not even said as a warning, really. They were merely a statement of fact.

"Yes," I said without hesitating. Then I realized I hadn't known that, not exactly, so I amended, "I don't care."

There was a long pause. Then, "Very well."

Larimar extended their fin. It took only a moment for me to realize what I was meant to do. With a deep breath, I extended my hand to meet them.

The second we touched, my senses were overloaded.

A blast of sunlight. Salt air. A ripple on a pond. The taste of fresh spring water. The darkness at the bottom of the ocean. The thunder of a waterfall. Gliding through a school of fish. Splashing through rapids. The birth of a dolphin calf. A toad resting in a puddle.

And something that spread through me, making my hair stand on end. Zapping every nerve in my body as it passed.

It was strength.

It was power.

CHAPTER EIGHTEEN

"Hey, there," Bergam said with forced friendliness as I opened the door. "You look like you're feeling a lot better!"

I stepped into the hallway. I was wearing a tank top, a pair of form-fitting athletic pants, and boots. My hair was still tied back in a braid. My book bag was slung over my shoulder, stuffed to capacity. Tucked beneath the collar of my shirt, hanging on its chain, was the larimar stone.

"I need to see Kieran," I said simply.

The Enforcer didn't miss a beat. "I'm afraid that's not an option right now."

His response was as I figured. It was all I needed to hear.

I had wanted to give him at least one chance.

I extended my right hand. Nothing happened, and Bergam raised a brow at me. I focused on my hand, centering my will, my energy, my focus. Every ounce of intention that existed in me.

"Maila, are you okay?" he asked, his confusion beginning to morph into concern.

Damnit. This was not how Larimar had said it would go.

I took a deep breath, flexed my fingers. Imagined relaxing the intensity of my focus, then reestablishing it. Refocusing.

I felt it the moment everything snapped into place.

Like a spark under my skin.

A moment later, the symphony of dozens of crackling and crunching noises filled the air as ice encased Bergam on all sides.

Heat had formed in my palm. Prickly. Tingling. In alternating moments, bearable and unbearable. It snaked down and around my wrist. I took another deep breath and let it flow through me. Imagined the air traveling through my veins, reaching every corner of my body. Imagined it fueling the fire that burned under my skin.

I didn't stop until Bergam was completely incapacitated. His head exposed, the rest of him a pyramid of thick ice. Larimar had been right—releasing their magic, which was rooted in the various forms of water, as ice had been the perfect way to disable without hurting.

Bergam opened his mouth wide as if to shout for help. But just as the first syllable was forming in his throat, I yanked a shirt out of my bag and stuffed it in his mouth.

"I'm sorry about this," I said. "But this is important. Are you listening to me?"

I felt like Nya that first night that she and Kieran visited my apartment.

He nodded.

"I don't want to hurt you," I continued. "But I will if I have to. I need to know where The Council is keeping Kieran. I'm going to remove the shirt so that you can tell me, and I need you to understand that if you don't, I will hurt you. And if you call for help"—I swallowed reflexively—"I will hurt you, plus whoever comes to help you."

I was grateful once again that that the hallway was empty, quiet.

Bergam exhaled through his nose. He blinked in what I hoped was understanding.

"I'm going to pull the shirt out now. And when I do, the only words I want to hear are where they are keeping Kieran." I paused for emphasis. Then I removed the shirt from his mouth.

"Before you do this," he said in a rush of breath. "There's something you need to—"

Without missing a beat, I shoved the shirt back in his mouth.

"I'm not very good at this," I said, holding up my right hand again. "But I did try to leave you some room to breathe. I can change that."

I had no idea if I could change that. Increasing the thickness of the ice, tightening its grip around his chest, seemed like something that would require a ridiculous amount of precision. With my luck, I would accidentally spear him through the lung. But he didn't need to know that.

"Let's try this again. Where is Kieran?"

Bergam was already talking the second the shirt cleared his mouth. "I'monyourside!"

I blinked. "What?"

"I'm on your side," he said, more slowly this time. He dropped his voice to a whisper. "If you're doing this, if you're rescuing Kieran and siding with the people from Ersa Estates—you do know that's what rescuing him means, right? How The Council is going to take it? Anyway, I'm on your side, Maila." I opened my mouth, and he immediately cut me off, "No time for questions. Go ahead, continue like I never said anything."

And then he was growling and cursing and calling me every profane name under the sun, while struggling against the barrier of the ice.

"Um," I began, trying to collect myself. He nodded imperceptibly, as if urging me on. "Be quiet and tell me where Kieran is?"

He sighed heavily, as if resigning himself to his fate. "He's being held in a storage room on the first floor," he said. "It's not ideal, but Leon felt it would be too risky to try to move him to Headquarters until we had a better idea what to expect. Moving him sooner would've invited too many questions and created too many opportunities for onlookers to become collateral damage."

"Where is the storage room?" My hands began to shake. Not from the magic, but from adrenaline.

"It's right across the hall from where we were before. The others were moving like they were going to take him out the exit on the opposite side of the room, but that was just to throw you off. They left out the same door we did."

I steeled myself to ask the question that terrified me the most. "Are they…torturing him?"

"I don't know." Those were the words he spoke, but he was subtly nodding his head yes. My heart sank. "You're making a mistake. Kieran is extremely dangerous. Even before the incident the other night, we were told never to engage with him one-to-one. You don't know what you're getting yourself mixed up in."

I knew I could have kept pumping him for information, but time was of the essence. I needed to get to Kieran as soon as possible.

"Thank you," I said simply. I held the shirt back up to his mouth, hesitating slightly, and he gave another subtle nod. I replaced the shirt, but left it loose, making sure he could breathe easily enough around it. Then I turned to run for the emergency staircase at the end of the hall, the same one we had taken the previous day.

But I halted abruptly as a flash of yellow caught my eye, beyond Bergam's shoulder.

Someone was standing at the other end of the hall, near the central staircase. Her billowy shirt was a pale yellow, her hair pulled into a low side ponytail that was draped gracefully over a shoulder. Her hazel eyes were wide, mouth hanging open. One hand still clutched the handle of a thermos, but her arms were limp at her sides.

"Brielle."

Even from where she was standing, I could see her throat spasm involuntarily. She blinked at me. Then she slowly, shakily held up the thermos. It was pink, and something about that made a lump form in my throat.

"I-I made you soup." Her voice was small. "You weren't at—so I thought, maybe, you were sick, and… what's happening, Maila? What is this?"

"Brielle," I began. "I don't have time to explain what's going on. But I need you to trust me. And I need you not to tell anyone. At least not yet, not until I've had time to finish…what it is that I'm doing. This is hard to explain, but I need you to remember who I am and trust that there's a good reason behind what I'm doing."

Earlier I had felt my words reflecting Nya's. Now they were reflecting Kieran's yesterday with The Council.

"Please trust me," I begged again. My voice faltered on the last word.

Brielle didn't say that she would. But she also didn't say that she wouldn't. She didn't scream or yell or take off running. And that was something.

I refused to look back again as I sprinted for the stairs.

Leaving Brielle as frozen to where she stood as Bergam, tears streaming down her face.

CHAPTER NINETEEN

I rushed down the stairs as fast I physically could, practically leaping from landing to landing. Meanwhile, Larimar's magic felt like it was sizzling beneath my skin. I hoped that just meant it was waiting, ready to be put to use, and not that it was doing some kind of irreparable damage to my body. Larimar had forewarned me that it was a possibility, especially considering that I had had exactly zero training with this.

There were no Enforcers posted in the stairwell, and when I burst through the door to the first floor and startled only two of them, standing by themselves in the long hallway, I realized that most everyone must have been called to handle the situation—the "battle," as Larimar had referred to it—with the Strangers. The door the two men were guarding obviously led to the storage room, because it was almost directly across the hall from the room we were in yesterday, as Bergam had said.

I held out both hands this time, focusing on releasing energy from both. Moisture began to build on my palms as if they were sweating. Then water began pouring steadily from them, creating two puddles on the carpet.

"What in the actual fuck are you doing?" one of the Enforcers asked, starting to walk in my direction.

I wanted to tell him his guess was as good as mine. What the hell was I doing wrong?

Then just as with Bergam, I felt something like click. Like Larimar's magic and my intentions had finally found one another. A cacophony of creaking and snapping filled the hall. Thick tendrils of ice climbed the two Enforcers.

Unlike with Bergam, genuine shock, horror, and fury paraded across their faces.

"You fucking bitch!" one of them snarled as I pulled another shirt out of my bag and stuffed it in his partner's mouth. I shoved a third shirt—my last one—in his mouth as he was gearing up to hit me with another slur.

I looked down into my bag, already knowing what I would find there. What was left of the bread that I had devoured earlier. A reusable bottle of water. And no more clothing, shirt or otherwise. If I encountered more Enforcers, I was going to have to cover them in ice fully and hope that it melted before they ran out of air.

I pushed between the two Enforcers trapped in their icebergs and tried the handle to the storage room. Unsurprisingly, it was locked.

I took a deep breath and again summoned Larimar's magic to my palms. Having used my right hand several times now to expel it, the burning sensation was becoming more intense. Like the circulation had been cut off to my hand and forearm, but worse. My left hand wasn't far behind. As I focused my breathing, my energy, my mind, my soul on the ice that was now forming over the handle and the lock within, a dull ache began to spread from the back of my neck to the front of my head.

"If you feel a headache setting in," Larimar had said. *"It means you are doing too much, too fast. You are still a human wielding another being's magic. Your body still has limitations."*

I didn't have time to care about limitations. I steeled myself.

There was a screechy, grinding, crunching sort of noise that seemed to be from metal bending in ways that it shouldn't.

Gritting my teeth, I focused on what I wanted the ice to do next. I curled my fingers into a fist, willing that physical motion to guide the ice.

I could have cheered when it did.

Clouds of steam began to rise from the surface of the ice. And then the surface became damp. Melting.

The ice was still dissipating into liquid water when I shoved the door open.

And there he was.

"Kieran," I breathed.

He was sitting against a wall, hands still bound behind his back. His legs were straight out in front of him, his ankles also bound. Tears of relief welled in my eyes as I observed that his chest was rising and falling. He was breathing.

Oh, thank you, thank you, thank you. He was alive. Kieran was alive.

But the tears of relief turned to tears of horror when I saw that his injuries were endless. It seemed there was no part of his body that wasn't covered in dried blood and the beginnings of bruises.

His eyelids fluttered open. Two dull gray orbs. Then they snapped shut, as if holding them open was too painful. His dry, pale lips moved as if forming words, but no sound came out.

I stepped closer, into the room.

A violent wave of nausea exploded in my gut, and the room pitched as if on a wild sea.

I heard an audible smack and felt a corresponding jolt of pain as I hit the sealed concrete floor, landing on my right side.

"Wards," a voice choked nearby. If Kieran weren't the only other person in the room, I never would have imagined that hoarse sound had come from him.

My head was spinning wildly. I willed Larimar's magic to do something. Anything. But I could practically feel it sputtering as the burning sensation in my palms died.

I had to get Kieran out of there. There was no other option. If I didn't pull myself together, we were both going to die. And I could make peace with my own death, but not his.

I squeezed my eyes shut and sat up, trying to orient myself. The nausea writhed in me like a great beast. Like the Leviathan, thrashing in the seas as it battled the Strangers. I barely managed to aim my head away from myself as I vomited.

I was still coughing up thick saliva, blessedly moving toward dry heaves, when I became aware of a shuffling, scraping sound. I allowed myself a quick look before squeezing my eyes shut again. Kieran had managed to get up onto his knees and was dragging himself slowly in my direction. With each movement, he exhaled sharply through gritted teeth.

I repeated to myself again that I had to get him out of there, bringing my mind back to the task at hand. At any moment, someone could see what I had done to the two Enforcers just outside the room, and it would be over for us.

I raised onto my knees. If Kieran could manage it in his state, I could, too. I braced a hand on each knee, forcing air into my lungs even as I gagged. I stole another look, barely peeling my lids from one another, and saw Kieran was almost within arm's reach. This "storage room," whatever it had once been used for, was compact. In fact, it couldn't have been much bigger than my bedroom.

We could do this. We could escape.

I extended my arm out in front of me, feeling for Kieran. It nearly dropped reflexively the moment it was raised, overcome with a sickening fatigue. I forced it to stay aloft with everything that I had. Then I pushed my eyelids open again.

Kieran was close. So close. Seeing that gave me a burst of strength.

I fell forward, bracing myself on all fours, and extended my right arm again. This time, my fingertips brushed against the fabric of his shirt. Whatever tattered scraps were left of it, anyway.

I yanked on the fabric, and he fell forward into me.

We were collapsed on the floor of a storage room, him covered in blood and me—despite my best efforts—likely covered in vomit, both of us struggling to hang on, but I had him.

And that was everything.

I leaned back as far as I could manage, bringing him with me, and began dragging us back toward the threshold.

This would have been a difficult task even without the wards to weaken me. Kieran was taller and heavier than I was, and I didn't have much upper body strength. But I could feel him moving against me, trying as best he could to help push us closer to the door. Each movement was minuscule, but we were making progress.

My left hand was on his shoulder, wrapped across his back. My right hand was on the door frame. I flailed my arm backwards, my shoulder straining in its socket. And then my fingertips were touching carpet. My whole hand was touching carpet.

This power was new, but when the burning sensation returned to my palm, it was already like an old, welcome friend. With every ounce of strength I had left, I flung myself backward, pulling Kieran with me. At the same time, I aimed my hand at the wall to the right of the doorway. The awareness of the connection snapping into place was instant this time.

Thank fuck.

I blasted the wall with a torrent of water so intense it catapulted us past the two Enforcers and across the hallway. My back slammed against the opposite wall so hard that it knocked the wind out of me.

I opened my eyes fully, grateful to be able to do so, and saw the two Enforcers still soundly trapped in their ice bindings at the door. Even with their mouths stuffed, I could tell their jaws were hanging open. Their eyes were almost comedically wide.

I couldn't tell if it was the sight of them or hysteria that made this the funniest thing I had ever seen. My diaphragm relaxed and my grateful lungs filled with air, only to have it escape again as I burst into laughter.

"What in the hell did you just do?" Kieran's voice was still raspy but less pained. He raised up to look at me. In the midst of his battered face, his eyes twinkled with amusement.

"Larimar's power," I managed to choke out. I was laughing so hard that I could feel tears forming. For the first time in a long time, they were welcome tears.

"Larimar's power," he repeated.

I could only nod, beyond speaking.

Kieran burst into laughter along with me, his body pitching forward so that his forehead leaned against mine. But his laughter was cut short by a sharp intake of breath.

"Are you okay?" I asked quickly, all humor vanishing in an instant.

"Could be worse," he gritted out. "Actually, I *was* worse until you got us out of there. Those wards were no joke."

I looked beyond the Enforcers then, through the doorway. I had been so focused on Kieran, I had missed them before. The black-inked markings of magic-dampening wards were scrawled across the floor, the wall, the ceiling. "They were awful," I agreed. "We're lucky that you're half-human, and I'm just a human carrying magic in my system. If we had been purely magical beings, we would've been fully incapacitated."

Reluctantly, I pulled away from him, moving to the wrists still bound behind his back. I used a similar method as with the door to crush and snap the hard plastic of the cuffs. It took a few tries, one of which involved squirting cold water in Kieran's face. When I finally got the cuffs off him, I frowned at the magic-dampening wards on the underside of the broken pieces. "I knew an enchantress assisted Cyllene with the barrier wards for the walls years ago, but I didn't know The Council still had access to these kinds of spells."

I glanced over at the two Enforcers, who were watching and listening closely. Their eyes were inscrutable.

"The Council has access to a lot of things," Kieran said with a sigh, rotating his wrists in slow circles. I finished breaking the cuffs on his ankles, and he flexed them as well. "But we don't have time to talk about all of that right now. We need to get out of here."

"Right." I moved to stand, but Kieran grabbed my arm.

"I know Addis said a lot of things yesterday. Thank you. For trusting me."

I gave him a small smile. "I'm not thrilled that you kept all this from me, but whatever this might have started as, I trust your intentions now."

I went to stand and instantly fell back against the wall. Kieran did the same, his legs buckling under him. His issue now was his lingering injuries. Mine was the toll that Larimar's magic was taking on my body. I could feel the creeping headache returning, this time with a vengeance.

"Hey," Kieran said quietly, his voice still raspy. He smoothed back a few strands of hair that had come loose from my braid, tucking them behind my ear. "I'm here now, so don't use magic again unless you absolutely have to. Don't overdo it."

"I'm not, don't worry." Here I was talking about trust, and I was lying to him. My head was pounding. But his fingertips brushing against the shell of my ear were certainly a nice distraction from that.

I didn't fool Kieran for a second. Wordlessly, he gestured behind him to the two men encased in ice, as if that proved his point.

"It's not funny," he chided as I was overtaken by another fit of laughter. "It takes a lot of magic to do something like that, and it will catch up with you quickly. You're human."

Before I could stop myself, I said meekly, "There's another one upstairs."

Another one who's on our side, apparently, I wanted to add. But not with the two others in earshot.

Kieran stared at me for a long moment. In spite of himself, his lips tugged into a smile. "Come on, Maila. Larimar's apprentice. Whoever the hell you are."

He grabbed my arm and pulled me down the hall toward the central staircase. He was trying to conceal that he was limping. I fell into step beside him and loosened my arm from his grip so he could use his to balance.

Clearly, we were equally worried about the other overexerting themselves.

When we reached the base of the staircase, I spotted two women descending from several levels up, engrossed in conversation. We needed to pick up the pace before anyone took notice of Kieran and his silver eyes. Or how banged up he was, for that matter.

He must have had the same thought, because even with his injured legs, he made as if to break into a jog, turning in the direction of the glass doors that led to the Knowledge Center.

That was when it hit me.

"Kieran, wait." He whipped around to face me. "Larimar told me that Nya and the others are trying to break into Cyllene from the beach. They're facing off with the Enforcers. That's why it's so quiet right now."

"I know." He gave a sad smile. "That's why I was armed. I was supposed to join them today. After I convinced you to stay in your room, no matter what you heard, and…" His throat bobbed. "And wait for me."

"Wait for you?"

"The decision was yours to make, Maila," he said softly. "I know we came on strong in the beginning, but…once we got to know you, there was never any other option. It had to be your choice if you wanted to help us or not. And if it was left up to me, you would be somewhere safe. Not involved in any of this. Not anymore."

The backs of my eyes burned. "So what is 'this,' Kieran?" I asked softly. We didn't have time for this, I knew. But after all of the lies—some outright, and some by omission—I deserved for someone to tell me the truth of what I was getting into this time. "What are you all trying to accomplish with this?"

The only hesitation from Kieran was the time it took to pull me into the shadows beneath the stairwell. "We're taking the city. Not forever, but just long enough to dismantle The Council and establish new leadership. Leadership that we'll be a part of. Everyday citizens will be included in that process, too, even though they'll initially be scared." He smirked that signature smirk of his. "I'm going to join my people, Maila. My offer still stands. You can follow, or you can stay out of this mess and wait for me in your apartment. I'll come find you. No matter what, I'll find you."

Then he was running again.

For a moment, I stood there. Speechless. Then with a deep breath, my decision already made, I hurried to catch up.

"Maila."

The voice made me stop in my tracks.

Addis was standing at the entrance to the hallway on my right, as if he had just come from there. His hands were in his pockets, the picture of casual. Relaxed. Unruffled. An easy smile highlighting the laugh lines in his aged but handsome face.

The smile didn't quite reach his eyes.

His chest was rising and falling almost imperceptibly faster than it should have been, as if he had been walking fast or even running and was trying to conceal it.

"Let's continue that conversation," he said, and it was almost as if he forced his eyes to crinkle, to appear amiable. "Clearly I see what you've done here, and I'm sure you think there will be consequences for that. But there's a lot happening right now. A lot of big revelations. Just a lot to wrap your head around in general, right? And I know you care very much for Kieran. But let's make sure you have all the facts before you do anything rash. It would be a shame for you to put yourself in danger unnecessarily, wouldn't it?"

I heard the creak of a door opening down the hall, behind him. Quinn, Westley, and Cato emerged and began heading toward us at a quick clip. I didn't know what The Council had been doing in that room or why. If it had been a meeting about the battle, about Kieran, about me, or all of the above. But I did know that Addis was buying time.

"I think I'll pass."

He frowned, but there was something calculated in it. A sudden intensity in his stare. He said his next words slowly. "My granddaughter would be devastated if something happened to you."

What? I thought I'd said it in my head. Then Addis opened his mouth to respond, and I realized I had said it out loud.

"Brielle."

I stared at him. He stared back.

The leader of The Council was Brielle's grandfather? And Brielle had never once, in our six years of friendship, thought that was worth mentioning? Apparently, I wasn't the only one keeping secrets.

I considered saying something else to Addis. But the rest of The Council had almost reached us, and in the end, I turned on my heel and raced out the door after Kieran.

I refused to look back. Yet I was waiting. Waiting for pounding footsteps behind me, for Cato to grab me by the shoulder and drag me back to the living quarters. Back to Addis and The Council and whatever fate awaited me there.

With a pang, I recalled Cato's many lectures over the years on the importance of enriching not only the mind, but the body as well. He could close the considerable distance between us in no time.

My adrenaline spurred me on, my heart pounding wildly with fear and anticipation.

Cato never appeared.

CHAPTER TWENTY

My lungs ached. I could feel a stitch forming in my side. Even injured, Kieran was faster than I was. I considered for a moment if I could use magic to help propel me along, but the throbbing in my head was my answer.

As the courtyard flew past us, I thought vaguely of the Wildlife Preservation department. What if one of them was out here right now, tending to the gardens, and saw us? What would they think? What would anyone think, for that matter? If everyone in Cyllene knew the events of the last twenty-four hours, knew what I had done, what would they say?

A sobering thought hit me. I was already thinking of Cyllene in terms of "they." Not "we." But wouldn't we all be a "we" if this worked out? If the Strangers were successful in occupying Cyllene, I wouldn't have to choose one or the other. I could still have Brielle, the Library, maybe even Zander's friendship again one day.

Why did I feel like I was lying to myself?

The gardens around us were highlighted in faint gold, picking up those first morning rays. The sun was rising, I realized. In fact, the sky probably looked spectacular on the beach, where our friends were fighting for their lives.

I willed my mind to quiet, to be still. To take in the courtyard. Just in case it was a while before I saw it again.

I took in the sight of all that greenery, carefully protected and preserved. The blending of so many shades—olive and chartreuse, lime and sage. And my personal favorite, emerald. Just like Irene's eyes.

The fresh scent of gardenias. Sweet and comforting and familiar. The scent that accompanied morning strolls to work with Brielle. Strolls that I had always taken for granted, but that I could now see myself missing if they never happened again.

Over the sound of mine and Kieran's panting, I could hear the soft misting of water. The solar-powered sprinklers strategically placed around the garden. Wildlife Preservation didn't have very many of them, but the few they did have were a huge source of pride. They would continue making advancements like that, continue trying to move forward. The Strangers would more than support that, I knew.

Mixing in my mouth were the taste of sweat and of blood. I wasn't sure where the blood had come from…if it was mine or Kieran's. I could also taste something else.

Rather than the salt of sweat, it was like the pleasant salt of the ocean. Fresh and healing and ancient.

The knowledge of what it was settled into my brain like a comforting hug. Larimar's magic.

And finally, the pounding of my boot-clad feet against the pavement. The stabbing in my joints at each lunge forward. The cramping, constricting ball of pain that was enveloping my chest as my lungs fought for air. The roiling beast of a headache, approaching migraine level, that was circling my head in laps. None of it mattered. Kieran was no longer a prisoner, and we were going to rescue our friends.

The corners of my mouth twitched in a sad smile as I observed my train of thought. Beginning with the gardens, and then steadily drifting right back to Kieran. To Larimar. To the others. I couldn't separate myself from them, even for a few moments. They invaded—no, they were *welcome* to enter my every thought.

A gap was forming between me and Kieran by the time we reached the entrance to the Knowledge Center, but he paused to hold the door. An opportunity for me to catch up.

"You. Don't. Have. To wait. On me," I managed to call out between gulps of air.

"I'm not leaving you behind," Kieran called back. "If you get captured, I don't think we're going to be able to pull some amazing stunt to break out of the wards again."

I wanted to remark on how unfair it was that he wasn't more winded, but I couldn't afford to waste my own breath. I ran through the door, and then we were both racing through the Knowledge Center.

I had guessed this was where we were going to be noticed. I was right. The atrium was mostly empty, but there was still a cluster of people standing around, faces pressed to the glass on the opposite end of the atrium. Every one of them jolted to attention at the sound of our feet slamming against the linoleum floor.

After taking in a few shocked expressions, I trained my eyes on the exit beyond them. There was nothing to do but keep running.

We were almost there when a woman shouted, "Don't go out there! Something is—"

We were already shouldering through the doors, leaving her warning to echo uselessly behind us.

We tore through an area that I had only visited a handful of times in my life. On the eastern side of the Knowledge Center, rather than smooth pavement that was easy to traverse, the doors opened onto hilly, uneven ground that forced us to slow our step. Contrasting against the aesthetically pleasing gardens of the courtyard, this stretch of land was not only not fussed over, but didn't give the appearance of being tended at all. It was a mixture of gritty sand, clusters of rocks, yellowing grass, and unexpected dips in the terrain. Packed with potential pitfalls. It wasn't long before we were half-running, half-hopping to get to the other side.

To the wall.

Except even from a mile out, I could see that it was not a wall. Not anymore.

If I wasn't already gasping from running, I would have gasped at the sight of the wall caved in. Massive chunks of concrete jutted up from the ground as if it had been quite literally blown apart. Suddenly, the loud noise I thought I had dreamt or hallucinated earlier made sense.

The hole must have been at least a quarter of a mile wide. Beyond, the terrain dipped down into a pristine beach. The sun was peeking over the horizon, turning the ocean a soft shade of turquoise and transforming the sky above into a rainbow of pastels.

A peaceful backdrop for what could only be described as utter chaos.

Swarming around and over the hole in the wall, like ants protecting their hill, were Enforcers. No, not just Enforcers. All clad in similar outfits, which even from a distance I could see were the waterproof coverings made from the marsh wolf pelts, were the Strangers. As we approached, I heard the clang of metal against metal and could begin to make out clusters of people engaged in combat.

But there were also other noises…grating, roaring noises. And flashes of light. Multi-colored lights, some of which resembled flame. My brain raced to understand what I was witnessing.

The distance between me and Kieran began to grow again as he launched into a full sprint, sailing over the dips and holes in the field, practically flying. Spurred on by horrors that he could make out in detail even from this distance. Horrors that were slowly but surely coming into focus for me.

There was blood. So much blood.

That unmistakable, ominous red was splattered across the craggy edges of wall that were still standing. Morbid shades of red, brown, and black covered the shattered chunks of concrete that, I observed as we got closer, were littered across the field even more thoroughly than I had first realized. People, some one-to-one and others struggling against each other in groups, were covered in gore.

Panic detonated in me. Before I knew it, the burst of adrenaline had me running right alongside Kieran.

Where was Nya? Were Cecil and Xiomara here? Surely Rubi, Wren, and George had stayed back…right? There were so many of the Strangers here. Way more than had gone on the mission to take down the Leviathan. And then there were the Enforcers. Was Zander out here somewhere?

Then the worst realization of all hit me. Not just figuratively, but literally, as my foot bashed into something solid and I sailed through the air. My arms and legs flailed for purchase, but my momentum had me careening. My arms and legs scraped across tiny rocks, sand, and the jagged edges of the straw-like grass. When I finally tumbled to a stop, I looked back immediately to see what I had tripped over.

A person. A person, who was not moving. A corpse.

A man, probably in his early twenties. Wearing that familiar Enforcer uniform, under armor that I had only seen the Enforcers don a few times in my life, mostly for ceremony. His arms and legs were sprawled limply on either side of him. His eyes stared unseeingly up at the lavenders and pinks of the breaking dawn.

I hadn't seen a dead body up close since Leon killed my sister. I wanted to scream, to cry, to vomit again, all at once. But all I could do was stare in horror.

Something whizzed past my face. Something so hot that my skin stung even after it had passed.

Tearing my gaze away from the Enforcer's body, I looked to see where the fire had landed. It was a few feet away, and it wasn't fire. Not exactly. Smoke coiled upward from tendrils of strange light. From a blaze that was at once purple and yellow and red and somehow also green. Like it was cycling through new colors every second.

My brain shoved the fear aside and snapped into survival mode.

What was this? And where did it come from?

I twisted around to see Kieran about thirty feet ahead of me, grappling with an Enforcer. The Enforcer had a weapon…that same strange, white gun, I realized. It looked just as menacing as the first time I saw an Enforcer brandish it.

The Enforcer was trying desperately to aim it at Kieran, but Kieran had the Enforcer's arm pinned so that it aimed only at the sky. In one swift movement, Kieran jerked the Enforcer's arm further, and a curse erupted from his mouth as he fell backwards. His arm was hanging unnaturally as he fell.

Kieran kicked in the direction of his face, and I cringed when the movement halted abruptly, letting me know his foot had connected with its target. He yanked the gun out of the Enforcer's hand and flung it in the direction we had come.

Then Kieran was shouting at me. "Maila, come on!"

I leapt to my feet, vaguely noticing that blood was trickling down my arms and soaking the knees of my pants. I couldn't feel the pain.

We were making our way through the outer edges of the battle now, to the heart of it. We passed several Enforcers, and unlike the first one we encountered, Kieran was on them too quickly for them to react. They were focused on the threat from the beach and weren't expecting anyone to approach from behind. I had no small sense of relief when I observed that each time, Kieran disabled the Enforcers without killing them, always tossing those mysterious guns to the side, far out of reach. I wasn't sure what the long-term plan was or if he even had a long-term plan for ensuring these Enforcers would no longer be a threat. But I wasn't ready to see him take a life, not just yet. And something told me he wasn't ready, either.

As we grew closer and closer to the hole in the wall, the yellows, browns, and greens of the grass gave way to ashy black. Charred, smoking patches where the fiery blasts from those guns had landed. Some of them still glowered with embers of that technicolor light.

"What are those?" I yelled over the din, as Kieran tossed what must have been the sixth gun behind over his shoulder.

"We call them Immobilizers," he grunted. "They're basically guns that are also effective against magical beings."

We came upon two more Enforcers, and Kieran repeated the pattern of pouncing while they were unsuspecting. In a single movement, he threw one to the ground, ripped the Immobilizer out of his hand, and used it to bash the second one in the face.

Movement in my left peripheral had me turning my attention to a third Enforcer. Approaching from the side, Immobilizer drawn. Aimed right at Kieran.

I ran straight for him.

He saw me and raised his brows. He looked younger than the men we had encountered so far. Possibly even a teenager. His unsteadiness reminded me of the boy I tried to rescue at the beach.

Speaking of him—was he here, too? It was amazing how quickly I had gone from only having to look out for myself to having so many other people to worry about now.

The Enforcer seemed conflicted about whether to keep his gun trained on Kieran, or fire at me instead. Before he could make up his mind, I held out my right hand and internally screamed at my brain to please just do what I was asking without any delays or screw-ups. Two seconds later, I was hurling a torrent of water in his direction. The pressure knocked him backwards and forced him to let go of his Immobilizer.

The strength of the blast knocked me back a step as well, but I recovered and was upon him before he could react. I held out my left hand, giving my right some time to recover, and watched with satisfaction as ice invaded every crevice of the Immobilizer, cracking and snapping it into several pieces.

The Enforcer watched with eyes the size of saucers. I couldn't tell if he wanted to run screaming or worship the ground I walked on.

"Get out of here and go home," I ordered in what I hoped was my most authoritative voice. Then I rejoined Kieran, who was already backtracking in my direction.

"Look at you!" he drawled. His voice was full of mock admiration, but there was also a glimmer of actual pride in his eyes.

"I think you owe me." I was too out of breath to sound as smug as I felt.

"I'm sure you'll think of a way for me to make it up to you," he said.

And I didn't know if it was his suggestive tone or the return of that smug smile that was so characteristically him, but my cheeks burned. It felt good to be distracted for a moment. He could say things like that because there was a future after this. We would get through this.

Both of us sobered up fast as we finally reached the tangle of bodies that was the center of the conflict.

My ears were instantly overwhelmed by the screaming and shouting and cursing that surrounded me on all sides, mixed in with the sharp clang of weapons colliding with one another. And the ever-present roar of, I now realized, the discharge of the Immobilizers.

The bodies on the ground, a mixture of the injured and what I hoped were just the unconscious, were so frequent that we could no longer move at even a slow jog. We were hopping over the arms and legs of the fallen. At one point, I heard a shriek as my foot accidentally landed on something that was not grass. But I had to keep going.

We weaved through the clusters of people, through the smaller battles whose results would determine the outcome of the big one. Along the way, Kieran continued to use the element of surprise to disarm the Enforcers, giving the men and women on his side—our side now— the advantage. He seemed to be the only one taking that approach, though. Our people, while not armed with Immobilizers, were using the weapons they had looted from the cave devils to strike what could only have been killing blows. Swords sliced at any exposed fabric between the plates of the Enforcers' armor, spears pierced unshielded eyes, maces cracked against uncovered skulls. Daggers slit bare throats.

Witnessing the carnage made me question, just for the briefest of moments, if I had made the right decision. I was on their side. But that didn't mean I thought the Enforcers deserved to die. That Zander deserved to die.

At the thought, I turned a circle, hoping to catch sight of him, yet also not hoping to catch sight of him. He could be here and still alive. He could also be here but unconscious and out of view. Or…worse, and out of view. He could also be somewhere else, on a special assignment like Bergam and the two Enforcers guarding Kieran had been. I hoped beyond all hope that it was the last one.

Unsurprisingly, visibility was too poor for me to catch sight of Zander. But I almost cried with relief as Kieran and I cleared a jagged chunk of concrete and were suddenly face-to-face with Nya.

"It's about time!" Nya yelled.

If not for the Enforcer that was charging right at her, readying his Immobilizer, I would have charged her myself and thrown my arms around her.

Her braids were pulled back in their usual ponytail. But rather than her usual tank top and shorts, she was wearing that gleaming gray-brown marsh wolf pelt, the material highlighting each of her curves and muscles, giving her the appearance of a statue. A shining paradigm of the human form. Gripped tightly in her right hand was a sword with a magnificent golden hilt, the blade already stained with blood.

I hadn't thought it was possible for her to look any more fearsome, yet here she was.

Absolutely terrifying.

Nya ran straight at the Enforcer, so close that I thought they would collide, then dove at the last second. She whipped the sword around at such an angle that rather than connecting with the protective plates across his shins, it caught the man in the calves, dropping him instantaneously. As soon as his Immobilizer hit the ground beside him, she was sheathing her sword in the gold scabbard at her side and grabbing the gun.

Kieran and I both looked on, open-mouthed, as she used the Immobilizer to fire three successive shots into the chaos. One soared out of view, but two connected with their targets, who immediately doubled over. They screamed and gripped their chests as light and smoke and that flame-like something blazed away beneath their frantic hands.

Nya aimed and attempted to fire again, but the Immobilizer just sputtered. Nothing came out but a thin tail of smoke and a few sparks.

"Seems like five's the max with these." She tossed the gun aside.

"How are we doing?" Kieran shouted back.

"The cave devils' explosives, whatever they were, worked better than we had hoped. As you can see by the fact that we're here and not still on the beach." Nya dragged an arm across her forehead, wiping sweat from her brow. "But right now, this thing could go either way."

With that, she headed toward another Enforcer, sword drawn. Kieran was right behind her, and I was close behind him.

The Enforcer fired his Immobilizer, but Nya dodged without slowing. By the time she was on him, he was dropping the gun and holding his hands in the air in surrender. Just as before, Nya grabbed the gun herself and was able to fire one more shot before it was spent. I wondered who the first three shots had been used on, and if the targets were alive or dead. Beside me, Kieran took down a burly Enforcer who was gripping his gun with meaty hands. He tackled the man to the ground and delivered a knockout punch to the face.

People on both sides started taking notice of what was happening in our small circle of the field. The Strangers acknowledged us with quick nods when they could, relief visible in their tired eyes at the sight of a few reinforcements. Meanwhile, a cluster of Enforcers shoved their way through, making a beeline for Nya and Kieran. I counted six of them.

As they broke through the crowd, gathered in a tight, impenetrable formation, I saw that there was no way that Nya and Kieran were going to be able to fend them all off without taking damage.

"Stand back!" I yelled at the two of them.

They paused mid-step, and I only had a split second to witness the confusion on their faces as I shoved in front of them, arms outstretched.

As I geared up to use Larimar's magic again, I could feel my hands, my head, everything screaming in protest. But I shut it all out as I zeroed in on the six Enforcers in front of me. I thought about doing my go-to move— surrounding them in a massive block of ice. But this time, I decided to try something new. Something that I hoped would be slightly less taxing on my system.

I lifted the six Enforcers in a swirling, raging mass of water. I lifted them five feet into the air. Ten feet. Twenty.

Then I let the water fall. And them with it.

The six of them connected with the ground so hard that it knocked one of them unconscious straight away. The remaining five cried out, water sputtering from their mouths and spraying from their nostrils, as their arms and legs took the brunt of the impact. Every one of them dropped their Immobilizer on impact.

Without missing a beat, Nya and Kieran swooped in and grabbed up the guns. They tossed several away, out of reach. Then Nya fired two, which were each fully loaded with five…blasts? Bullets? I still wasn't certain what made up those blazing balls of light and power.

Kieran stared at one of the Immobilizers for a moment, seeming to weigh something in his mind. Then, without another moment's hesitation, he mimicked Nya's movements—one hand steadying the barrel, one gripping the trigger—and trained it on the chest of a nearby Enforcer. The technicolor sphere that he let loose found its mark, and the Enforcer toppled to the ground, giving the dagger-wielding woman in front of him the upper hand.

I watched the whole event numbly. There was no room for my judgment here.

It was war. It was kill or be killed.

"So," Nya shouted behind me, clapping a hand on my arm. "I'm going to take a wild guess and say you know you can wield magic now."

"They called her a 'Conductor,'" Kieran called back, discharging a few more well-aimed shots and tossing the empty gun to the side.

Nya's answering laugh was so normal, so not a part of the horrors that were happening around us, that it soothed me to hear it. "Always with the creative names!" she roared. Then added, "I still like ours though—'Badass Magical Human.'"

I laughed in spite of myself.

Nya and Kieran sprinted off again.

Turns out, lifting six adult men in raging mass of water was no less taxing than generating mini mountains of solid ice, which felt very much like a "No, shit" moment for me. My vision was pulsing now with the pounding in my head. But I managed to keep up with Nya and Kieran, and in a matter of mere minutes, the two of them felled four more Enforcers, saving one man on our side who had been knocked to the ground. His eyes were shining with tears when Nya helped him to his feet, but he didn't waste any time in rejoining the battle, returning the favor by coming to the aid of two more people who were being overpowered by Enforcers.

Although neither of them were enjoying the task at hand, it was clear that Nya and Kieran were in their element. They were not only excellent fighters but excellent partners. She had his back, and he had hers, in the truest sense of the phrase.

I flexed my aching fingers and wrists, readying myself for when I would be needed next. We were going to make it through this. Together. There was no alternative.

The sun's movement across the sky was the only thing that kept me from losing all concept of time. It finally drifted above the waves, highlighting them in vibrant gold, and then the sky became a clear, cloudless blue.

Nya, Kieran, and I took a moment to pause and try to catch our breath. The air reeked of sweat, blood, and charred flesh.

"How much pain are you in?" Kieran asked, scanning me from head to toe.

I didn't have it in me to lie this time. "A lot."

"Turning that whole section of Enforcers into an iceberg must have taken a lot of magic," Nya mused, observing the giant block of ice that glittered on the other end of the battlefield. The heads of Enforcers—twelve at last count—poked out of the ice in various spots, their expressions a mix of absolute bafflement and frustration. If I weren't so focused on trying to remain standing, I probably would have found the sight hilarious.

Kieran placed his hands on either side of my face, tilting my head upward and forcing me to look him in the eye. "You need to stop using magic."

"I don't think I have a choice but to stop, unfortunately." My hands, wrists, arms, and shoulders raged with flaming pins and needles. I attempted to lift my hands as if to summon Larimar's power. Not only was the movement excruciating, but that sensation that had been becoming more and more familiar, the feeling of magic welling up in me and preparing to dispel, was almost entirely gone now.

"Find somewhere to hide and rest," Kieran ordered. Then he added softly, "Please."

I opened my mouth to respond. As I did, an Immobilizer blast blitzed past, an inch from Kieran's shoulder.

We all whipped around at the same time to see Zander, the barrel of his Immobilizer smoking.

I didn't know whether to weep at the fact that he was alive and—aside from the angry gash on his head from the fight with Kieran and some dried blood crusted on his face and hands—seemingly unharmed, or weep at the fact that he had just come within an inch of killing Kieran.

"Get out of the way, Maila!" Zander was in full Enforcer mode. There was nothing warm or familiar in his voice, only the hardness of someone who was fighting for his life. Fighting for the lives of his friends and companions. Just like us.

"Zander, don't—" My words were lost from the moment they left my mouth.

In a flash, Kieran had lunged from where he crouched next to me, and he and Zander were trading blows. Kieran knocked the Immobilizer from Zander's grip, but my relief didn't last long. The punches and kicks they aimed at one another, targeting vital organs, seemed almost as deadly. In the flurry of flying limbs, Kieran managed to get an arm around Zander's neck, slamming him to the ground with enough force that I could hear the thud over the chaos around us.

But it wasn't long before Zander had wrenched free, and the two were tumbling over one another, grappling on the ground just as they had before, but now I was watching it play out fully before my eyes.

"Good to see you again, Maila."

That voice. My blood froze in my veins. I was no longer on a battlefield. I was on the front lawn of my house. The blur that was Kieran and Zander faded away. The Enforcers battling around them were the Enforcers gathered in my front yard. The faces twisted into battle cries melted into faces twisted with grief and guilt. And there he was, close enough to touch.

Leon.

"I would say I'm surprised you're not in your apartment where you're supposed to be," he said nonchalantly. As if people weren't killing each other on either side of us. "But lying, deceiving, and sneaking around seems to be what you're best at these days."

Up close, his blue eyes were the same as I remembered. Unremarkable. But the pure revulsion in them, so at odds with his level tone, pierced all the way down to my very soul. I had to avert my gaze, and it was only when I did so that I noticed his hand. Tangled in Nya's braids. Holding the barrel of an Immobilizer to her temple.

"It's a shame that you couldn't understand," he continued, "that I only do what is in the best interest of Cyllene. Someone has to do what others will not. Someone has to keep us all safe."

He wrenched Nya's head so that she stumbled to stay upright. Her face was schooled into that calm, quiet defiance that was so familiar, I could still see it with perfect clarity when I closed my eyes. Irene's face, at the end.

"But here's the thing," Leon went on, still in that easygoing voice. Like we had all the time in the world. "There's something else that you need to understand, too. And that something is that some of us are *really fucking sick* of your shit. We are sick of catering to a moody, bratty little girl just because she *might* be able to do some good for our city one day."

My legs were trembling. In my head, I screamed for Kieran. For Zander, even. For someone. Anyone.

"You have this ability, sure. Good-the-fuck for you. But you're never going to do anything useful with it, Maila. I've known you from the time you were a child. Even then, your parents catered to you. Irene catered to you. What a spoiled little thing you were!" He laughed, and the sound was like metal crunching. "I tried to tell the rest of The Council that if we were going to waste any of our valuable time on you, we needed to do it early. Work with you, train you, figure out what you were capable of. See if there was even any hope for you, or if we just needed to cut our losses and forget your fucked-up family ever existed in Cyllene. Even you would agree that makes sense, right? More sense than letting the years go by, with you doing whatever useless shit it is you do with Cato in that library?"

There was a pause.

"Answer me. It doesn't make sense, does it?"

I opened my mouth to speak, but all that came out was a garbled noise. I shook my head.

"Right. It doesn't make sense. All the time I put in with your family…I mean, fuck me, all that time I spent with two little girls, trying to stay close, keep tabs on you, get you ready for that next step…and damn if it all hasn't gone to waste. First with your mother, then Irene, and now you." The whites of Leon's eyes were visible the whole way around now. His jaw shifted from one side to the other, teeth scraping between his words. "Even now, we're all supposed to bow before you, Maila. Our almighty Conductor. Our great weapon. Maila wants to work in the Library? Let her. Maila wants to learn all about magic down in the basement? Let her! After all, she's a twenty-year-old girl. No, even better! Ten years old, when we first assigned you to the Library. A little girl needs to know the secrets of our city, right? So she can run off and share them later in life with some Stranger boy she's fucking? But even that's forgivable. Anything goes when it comes to Maila Gray."

I stole a glance in Kieran's direction. That split second told me that he saw what was happening and was scrambling to get to us. But Zander, either oblivious or fine with what was happening, used the opportunity to land a punch that made Kieran's head snap back with an audible crack.

"Look at me when I'm talking to you!"

Leon's scream shattered any ounce of resistance that was left in me. I collapsed onto the ground, my chest heaving with sobs.

"That's what I thought!" His face was contorted in rage now. "A coward. A meek, sniveling little girl. You're not some great weapon. Your mother, your father, your sister… they had that fire. They were fighters until the bitter end. Until *I* put an end to them. But you. What a fucking joke."

He threw his head from side to side, cracking his neck. Rolling his shoulders. Gun still trained on Nya. Her eyes glistened with unshed tears, and I knew because I knew her that they weren't for herself.

"A few others on The Council—Addis and that insufferable prick Cato—seem to think you're worth keeping around, no matter what shit you pull," Leon snarled. "So unfortunately for me, I have to rescue your ass from this mess you've gotten yourself into, and take you back to them. But before I do…I think it's important for you to understand that your behavior has consequences."

He was grinning then, his teeth a menacing slash of white across his demented face. He ground the barrel of the Immobilizer into the side of Nya's head, making her grit her teeth.

No, no, no, no.

It couldn't be happening again. I had relived this so many times. I had turned it over and over and over and over. Played out every possible scenario. Every possible way that I could have saved Irene, but didn't.

Leon's face was absolutely glowing as he savored my realization of what was about to happen. "They say if you lie down with dogs, you get up with fleas. Maybe you'll think about that the next time you want to take up with someone like this one here or choose to get fucked by some delinquent." He tossed his head to the side, in Kieran's direction.

And then time screeched to halt.

Leon's finger moved for the trigger.

Nya tilted her chin upward. Ready. Accepting.

I lunged.

Not only with the strength of Larimar's magic. With the strength of all that was in me, all that had been simmering beneath the surface for ten long years. That living, breathing thing that had consumed me. Left me drowning in unbearable grief. The thing that now said I would not endure this again.

I crashed into the two of them so hard that Leon lost his grip on Nya's shoulder. So hard that Nya lost her footing, falling onto her back.

A gurgle erupted from Leon's throat, breath and blood and everything in him strangled by the spear of ice that pierced straight through him, goring the front of his neck and chest and splintering out his back like some obscene icy growth.

Larimar…forgive me.

Leon's blue eyes, just as cold as the ice that now skewered him, flashed with what could only have been the terror of certain death.

And then there was a boom. A flash of light.

Leon's last fuck-you, to me and to us all, as he pulled the trigger.

In that moment, that last fraction of a second, I let my gaze drift beyond his gun. Beyond the arm that held it in position. I let my gaze drift across the grass to the silver eyes that I already knew were trained on me. And I let my own eyes fill with everything that I felt for him. Everything that he meant to me. Even as his own widened in horror.

There was an instant of pain. Scalding, clawing, all-consuming pain. Pain that tore me in two. Pain that became everything I was, all that was left of me.

And then this time, truly…

There was nothing.

CHAPTER TWENTY-ONE

I was floating on water. Crisp, cool water. Clear as the air. Clear as the sky overhead, a cloudless arctic blue. I dragged my hands through the pristine liquid ever so slowly. There was nothing above me. There was nothing below me. It was just me, drifting on the surface of sunshine itself.

Nothing to fear.

Nothing to grieve.

Nothing but crystalline peace.

I drifted for a time that was long and a time that was short. I drifted endlessly. I drifted forever.

A gentle ripple next to me. Larimar.

Their face, always a sight to behold, was prismatic.

Warm, welcome tears gathered in my eyes at the sight of it. At the sight of such loveliness. At the sight of my dear friend.

"I cannot interfere in human conflicts," Larimar said, their face expressionless.

At their words, grief bloomed in me, though it was not my own. Grief so intense that my tears of joy turned to bitter weeping.

I extended my hand to rest upon Larimar's fin. It was as smooth as silk and reminded me of how I felt when I rested comfortably upon the ocean floor, the surface above like a glittering sky. I remembered it, though the memory was not my own.

"You've already told me this," I said. "And you've done more for me than you could ever know."

Larimar lifted their head skyward.

Storm clouds were rolling in. The clouds' underbellies flickered with lightning, but what sounded in their wake were screams. Faraway screams. Screams of anguish.

I was floating, and I was gliding.

I was present, and I was escaping.

Larimar was beside me. "It is not over."

Something tugged at my memory. This memory was my own. I wanted to forget.

"But I'm here now," I cried. This time the weeping was mine and mine alone. The salt of my tears blended with the salt of the ocean.

My tears echoed for miles.

They echoed without ceasing.

Larimar's face was expressionless. Then their face was alight. Not just with their kaleidoscopic beauty, though that was there. It was something else.

And then I was a small thing, a piece of light itself, resting in Larimar's fin.

"Be safe," they whispered, and I felt the intensity of their grief once more as they released me.

A speck of light.

A seed of hope.

"Maila! Oh, my God. Oh, my God. Maila, Maila!"

Nya's screaming had my eyes flying open. Heart pounding.

"Kieran, stop! *She's alive!*"

It was night. Had I been unconscious that long? There was a storm raging above, the likes of which I had never seen. A hurricane. Worse.

Nya's face appeared over mine. Even in the darkness, I could see that her eyelids were swollen from crying, and her chest was heaving with rasping breaths. I became aware of a weight on me. Her body was covering mine.

"What happened?" I asked. Or tried to ask. My words were swallowed up in a gust of wind. Its howl was enough to leave my ears ringing.

"Kieran, please!" Nya screamed at something behind me.

It clicked into place. Kieran. Kieran was there.

Snapping out of my stupor, I tried to sit up, but the weight of Nya's body held me down. The air was thick with something like humidity but denser. More ominous. I struggled weakly against Nya's grip, pushing on her arm until she finally lifted it.

Her cheeks were wet with tears, and she was shaking, but her expression was full of hope. "Tell him you're okay." Her voice was barely audible over the violent gusts. "Tell him, Maila!"

I raised myself and instantly knew Nya was wrong.

I was not okay. I was dead. Because there was no other way to make sense of the scene before me.

It was not nighttime, because what was above us was not the night sky. It was black, solid onyx. No moon or stars or even a cloud to be found. It was not storming, and yet something like wind, ear-shatteringly loud, was ripping across the battlefield. Across the ground. Across everything. Chunks of dirt and grass, the loose pieces of concrete that had once been part of the wall, even the wall itself...objects were being lifted on this mysterious wind, only to disintegrate into nothingness. As if they had never existed to begin with.

Holy shit. Was that the roof of the Knowledge Center?

Before I could comprehend what that meant, my eyes landed on something else. Someone else.

Leon.

If not for those blue eyes that stared upward, unseeingly...those miserable eyes that I would never forget as long as I lived…I would not have known it was him. The corpse I had left behind was destroyed. Obliterated. As if it had simultaneously been incinerated and torn limb from limb.

As I watched, the remains began to lift and sway as if in a funnel cloud. Carried upward by that strange wind. Then they disintegrated. Leaving nothing behind, not even ash.

I might have rejoiced, but it was happening all around me. Enforcers. Strangers. People on both sides. Bodies were scattered everywhere, as far as I could make out. And they, too, were floating up on the wind and disintegrating.

Nya gripped my arm so hard that I cried out. "You have to stop him!" she shouted. She jerked my shoulder, forcing me to look behind me.

In the midst of the felled bodies and the field that was turning to nothingness, Kieran stood as still and as straight as if it were any other day. His arms hung limply at his sides. His clothes were in tatters that whipped frantically around him, barely concealing his body.

His *healed* body.

All evidence of the scuffle with the Enforcers when he jumped the wall, the torture that he had endured from The Council, the wounds from battle…it was gone. His hair, as dark as the sky above, was being tossed in the wind in the same manner as his scraps of clothing. A few strands brushed across his face. Across his eyes.

And therein was the only indication that something was not as it should be.

His eyes often gave the appearance of glowing. But this time, there was no denying that that was actually what was happening. As iridescent as Larimar's skin, the light they reflected was coming not from outside, but from within. And despite their beauty, there was something dire in them.

"Kieran!" I called out to him.

He didn't react.

"Kieran!"

Still no reaction. Not even a twitch. His eyes stared out at the horizon, unseeing.

"*Kieran!*"

I was comprehending now the full gravity of our situation. The reason behind Nya's panic.

This was all his doing. And he was going to destroy us.

He was going to wipe all of us—no, all of Cyllene—off the face of the planet. Or worse. What if it didn't stop here, with us? What if this thing, whatever we were witnessing, just kept going? Taking everything and everyone down with it?

I turned fully onto my stomach and dragged myself closer to him. Nya followed suit. When I was within reach of him, I grabbed hold of his ankle. Then his knee. And slowly, carefully, I was standing. Bracing myself against him to keep from getting carried away. Turned to dust.

Nya was slamming her fist against his leg, outright punching him. It was such a Nya thing to do, it made my heart ache.

I pulled myself up another inch, and then another, until I was hugging Kieran's chest.

"*Kieran!*" My voice was a small shriek lost in the larger, ear-splitting shriek of that dark wind. Behind him, in the distance, that once-turquoise sea was as black as tar. It thrashed violently, like a caged beast readying to escape its captor. "Kieran, please! I don't know what's happening, but please follow the sound of my voice and come back to us. Please…"

I was talking to myself, and I knew it. He couldn't hear me.

I pressed my face into his chest and willed the utter destruction around me to disappear. Even though his skin was chilled, there was also a warmth to it. The same warmth that I felt that morning in my bedroom.

My bedroom.

Where while I was on top of him, I had unknowingly started draining his power.

I knew what I had to do.

Still holding onto Kieran with everything I had, I closed my eyes, took a deep breath, and cleared my mind of all but one thought.

I imagined Kieran's magic as a tangible thing, something I could reach out and grab onto. I listened for it and focused my thoughts, my energy, my being on calling out to it.

During this process, I felt an absence, something departed, and I understood that Larimar's magic, as well as the side effects of using it, were gone. But those last remaining remnants had healed me.

I allowed myself only a moment of gratitude, only a moment to consider what would have become of me if not for them, and then I set those thoughts aside. There would be time to be thankful later. When I could add being thankful that *all* of us were saved to the list.

I waited. Visualizing that thing…that tendril of darkness…like ink spilled across a sheet of paper…

There.

I saw it. I was seeing Kieran's magic.

I followed the same steps I had followed when Larimar lent me their magic. I took another deep breath, steadying myself as much as I could in these circumstances, and then I reached for it. Not with my hand, and not with my mind either. I reached for it in a way that I couldn't quite explain.

When I connected with it, it felt different from Larimar's magic. That was to be expected, right? I felt a prickly sensation all over, almost like something was exploring, testing. Deciding.

This wasn't just different, it was very different. What exactly was happening to me?

I no longer felt Kieran against me.

My eyes flew open, and I was standing on an unfamiliar hill. At night. Alone.

I couldn't begin to understand what had just happened. Where was I? Was I physically here? Or only mentally? Spiritually?

It was night. True night this time, with a star-filled sky. And I was standing on a hill. A dune. Covered in tall, spiky fans of marram grass.

I half-walked, half-slid down the sand until I reached level ground. All that lay ahead of me was a quiet beach. The ocean was so calm that aside from the gentle shifting of the water right at the edge, lapping at the sand, it resembled a sheet of midnight glass.

Sitting in the sand, out of reach of the water, was a boy. He was facing away from me. But as I approached, I noted that he couldn't have been more than seven years old. He sat with his legs pulled into him. His dark hair was short, but shaggy. A few tufts hung in his eyes.

His gray eyes, tinged in ethereal silver.

"Kieran?"

The boy wouldn't look at me. But he said, "What?" in a small voice that was both familiar and unfamiliar.

"Do you mind if I sit down?"

"It's not my beach. Do what you want."

I sat down beside him and pulled my legs into my chest, mirroring him. My eyes drifted over his face. The little nose. Cheeks that had a slight pudginess to them. A jaw that was still softened by youth. My heart swelled.

We sat in silence for a while. He refused to so much as glance in my direction.

Eventually, I spoke. "Kieran. Why don't you tell me what's bothering you?"

He snorted. "What do you care?"

"I care," I said, turning away from the ocean to face him. "Because I care about you. I want to know what's bothering you, so I can make it better."

"Okay," he drawled sarcastically.

I had to resist the urge to roll my eyes. So the sarcasm wasn't a new thing for him, then.

"I mean it," I said patiently. "I care about you, and I don't want you to be upset. I want you to be happy. In fact, I want you to be the happiest person on the entire planet." He tried to stifle a laugh. A real one, I detected. I kept going. "I want you to be so happy that you don't know what to do with yourself. So happy that you get bored with it and actually wish you were sad sometimes, just to change things up."

He chuckled then, and his eyes darted to mine warily. Then he resumed staring out to sea, all traces of laughter gone. "You shouldn't bother."

"Why?" I shifted so that I was sitting cross-legged, tilting my head toward the sand until I caught his eye.

"I think I'm just supposed to be by myself," he said with all the authority of a seven-year-old. When he continued, his voice was soft. "Everyone I care about always dies. My mom, my dad…and now you."

I swallowed. "So your mom and dad died, then?"

"Yeah. My mom first, my dad second. My mom died because she was sick. My dad died because his family didn't like me and my mom. They said he had more important things to do."

"That's hard stuff," I said quietly. "Especially at your age."

"Yeah." He nodded, his dark hair bouncing. "But your parents died, too. And your sister. That's even more people."

I went still.

"When you told me they all died," he continued. "I was sad. It's sad to be alone. It's scary sometimes, too. Like maybe I'll get eaten by a marsh wolf or something, and no one will even care because I'm all alone anyway."

"You're not alone, Kieran." My voice was a whisper. "Larimar's magic saved me somehow. I'm not really sure how it's possible, honestly. But the important thing is that I'm not dead. Or at least, I'm not anymore. I'm here. With you."

He turned to face me fully then. His eyes were that blending of bright silver and muted gray. Hope and fear. "Why do you care so much about me?"

I took his small hand.

"Because I love you, Kieran."

I was back on the battlefield, clinging to Kieran's chest.

The wind was still roaring around me.

Then it was silent, and I wondered if the roaring had finally shattered my eardrums. Still squeezing my eyes shut, I was too afraid to hope for the alternative—that it was finally coming to an end.

I don't know how long I stood there before I tentatively opened my eyes and tilted my head up to Kieran's face. He was already looking down at me. The sun, emerging from the ominous black overhead, was reflected in his eyes. A gradient of silver and gold. The colors began to tremble. His eyes were filling with tears.

"I watched you die," he said softly. He traced my face with his fingertips, studying every inch of it. As if he were seeing me for the first time.

I placed my hand over his. "I know, but I'm here now."

Kieran smiled back at me, and it was brighter than the sun. There was no sarcasm in it, no wryness. Just joy.

The most beautiful thing I had ever seen.

Then he fell forward slightly, and Nya was beside me, helping hold him upright. A spike of dread shot through me. Kieran's head rolled back, his eyes fluttered closed. Then his breathing slowed, becoming automatic. Relief flooded me as I realized he was just unconscious. Asleep.

"I guess I would be exhausted, too, if I just annihilated half the fucking bay," Nya muttered as we lowered him carefully to the ground.

At her words, I stood abruptly and turned a circle, taking everything in.

Devastated.

That was the only word that came to mind as I beheld what little remained of the field, of the wall, of...the Knowledge Center. My stomach turned over.

People on both sides—the Enforcers and the Strangers—were doing the same as I was, standing and surveying the destruction. Helping one another to their feet. I had cried so much lately, I didn't think I had any more tears left in me. But seeing that there were people alive, that others had been huddled on the ground just like us, waiting for the chaos to subside, brought fresh tears to my eyes. I couldn't allow myself to think just yet of those who didn't survive.

My gaze drifted to the beach, and I relished the sight of the ocean, blue and bright and calm under the midday sun. No longer a roiling black mass.

I started.

Where the grass transitioned to sand, outlined in an almost ethereal glow by the sunlight reflecting off the water, was a figure. A figure cloaked in black.

Silver eyes stared out from the shadows of its hood.

It stared at me unblinkingly. Then it inclined its head toward me and vanished.

The next few hours eroded my sense of relief, leaving nothing but heartache in its place. The Strangers had failed. That much was clear. With at this point uncountable people injured and dead, there simply weren't enough warm bodies to keep pushing to take the city. And frankly, it wasn't even clear how much city was left to take anymore.

The only small mercy for all was that there was an unspoken cease-fire as both sides tried to get their bearings.

Initially, there were shouts and tears and tight hugs as friends found one another still standing, talking, functioning. Still alive.

Then came the realization that that dark power, Kieran's magic, had disintegrated all the bodies that were lying deceased on the field. Some remarked that this saved the trouble of digging graves for hundreds upon hundreds of people, but others mourned the fact that they would not be able to give their companions a proper burial.

Then people began to identify others who had been alive before the start of the chaos, and who, while still living, breathing, screaming, had been carried up by the current of Kieran's power and reduced to nothing. Not even to dust.

Nya and I managed to drag Kieran's unconscious body to the beach, depositing him safely in the sand with the group of injured men and women that was beginning to assemble there. As we moved on to reunite with members of our group and tend to the wounded, I began to overhear the stories. One Enforcer shared with another how his comrade had been lifted skyward before his very eyes, his mouth still twisted in a wail as he disintegrated. Another shared how his whole group had been carried away by the wind while he clawed at the grass and dirt and held on for dear life.

But the stories from our side were the most uncomfortable. Stories from people who knew Kieran, who were friends with Kieran. Who considered him one of them. On their side. And yet he had destroyed members of their group. He had destroyed people who, according to the accounts we were given, had worked alongside him during long days at camp. People he had trained with. People he called friends.

When Nya and I finally encountered Cecil, there was a much-needed celebration.

Despite being covered in burns and having half his beard singed off from the kiss of barely-dodged Immobilizer blasts, Cecil was alive. He lifted Nya off the ground with his hug. Then he gave me a hug that was more careful but no less hearty. We joined him in wrapping the wounds of those who had fought near him.

Then came the discussion of what had just taken place. And even he, I saw with a sinking feeling in my gut, had a hardness to his expression. I could see that even though the battle was over, conflict still raged powerfully within him.

"We were winning, Nya," he said, his voice low. He seemed to have forgotten that I was standing there, and in that moment, I was grateful. "We were going to do it. After...after all of it, after everything, we were going to do it."

For the first time since meeting him, I didn't hear the friendly, good-natured tone of a man who drew terrible maps and adored his infant daughter. I heard a warrior who had put everything on the line for the betterment of his people and had lost.

At one point later while wrapping a man's leg, my eyes and Nya's met. Neither of us had to say anything. We were both thinking that there was still another battle to come.

The battle between those who understood that what happened was out of Kieran's control, and those who would not so easily be able to forgive and forget.

As we were preparing to move on to the next group of injured, Nya caught my arm. When she spoke, her voice, hoarse from screaming, was pitched even lower. "I think you need to go be with Kieran. Keep an eye on him."

I swallowed and nodded. "Nya…what was that?"

She knew my meaning. And she didn't bother hiding the fear in her eyes. "I don't know, Maila. Ever since we found Kieran in the woods and took him in, we always wondered if he had other abilities besides just the enhanced vision. I guess we assumed he did, and they were dormant. But what happened today was…beyond what we had ever guessed." For the first time since she broke into my apartment that night, I saw something like real fear in Nya's eyes. "You were dead, Maila. Before Larimar's magic revived you and brought you back to us, you weren't even…" She winced as if the memory was a physical sting. "You weren't even recognizable."

The reality of what that must have been like for her and Kieran settled over me.

"When Kieran saw that," she continued. "Everything went to hell. He…he lost it. It was like suddenly he was so strong. Inhumanly strong. And I couldn't even keep up with what was happening. He knocked your Enforcer friend out of the way like it was nothing, and then he just unleashed on that horrible man. Even when he was obviously dead, he just kept going and going and going… and the sky was so dark, and I thought a storm was moving in or something…"

She trailed off. I didn't press her to continue. I understood enough about what had happened, and the raw terror that came over her expression as she recounted everything wasn't worth satisfying my curiosity about the details.

"Do you have his power, then?" she asked. "Temporarily, I mean."

"No," I replied, and I was thankful that was the truth. "I didn't actually take his power. I think I just used my ability to communicate with him somehow. To break through to him. I don't really understand it, honestly."

We were both silent for a while. Then I remembered our reason for pausing—Kieran. I needed to go be with him. Maybe even protect him, if people's reactions so far were any indication.

I moved to turn, then realized Nya was still gripping my arm. She grabbed my other arm, squeezing them both so tightly that she nearly lifted me off the ground.

"Don't ever do that again."

I had never heard her voice sound so small.

"What do you mean?"

"You know exactly what I mean. Don't you ever do that again, Maila." Her eyes were glistening. I knew she would fight letting those tears fall with everything she had. "Next time, you let me die."

When I spoke, my voice was just as small. "You know I can't promise that."

"You have to," she snapped, releasing me. "Or I fucking swear I'll follow you into whatever afterlife you're in, and I'll kill you again myself."

Without another word, she strode away.

I watched her hurry toward a cluster of Strangers, all injured and trying to assist one another in patching wounds.

Standing amongst the others, cradling her left arm and leaning heavily on her right leg, was Xiomara. Like the rest of us, she was covered in dirt, ash from the Immobilizers, and dried blood. Some of the blood looked to be her own. But I sighed with relief when she almost tackled Nya to the ground, embracing her with her good arm. She was going to be just fine.

I spun in the direction of the beach. Or started to, at least.

In the distance, beyond the spot where Nya had just been standing, were the remains of the Knowledge Center. The first three floors still mostly intact, the rest a gaping void of nothingness. Just blue sky where immeasurable records and projects and supplies had once been.

Where the bulk of the Library had once been.

My safe space.

With the books that had been my friends, my teachers, my world, for so long.

I had known when I called on Larimar that there was no going back. This was a physical testament to that. But was it the right decision?

Was there even a right decision to be made?

As if on cue, something else came into focus.

I couldn't say if he had been there all along, or if he had been kneeling and only just stood. But I was motionless as I stared across the scorched field. Beyond men and women from our group, leaning on one another for support as they made for the beach. Beyond the Enforcers that were now assessing their status and providing first aid to one another, following a protocol that had undoubtedly been laid out for them in advance. I stared past it all, unseeing, into the amber eyes that stared back at me.

Like two blazing infernos in both color and intensity, Zander's eyes could have pierced my own. Burned straight through me. There was some relief there, and I remembered then that he had watched me die, too. But I watched the relief slowly dissolve, and in its place was nothing but profound sorrow and betrayal.

His armor was askew, barely hanging on. Between plates hung shredded wisps of cloth. His face was smudged with blood and ash. I took it all in, while at the same time, only seeing that stare.

I didn't go to him. I didn't try to speak. The thought that there could even be a possibility of repairing our friendship was laughable. Regardless of what I believed was right, and what I believed was wrong, I had participated in destroying everything *he* believed in.

His companions were injured and dead. His city was in shambles. That quiet woman that he had always carried a torch for was right there at the center of it all. And with another man, no less. As if all the rest wasn't enough for a lifetime's worth of despair.

I considered it a consolation that he was alive. It was the most that I was allowed to hope for. And with that knowledge, I turned and headed for the beach.

To Kieran.

To the Strangers.

To my future.

CHAPTER TWENTY-TWO

The expressions on the Strangers' faces as we stepped through the gate, back into Ersa Estates, will be burned in my memory forever.

Not the faces of the Strangers who fought. They had had half a day of trudging through the wilderness, injuries slowing us down, to process the outcome of the battle. Half a day of weary bodies dragging through the underbrush, just as much as they dragged the wounded on makeshift gurneys behind them.

What will be burned into my memory is the moment when what was left of the Strangers' army crossed into camp, bleeding and broken, and nearly a hundred waiting faces all fell at once.

Today was supposed to change things for the Strangers. But their circumstances had changed only in that there were fewer friends and fewer loved ones to ease the burden, both literal and figurative, of their daily lives.

It was a world-shattering loss.

As we hauled the injured through the street, Nya and I stayed close to Kieran. And we remained close as Cecil helped us carry him into one of the houses near the bonfire, into Kieran's room.

When Cecil left, neither of us moved to leave with him.

Let's call it what it was—we were guarding Kieran. And we both knew it.

"Do we need to worry about his roommates?" I asked as I took in the space. I don't know what I had expected of Kieran's bedroom, but it was much the same as Nya's—crumbling walls, carpet so stiff that it no longer felt like carpet, the pervasive reek of mold and mildew. What made his room different, though, was the number of people sharing it. Rather than a mattress, the room was strewn with sleeping bags. Six total, including Kieran's.

"I don't know," Nya replied. Hearing her so uncharacteristically uncertain was all the answer I needed.

We sat against what remained of the wall on either side of Kieran's sleeping bag. As the room darkened with the setting sun, I tried to think of something to say. It felt like there was so much that needed to be said, while simultaneously, here was nothing worth saying after all that we had just endured.

At some point, footsteps sounded in the hallway, and we braced for one of Kieran's roommates to enter.

But it was just Wren. She was sniffling as she embraced Nya, her long lashes wet with tears. When she pulled Nya into a passionate kiss, I had to stifle a smile. Nya might have been avoiding calling what they had a relationship, but it was clear to me now that that was just semantics. There was no mistaking the way they felt about each other.

Not long after, footsteps sounded in the hallway again. Then Cecil's hulking form appeared in the doorway.

"Maila," he said. "Someone wants to talk to you."

I furrowed my brow. "Who?"

"You haven't met her yet," he said. "Her name is Sigrid."

I was finally going to meet Sigrid. The Strangers' enchantress.

As Cecil and I made our way down a side road, perpendicular to the cul-de-sac at the center of camp, I considered the limited information that Nya and Kieran had shared about her. She helped the Strangers with basic spells, potions, and brews. And she had refused to meet me during my first visit to the camp.

Now, I had only been back at the camp for a few hours, and there was apparently a sense of urgency to talk to me. I didn't know how to feel about that.

"Did she say what she wanted to talk to me about?" I questioned.

"She did. But I think it would be better for you to hear it from her." Cecil flashed a reassuring smile.

I glanced around us. I hadn't spent any time on this street. I had only seen it from a distance during my first visit. But it was the same as every other street in the skeleton of the neighborhood. Every decaying house was slightly different from the next, yet also just the same.

Even though we were walking in the opposite direction from the fire, the musky smell of burning brush still hung in the air. I breathed it in and felt a pang in my chest, remembering the last time I breathed in the scent of the bonfire with Cecil beside me.

"You knew that Irene could wield magic."

Cecil's sigh sounded pained. "I did."

"And that I have the same ability."

"Yes."

He seemed to be expecting me to say something else. When I didn't, he continued, "I couldn't share that with you when we talked that day. It was too much, too fast." He paused in front of a house with gray siding. Or at least, it was gray now. It was unclear what color it had once been. "I think you'll find that Sigrid will be able to answer a lot of the questions that you have."

He led me through the door without knocking.

The first thing that hit me was the smell. Or rather, many smells at once. The mingling of fresh herbs, something medicinal, and something strongly floral. Together, the mixture burned my nostrils.

We were standing in a front room that made Cato's office look plain and pristine by comparison. The walls and floors had the same rough appearance as the other houses I'd been inside in Ersa Estates. But rather than the barest of furnishings, this one was packed to the brim with all manner of objects. Some made sense to me, for an enchantress—the shelves of bottles with contents that were all the colors of the rainbow; the collection of stones and other talismans that littered mismatched tables of varying sizes; the spell books strewn among everything, each one seemingly opened to the spell that was last used. But there were also decidedly human objects as well, many of which were old, obsolete electronics that I knew only from books. Things like toasters, hot curlers, and even a lawn mower. There were boxes with cracked glass screens that had once been computers or televisions… or maybe there was a mix of both. It was difficult for me to distinguish between the two.

"Admiring my collection?"

The voice was as smooth as silk, and it was a perfect fit for the person it came from. She stood in the corner of the room, and the first thing I noticed about her was her hair, which alternated between streaks of raven black and snow white. Her skin was pale but still had some warmth to it, with undertones of gold. Which was the perfect complement to slightly upturned gold eyes. In contrast to her striking features, she wore a simple black dress that billowed around her ankles.

"Yes," I said finally. "It's incredible."

Cecil gave me a quick wink as moved toward the door. "I'll leave you two to it."

And then we were alone.

"Come, have a seat." Sigrid gestured to a small table by the gaping hole in the wall that was once a window. Fabrics of all different colors and patterns had been pinned over it to keep out the elements.

I sat down in the open chair, and she cleared a stack of books from the chair across from it. When she sat, the corner of her delicate pink lips turned up in a knowing smile. "Am I what you expected, Maila? Do I match the descriptions your Library gave of witches?"

"Yes," I answered immediately. There was something unsettling about her, but also something fearsomely beautiful. Just as the encounters that were detailed in the basement journals had described. "Except your kind are referred to as 'enchantresses,' not 'witches.'"

Sigrid's laugh was like a song. "How surprisingly inconsistent! I've never known humans, and particularly

Cyllene, to go with the least degrading term for a magic user."

I couldn't argue with that.

"Let's not mince words, Maila." Her tone was firm, but not threatening. "I didn't want to meet you before because I'm not quite as trusting as some of the others in our camp. Twenty years is a long time to live in a city. To nurture relationships with its people. To have every day, every action, every aspect of your life intertwined with its belief system."

"My beliefs are my own," I answered just as firmly. "And not everyone in Cyllene is bad."

"I agree with both of those things. That's why I decided I was ready to meet you." She took a deep breath. "I know Cecil shared with you that he knew your sister, Irene. I knew her as well. After she confessed to him that she could wield magic, he started bringing me with him when they would rendezvous. She supplied us with food and other essentials. In turn, Cecil shared books with her. And I supplied her with the knowledge she needed to hone her abilities. It was a great partnership while it lasted."

The note of regret in her voice made my throat tighten.

"I'm guessing you know now the truth of our history with Cyllene. The fact that the people here, and those that came before them, have always been at odds with the city that shuns them. The city that celebrates the people it can control and exiles the people it cannot." She leaned forward, raven and snow-white strands pooling on the table in front of her. "You also know your abilities now. That you were sought out by us for your brain and the knowledge it contains, but also for your abilities, which we knew from Irene were—even though dormant—just as magnificent as hers."

The reminder that Irene never shared any of this with me herself made me shift in my seat. "Yes," I confirmed. "I know all of that now."

Sigrid leaned back, absently twirling one of the silver bands that decorated her fingers. "Tell me, then. What can I answer for you? What do you want to know?"

As always, a million questions ran through my head. But I settled for, "Why are you here? In Ersa Estates, I mean. Why is an enchantress willing to help the people here?"

Her eyes softened. "Because they need me. Contrary to what others from our world may think of humankind, I have a soft spot for creatures who are suffering. And maybe…maybe I see a bit of myself in them. Sorrow isn't an emotion reserved exclusively for humans. Magic users have the same conflicts, the same power struggles." She smiled ruefully. "Some of us feel like we're always on the losing end of things, too."

It wasn't the response I had expected. It made warmth blossom in my chest.

Before I could think better of it, I suddenly had the urge to speak exactly what was on my mind. "I want to know what all of this means. What I can do to make things right for Kieran, and Nya, and Cecil. For everyone in Ersa Estates. I don't hate Cyllene, and I certainly don't love what this group did to it today. What *we* did to it today. But I also want to make things right for them." I paused, trying to collect my thoughts. "I need to know what my role is in all of this."

The smile she gave me pinned me to my chair. "One day soon, you will."

As I walked back from Sigrid's later, my heart felt full. We had talked for hours about magic. And unlike my conversations with Cato, nothing was off-limits. It was strange, but in spite of all that had happened today, I had this feeling in my gut that things had happened exactly how they were supposed to.

I couldn't explain why. And maybe, if I tried to look deeper to understand it, I would find that it was just the sense of validation and camaraderie that had formed in me as Sigrid and I spoke. But I wasn't going to question it.

I rounded the corner from Sigrid's street and froze. It was late, and the chairs around the fire appeared to all be empty. But one figure stood in front of the flames, his back to me.

Kieran.

Relief and joy brought a grin to my face. He was awake. He was alive.

But he didn't turn as I approached. Or when I stopped beside him. Just like the seven-year-old version of him that I had spoken to, his eyes were trained straight ahead. As if nothing else around him existed.

Icy fear clenched in my gut. "Kieran?"

He still wouldn't look at me. When he spoke, his voice was flat. Empty.

"Maila. What the fuck did I do?"

CHAPTER TWENTY-THREE

Sunlight filtered through the branches of the gemstone willow, glittering on the jeweled leaves like a prism. Reflected light painted the grass, the trunk of the tree, our faces.

There were no words to describe it, and I marveled at the fact that the authors of the books in the Library had tried. When a breeze passed through, the leaves tinkled against one another like true peridots. In the gap between the branches and the grassy hill that the willow sat upon, the view of lush green fields extended for miles before turning to the hazy blue of the ocean on the horizon.

The section of ocean off the southern coast.

We hadn't returned to the shore near Cyllene since the battle. Even though it had only been two weeks, it felt like it was a lifetime ago. I didn't know when I would see Cyllene next. And after all that had happened, that was fine with me. There were too many wounds, and all were too fresh.

"If I'm being honest, I thought this was going to be kind of a waste of time," Nya said with a yawn. She shimmied down the trunk until she was almost lying down, then folded her arms over her chest and closed her eyes. "But this is nice. I think sometimes you get so used to seeing certain things, that you forget how to appreciate them."

"I guess I'll agree with you," Kieran said from my other side, his voice full of mock reluctance. "It's not so bad taking an afternoon to sit under a sparkly tree."

I smiled and lowered my head to rest against his shoulder. Maybe it was Nya's influence, or the peace that I felt sitting under the gemstone willow with her and Kieran, but my eyes were suddenly heavy. I tried to resist closing them, not wanting to miss a moment. But the resistance was short-lived. Kieran's fingertips traced lazy circles on my leg, and soon I was starting to dream.

"I do want to add, though," Nya spoke up again, startling me awake. "This is still nowhere close to enough to make it up to you for saving my life."

"You're not supposed to make it up to me," I murmured, eyes still closed. "I did what I wanted to do. But seeing a gemstone willow up close—a big one, like I had read about—is huge for me. And I appreciate it." After a moment, I added, "I appreciate both of you."

"I'm glad we could make it happen." Nya's voice was soft.

Kieran responded by kissing me on the head. I reveled in the touch. The press of his lips against my hairline, the warmth of his body against me, the fingertips that still danced absently across my skin.

I wished it could always be like this.

In the time since we had been back in Ersa Estates, I had settled in with Nya, the same as when I had visited before. And I filled my days with finding ways to be useful. Acting as an assistant to the healers, learning how to tend the vegetable garden, helping Wren and the other cooks prepare daily meals…sometimes just awkwardly following Nya around camp, not knowing where else to go or what else to do.

The highlight of every day was always the hour that I spent each evening at that little table in Sigrid's front room, learning the basics of wielding magic. Or as Sigrid would say, learning all the ways that I could've killed myself and everyone around me by going from zero to borrowing magic from an ancient water spirit. And how to ensure it was not just dumb luck but actual skill that saved me next time.

"I wish it could always be like this." Nya voiced my thoughts aloud.

"Same," Kieran said. He was keeping his tone light, but I could hear what lurked under the surface. Everything in me wanted to press a kiss to his shoulder, but I knew he would understand the meaning. And I knew, more than anything, that he didn't want my pity.

The fallout after Kieran detonated in Cyllene was as expected. Everyone understood that what happened was out of Kieran's control. Everyone understood that the magic he possessed was greater than anything the group had ever imagined, and that this made him an invaluable ally.

And everyone resented him more and more with each passing day.

Bitter over the lives lost. Lives that should have been given up to Enforcers while furthering the group's cause. But never as random casualties of a force that couldn't be controlled. Never at the hands of a friend.

And there was always that question, the one that permeated every hour of every day since our return—if not for Kieran losing control, would the Strangers have won? Would we all be in Cyllene right now, spending long but rewarding days carving out a new structure, a new system, a new home for everyone?

I knew Kieran's grief was unfathomable. And having lived under the oppressive shadow of my own grief for so many years, I had promised myself that I would be whatever he needed me to be while he weathered it. If only he would want me, need me. Let me be that person to pull him out of the darkness and remind him how wonderful life could be, the way he had done for me.

My thoughts had me sitting up, suddenly too restless to doze. I tilted my head to look at him. At the movement, he turned to look at me, too. Whatever he saw in my eyes had his narrowing, and a slow smirk spread across his face.

"What are you thinking about?" he asked.

It was everything, seeing that smirk. Seeing him look and act like himself. But I kept my tone nonchalant. "Wouldn't you like to know?"

"I can tell you who doesn't want to know," Nya interrupted, raising her hand in the air.

I laughed, and my heart swelled as I heard Kieran's chuckle beside me.

It was moments like this that made it all worth it to me. Moments that made me feel like I was truly living. No longer just surviving. Yes, some of the things life had thrown at me were scary and sad and frustrating. At times, even heartbreaking. But there were a lot of wonderful things, too. In trying to protect myself from life's heartaches, I had also protected myself from life's joys. But not anymore.

As the sun began to dip behind the tree line to the west of us, we stood and stretched. The sky was turning to shades of gold and tangerine, and when the light hit the swaying branches of the gemstone willow just right, the leaves transformed from peridot to topaz.

When we passed under the jeweled curtain, I paused, running my fingertips along a strand. I would never stop being amazed at how each briolette-shaped leaf felt like any other leaf, on any other tree.

I smiled at the gemstone willow. I was pretty sure it wasn't sentient, but I hoped it knew, somehow, how much I appreciated the beautiful afternoon that it had gifted me. With the two people who mattered most to me.

I followed Nya and Kieran down the hill, toward the field and the forest beyond. We were heading home.

And we were heading there together.

ACKNOWLEDGMENTS

I always have to give thanks first and foremost to God. Life is full of joys and sorrows, and I'm thankful when He blesses me with a time of joy.

Thank you to my husband, David, for being my first reader, my cheerleader, my real-life "book boyfriend," and my best friend. Thank you for talking about my characters like they're real friends of ours, and thank you for all the times you said, "I've got this—GO WRITE!" This book absolutely would not exist without your support. Period.

Thank you to the amazing Megan Records for the developmental edit and copy edit. And most importantly, for helping me take this book to the next level. I will never forget the excitement I felt while reading your feedback, knowing that you really "got" the story. I hope we can partner on more books in the future!

Thank you to MIBLART for absolutely nailing the cover design! Working with your team has been a wonderful experience from beginning to end.

Thank you to my mom for being my biggest fan, all the way back to my *true* first book, Coco the Monkey's Birthday (Seven-year-old me would be amazed at where my love for writing has taken me!). Thank you for always surrounding me with books, for instilling in me a love of learning, and always being there to encourage me when I doubted myself.

Thank you to my brother, Kent, for being the best brother I could ever ask for. I hope we can celebrate this book the way we always do—by eating sushi until our stomachs are about to explode.

Thank you to my dad, who I know is looking down on me and is proud of me for making this lifelong dream of being an author come true. I love you and can't wait to see you again.

Thank you to Ellie for reminding me just how much I love fantasy and romance (and as a result, helping inspire this book!), for cheering me on, and for being my book buddy!

A massive thank-you to anyone who has taken the time to read this book—I don't think there are adequate words to express how much it means to me that out of all the books in the world, you spent your valuable time reading mine. It means *everything* to me.

And last but not least, to Ariana—there is no job, no role, no purpose in my life that will ever give me more joy than being your mom. I can't wait for you to read this when you are thirty-five (and not a day sooner).

ABOUT THE AUTHOR

Tara Straight is a Stetson University graduate and lifelong bookworm. If she's not writing about fantasy worlds with swoon-worthy romances, she's probably reading about them. Having spent most of her life in central Florida, some of her greatest joys are walking on the beach, visiting Florida's many springs, frequenting the theme parks, and attending comic and anime conventions. No matter what she may be doing, you can guarantee it is with her husband, daughter, and daughter's stuffed pink bunny in tow.

Learn more at:
TaraStraight.com
Instagram, TikTok, and Threads @tarastraight